The World of Juno

Additional Content by Brent Lambert and Nick Bright

Space Wizard Science Fantasy
Raleigh, NC
www.spacewizardsciencefantasy.com

Publisher's Note: This is a work of fiction. Names, characters, places, and incidents are a product of the author's imagination. Locales and public names are sometimes used for atmospheric purposes. Any resemblance to actual people, living or dead, or to businesses, companies, events, institutions, or locales is completely coincidental.

Cover by MoorBooks
Illustrations by Katie Cordy
Copy Editing by Heather Tracy
Book Layout © 2015 BookDesignTemplates.com

The World of Juno/Daniel Eavenson, William C. Tracy, Heather Tracy.— 1st ed.
ISBN 978-1-7350768-9-8

#20

The World of Juno

A SECONDARY WORLD HISTORY AND ANTHOLOGY

Created by Daniel Eavenson
Edited by William C. Tracy & Heather Tracy

CONTENTS

The Observers and Solar Magic 6
The Species and Gods of Juno 12
The Kuhifadi 14
The Uchafumlaji 18
The Ngisikaa 22
Kimmasi: The Remembered One 24
Akkakuh: The Light of the Sun, The First 28
Onukuh: The Love of Life, The First Child 30
Unzulaja: The Night Serpent, The Slithering Dark 32
The First Age of Juno 34
The Line Between Light and Darkness 36
Hirolajak - Child of the Night, The Shadow 48
Ergalfadi - The Cloak of Death 50
Obakka - The Membranous 52
Fooon 56
Chulan's Honor 66
The Second Age of Juno 88
Obarikaa - First Child of Magic 90
Dalkka - The Work of Creation 92
Hursagkaa - Love Among the Gods 94
Elegy Of Light and Shadow 96
Ashfall on Jade 108
The Third Age of Juno 124
The Tour 126
The Fourth Age of Juno 158
Chasing Kusongangani 160
An Honest Life 188
Bait 220
God of Two Heads 250
Jackal 270

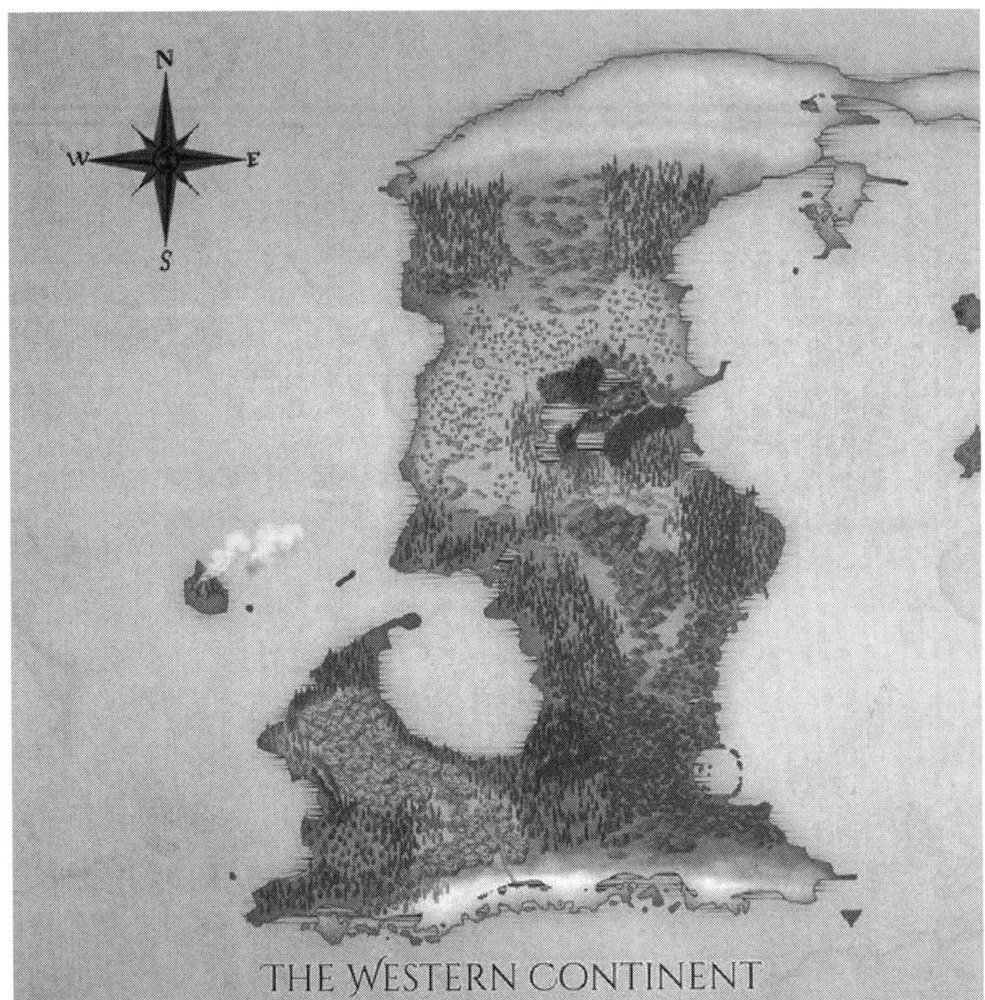
N
W
E
S
THE WESTERN CONTINENT
0
1000
2000
3000
4000
5000
Kilometers

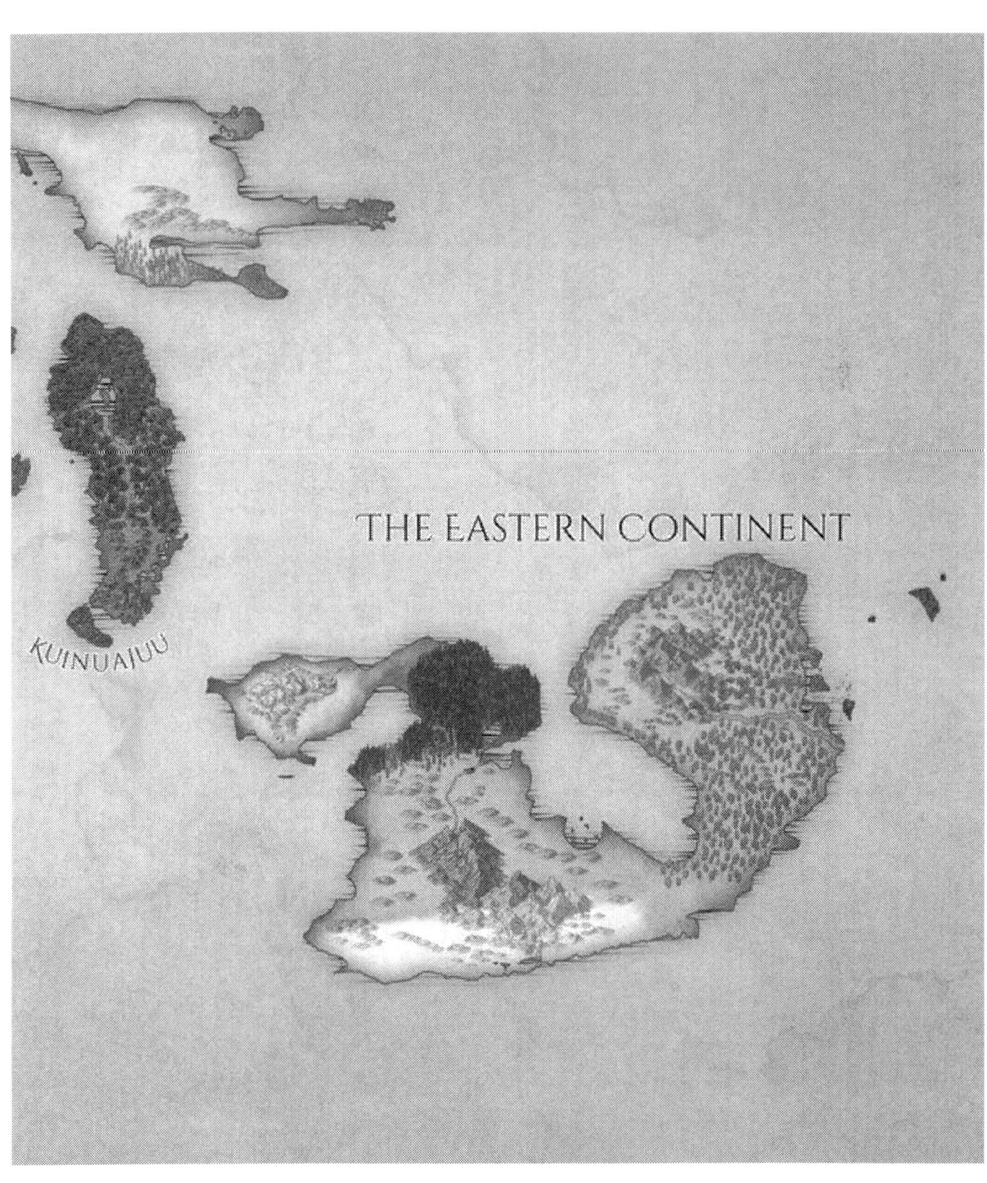
THE EASTERN CONTINENT
KUINUAJUU

Introduction

I'd had the idea for a shared world for a while. I wanted to create a playground for other people to create in. Often, I would read something that really moved me or sparked the inspiration that's chased me most of my life. It would lead to a short story or a novel idea, but I couldn't write in the world that inspired me with the same freedom as the original creator. Many times, there are worlds I want to explore not only by reading what the original creator envisioned, but also by my own creations and additions to the world. Ultimately, and with good reason, those creators want to control the worlds they created.

So, for a long time, the shared world idea sat in the back of my head with a kind of "wouldn't it be nice" tag attached to it. And I went about creating my own things, writing novels and stories that, for the most part, only I would read.

I met Julie Leahy in November of 2011. We were both writing novels for National Novel Writing Month at the local library. I'd like to believe that we both kind of knew, even in that first meeting, that we were going to be together. But because we were both who we were, we pined for each other for years. We helped form a local writing group in that time and surrounded ourselves with wonderful creative people. We were all of us creating worlds and showing them to each other, but only in the walled gardens most people are used to.

Finally, in 2014 we started dating. In 2017, we got married. About three weeks after that she was diagnosed with stage four cancer.

Our life became an escape after that. We were running with our creative lives, both of us trying to write as much as we could both together and as separate authors. In that space—with both of us delving as deeply as we could into each other's worlds and collaborating to make space for a lifetime of creation in just five years—the idea for JUNO came to me again.

On June 1, 2021, my wife, Julie Leahy Eavenson, passed away.

She was an amazing teacher, partner, and artist. And in all those capabilities, she tried to instill creativity and positivity in the people that she met.

A month after she passed away, still deep in my grief, I decided to try and create something to honor that part of her. I created the JUNO blog on my website. I reached out to people who I knew shared the creative spark Julie and I both reveled in. And I found so many gracious people to offer up their time and creative energy to this project. JUNO became not just a way by which to remember her, but something others could find creative soil in. Eventually we added open submissions to the project, and finally this anthology you are reading right now was born.

I would very much like to thank our first round of contributors. C.R. Rowenson, who created our original solar-based magic system. Bill Tracy, the founder of our three sentient species and our first historian who created most of the events on our current timeline. Katie Cordy, who created our first art pieces featured on the cover and inside this anthology. Nick Bright and Brent Lambert, who created our divine pantheon. Without them I don't think we would have had the momentum to make it this far, and I'll be forever grateful.

I hope this world of discovery and creativity is one Julie herself would love to create in, but I know for certain she would be excited for all of you to join us in the World of JUNO. Please come to WorldofJUNO.com and contribute your own part of our growing world. Let these first stories serve as inspiration for your own. We hope to see you there.

—Daniel Eavenson, October 2022

5 *The World of Juno*

The Observers and Solar Magic

Time: From the arrival of the Observers to this solar system until the beginning of prehistory.

JL1372 – Report Log
Day 2K

This is Primary Observer, identification JL1372. Our preliminary survey of the system currently waiting on primary designation is now complete.

The sun. Currently designated as simply Central Helios, is blanketing the system with power. Not simply the solar energy of common stars, but with the power to move beyond the common laws of physics and probability. Through the light of Juno's single star, the impossible becomes the ordinary.

Our analysis can only guess to the paracausal nature to the energy released by the star, but we assume it must be exotic to some extent. Whether the energy will cause spontaneous change or whether there is purpose to the release we cannot say without a significant amount of data.

While the strangeness of the light of Juno's star is unique in the universe, it is also, quite simply, light. Light means life and heat, and so it is that the strangeness of Juno is often met the same way. Absorbed into the firmament, flora, and fauna of Juno. Just as they soak up light and turn it into growth, the power of Juno's star slides in and under and around the light, burgeoning and bristling in the cells and the veins of the world and its children.

We don't yet know what effect the power inherent to the light of this star will do but we wait with eager hearts and minds to see what becomes of this unique world.

JL1372 – Report Log
Day 375M

Finally, a result. My scans of the system around Juno have finally shown results other than normal interstellar content. It seems that the metals in the closest asteroid belt of the system have abnormal crystallin formations. At last, the local cosmology is reacting to the exotic energy of the star. It only took a few hundred million days.

The crystals are mostly of iron and nickel, as those are the most abundant resources in the asteroids. But I have seen evidence of gold and tungsten growth as well. The energy is encouraging the alignment of the molecules to provide for collection and retention of the sun's energy. This includes the heat and light retention normal to the material, but also to the exotic energy. The effect mostly consists of collection, and some of the crystals have grown quite large, relative to the usual minute crystal structure of these naturally occurring metals. Paradoxically, though perhaps perfectly normal at the energy source's origin, the size of the crystal is not directly relational to the amount of energy stored.

Having brought some crystal structures in for analysis, we can make assumptions on the impact this is likely to have on Juno and the life beginning to develop in that last few 1.9-M.

Though the metallic nature of the material would suggest fractal growth patterns, instead things have progressed per organic growth. This might mean the energy itself is more compatible with organic structures, and forces metallic objects into similar natures. We will look for upcoming reports from analyst BT1272 and the efforts to catalog the surface of Juno.

```
BT1272 - Report to Observation Supervisor
Day 10,186M:
```

In the sun-drenched plains of Juno there now live many animals, lithe and fast, soaking in the exotically charged rays of the sun. Most of the creatures on this planet live in the daylight, though there are those that skulk in the night as well. This planet has wrought a unique feature on its diurnal denizens: "Kuh," a clear membrane able to divert the blistering rays of the sun into a more beneficial use. Some animals have many, all over their bodies, while others have few. Most who live in the day have learned to harness the sun's energy for many uses, including releasing bright flashes of light, or a burning ray to ward off predators. They may also heat areas of their bodies to remove invasive insects trying to suck the energy from Kuh. Still other animals can sap what is stored in a membrane for regeneration of wounds or even rarer, heal others. There are those who feast on plants, while others depend solely on the sun's energy to live. Very few of the diurnal animals have a need to eat other moving creatures. That is left to the night's children.

Plants on Juno also have rudimentary Kuh—though simpler than the animal version—developed solely to convert sun energy to nutrition. They cannot release energy as animals can, but from observations, the plant Kuh often seems to be the tastiest or most nutritious part. Because of the resource-poor ground of Juno, most roots do not store nutrients within. New plants or seeds will burst forth from Kuh on the parent plant, either falling to the ground nearby or carried away on the wind. Small insects who feed on the energy of plants are vital to reproduction, by mixing energy from different plants in their reproductive Kuh.

However, when night falls and Juno's sweltering, unique sun vanishes from the sky, the nocturnal predators appear, larger beings that use various other means to catch their prey. They don't have Kuh and may even be burned by sunlight. Instead, they take what they need by trapping diurnal creatures while they are asleep, sometimes rising from tunnels built underground to surprise their victims. Many night creatures are blind or have undeveloped eyes, but their other senses are excellent, especially echolocation and vibration mapping. Even when awoken in the day, these powerful beings are still dangerous, rising up to kill when land is disturbed, plants are pulled up, or trees are felled.

Time will tell how life develops in complexity on Juno.

11 *The World of Juno*

The Species and Gods of Juno

Time: Prehistory (PH). It is many billions of years since the solar system formed, and some unknown fraction of that time since the source of the sun's exotic material arrived at Juno from another aspect of existence. The Observers arrived later, witnessing the development of life on Juno.

PH 1,000–2,000: Kuhifadi/Uchafumlaji emerge, created by the gods.
PH 1,900: Akkakuh fully merges with Juno's sun.
PH 2,000: Onukuh/Unzulaja created.
PH 50,000: Hirolajak and Ergalfadi created, death comes to Juno.
PH 70,000: The first Ngisikaa gains sentience by pooling memories of others.
PH 90,000: All other gods have been created.
PH 125,000: The gods walk among the sentients.

Katie Cordy

The Kuhifadi

```
BT1272 - Report to Observation Supervisor
PH 20,583, Day 45:
```

One clever animal has risen above its origins, becoming more that its progenitors while thinking of ways to outwit the nocturnal predators, finding greater use for the exotic matter—dare I call it "magic"—given freely by the sun. The Kuhifadi share a name with the all-important sun-membrane, as it is that on which their civilization is based.

The Kuhifadi as a people are dark, almost blue skinned, with transitions to a golden, sun-baked color around their membranes, of which there are many. There are Kuh scattered around the body, though mainly on the hands, feet, fingers and toes, chest, back, cheeks, top of head, and under the eyes. Where animals simply process extraneous heat from the sun, the Kuhifadi continually search for new secrets to their magic. Their Kuh leaks magic in the visible spectrum, making a charged Kuhifadi's form literally glow, but the Kuh can be covered with a special type of black-out fabric that stops any solar leakage. While most Kuhifadi are dark-skinned, some lighter-skinned people exist in very northern and southern longitudes. But all have thick strands of hair, growing mainly on the top of the head and a few other places. There are several Kuh on the tops and sides of the head, and hair does not grow there. Kuhifadi generally don't let their hair grow long enough to obscure the Kuh.

The Kuhifadi spend most of their lives unburdened by concepts of what gender roles a particular person may play in society. When anyone can shoot a beam of fire at a rampaging night-beast, or sooth an unfortunate burn, there is less pressure to say some members are not suited for combat, and others not suited for raising children. In fact, when deciding to reproduce, a couple or trio must absorb much energy through their Kuh first. They then trade energy from a special regenerative Kuh in the lower belly. The energy release is quite pleasurable both for the "Releaser(s)" (he/him) and the "Gatherer" (she/her). The Gatherer then gestates a child within that special Kuh until the membrane ruptures and releases the child in a font of energy. This is the only Kuh with the ability to heal after rupturing, allowing a Kuhifadi (normally they/them pronouns) to have more than one child.

Kuhifadi have never worn many clothes, except as needed for protection and modesty. The more opportunities for their Kuh to gather sun energy, the better, and often animal leather includes the membranes of that animal, strategically placed so the Kuhifadi's Kuh can still receive sun energy. Sewn or otherwise fabricated cloth will also include added animal membranes or plant membrane equivalents.

The Kuhifadi tend to build above ground or on stilts to avoid the ever-present nocturnal predators. They prefer to be in the sun whenever possible, replenishing their reserves of magic. This leads to open, flower-shaped floor plans. Traditionally guests are brought to the highest point of the dwelling as a measure of ensuring their safety. Most receiving rooms and guest areas are located at the top of buildings.

The Uchafumlaji

BT1272 - Report to Observation Supervisor PH 26,421, Day 12:

Where there are creatures of the daylight, there are also creatures of the dark, and just as the Kuhifadi did, another species has risen above their fellows. The Uchafumlaji are evolved from large nocturnal predators lacking the Kuh, who survived by tracking sleeping diurnal creatures and trapping them so they couldn't run away. Contrary to what one might think of creatures that move in the dark, the Uchafumlaji are not always concerned with stealth. They prefer intelligent tracking and traps, and cunning inventions.

The Uchafumlaji are massive—one and a half to two times the height of Kuhifadi (and larger than your average Observer as well). They have powerful hands and feet they use to tunnel through dirt, and they are very intelligent, when engaged in conversation. Contrary to the Kuhifadi, their skin is thick, pale to albino, and covered in armored bumps and scales. Their head is thick and rounded, somewhat like a porpoise, good for tunneling through the ground. Standing in the magical sun for too long will cause them pain from the solar energy beating on their skin. This is, in fact, why diurnal animals evolved the Kuh in the first place: to manage the harsh sunlight.

These massive beings are separated into four genders, two of which are solely for reproduction and are rarely seen above ground. The other two genders are both referred to as “they” or “he” and while one gender—the ufriach—is more suited to digging, the other—the chugundach—is generally smaller and more suited to running down prey. Evolutionarily, the two types would work as teams to take down animals.

Lacking the excess energy from the sun, nocturnal creatures such as the Uchafumlaji are generally slower to reproduce than diurnal ones. They find various ways to do this, often using an exchange of built-up bodily fluids, but this happens deep in the lower levels of their cities by the reproductive genders, and is rarely spoken of.

Katie Cordy 2022

The Ngisikaa

```
BT1272 - Report to Observation Supervisor
PH 75,957, Day 284:
```

After many years of searching, I have discovered one final sentient species. They are Juno's odd creatures out, rare and ephemeral, existing on the edges of civilization. These are the Ngisikaa, fragile, glass-like creatures resembling a crab body with a squid attached to the top. While their eighteen appendages (eight legs and ten upper tentacles) might prove off-putting to other species when they finally meet, their whole bodies glow with solar energy in a beautiful display, as every surface on their body can absorb that energy, unlike the Kuh.

The Ngisikaa seem to be evolved from a unique offshoot species in the genetic record almost erased by a meteor impact (see cross-referenced report by RG1212). There are only two remaining types of these creatures: one animal (ngisikaa) and one sentient (Ngisikaa). The sentient Ngisikaa are much brighter than their non-sentient siblings because they have unlocked a method to crystalize the highly energetic solar energy into memory modules. This one accidental discovery caused the uplift of the first few sentients and their eventual civilization.

These creatures do not have a concept of genders per say, as they reproduce by pooling memory crystals from donor sentients into one of the non-sentient ngisikaa in a kind of natural uplifting, until it gains sentience. The ones involved in this process are considered female, heralding the elevation of a new member of their society. The rest of the species is genderless and uses xie/hir pronouns to refer to themselves.

While the Ngisikaa do not have the Kuh found on almost all other diurnal animals, their crystalline skin has a different method to defend against the solar rays. Directly under the translucent skin is a layer of crystal that converts the magical solar energy into engrams of thought, constantly capturing what the individual experiences. Their entire body is capable of this transference, even down to individual tentacles. In the non-sentient version, this conversion is only used for nutrition.

Nearly all Ngisikaa currently live on one small island between the two main continents of Juno. Because of their unique reproduction, the main body of their species is restricted by the regions in which the non-sentient versions can survive. Because of these restrictions, they have even less technical development than the Kuhifadi, and much less than the Uchafumlaji, but because they constantly store their experiences, the Ngisikaa have fantastic memories and calculating abilities.

Kimmasi: The Remembered One

NB0218 - Report on God of Memory (unverified)
PH 93,862, Day 67:

We have allowed the creature, which has identified hirself as Kimmasi, entry to our observational station in the Asteroid belt of the Juno solar system. It has been difficult to keep Kimmasi in the areas we designated and cleared for hir presence. Xie has escaped hir minders on several occasions and been found inspecting various, and sometimes sensitive, locations on the station. On at least one occasion the entity was seen wandering on the hull of the station in complete vacuum. There does not seem to be any malice in these diversions. The entity seems to be as curious about us as we are about hir.

Kimmasi appears very similar to the Ngisikaa species of Juno, however, xie is much smaller than the average specimen that we have so far observed. Like all Ngisikaa, Kimmasi has an array of crab-like appendages for movement and tentacles for interaction. Unlike those creatures, Kimmasi has at least three times as many appendages, at least fifty-four according to scans, though the number seems to fluctuate perhaps according to Kimmasi's direction or some other characteristic as yet undetermined. Each appendage is tipped with a knife-like edge and dagger point, formed from the memory crystal common to sentient Ngisikaa colonies.

Conversing with Kimmasi is...disconcerting. Often it seems as if we are remembering a conversation that has already taken place rather than having an active conversation in the present. Though many have reported and recorded audible conversation with Kimmasi, the entity does not seem to possess an orifice for aural communication.

I have encouraged BL2004 to allow the conversation of the interview to flow somewhat naturally, if possible, to avoid the connotation of an interrogation.

`Interview conducted by BL2004:`

BL2004: Thank you for agreeing to this interview. Perhaps we should begin with how you define yourself. Do you consider yourself a god?

Kimmasi: We do not have this word.

BL2004: A divine being. An entity that has been created outside the normal evolution of their environmental habitation. Commonly with powers and abilities far outside the norm of other species within the same environment.

—Kimmasi does not respond.—

BL2004: Do you have a reason for coming to this facility?

Kimmasi: To learn. To experience. To greet new friends. To teach as well.

BL2004: What do you have to teach us?

Kimmasi: History. To start. Then more. Juno should be recorded. Cataloged. Memorized.

BL2004: Were you always as you are? In your current form?

Kimmasi: I exist. And have always done so.

BL2004: Right...you pre-date life on Juno?

—Kimmasi does not respond.—

BL2004: Do you know why "Juno" is the same in all languages?

Kimmasi: Because it is the same, regardless of observation. *—flagged for follow up investigation—*

BL2004: Where would you like to begin? What part of history would you like to discuss first?

—Note from NB0218: *At this point in the interview Kimmasi pierced one of BL2004's external communication ports with a bladed tentacle. Before it could be removed a massive data transfer occurred both in BL2004's internal memory and ship memory stores. We are still working to decipher and catalog most of this data. BL2004's status is currently in a continual diagnostic mode. Kimmasi has been returned to the planet Juno.*

27 *The World of Juno*

Akkakuh: The Light of the Sun, The First

NB0218 – Report on the source of the exotic solar material
PH 93,862, Day 92:

After the download of information from the entity Kimmasi, Observer BL2004 began to audibly narrate many entries they were given. In an attempt to maintain the information in the format received, I, NB0218, present this:

Akkakuh is not a native of Juno. He remembers the darkness from before heat and light and mind defined the universe. Many believe he created Juno from the deep loneliness of those memories. He nourished life on early Juno, but his power was too great. Often, early life forms crumbled to ash in the wake of his divine presence.

So Akkakuh, feeling both grief at the loss, and the memories of loneliness, set out to lessen his touch on the new planet. He merged with Juno's star and the strange energies that touched our world from beyond. He became formless and yet all-encompassing of form. He suffused himself into the world that soaked in his light. But still the strength of his power was corrosive to any who sought to absorb his life-giving strength. And so, he brought forth the Kuh. The fold of exotic-matter that allows for life to hold his gifts and the powers of Juno's star.

When his all-powerful presence is perceived away from the star, he has the appearance of one of the Kuhifadi but with skin of a bright yellow. At times, looking upon him is as looking upon the sun with uncanny light leaking from his form. Often, he is seen with an array of arms that radiate from his body like the light of the sun. In his chest, is a single large Kuh membrane. It is said that his presence fully charges any and all Kuh around him, and so he is often sought by those who seek power and the use of Juno's magic, or for healing, to those that have damaged or exhausted the power of their Kuh.

Onukuh: The Love of Life, The First Child

```
NB0218 – Report on the first apotheosis
PH 93,862, Day 134:
```

After Akkakuh abandoned his physical form, and sought to generate life and the propagation of the Kuh, he found such actions were now too much for his diminished capacity. Though with his full power this would be trivial, such power often destroyed the life he created as he brought it forth.

To bring order and leadership to the world, he created a descendant. He chose a form similar to the fledgling sentients of the Kuhifadi. With a need for greater power than a mortal, he suffused Onukuh's form with a multitude of Kuh—nearly covering her entirety. Finding a need for diverse opinions he gave his child two heads. Problems started immediately.

Onukuh did not feel the sense of purpose in her existence that Akkakuh had. Managing life on Juno was her job. She felt that her role was as guardian, but she had no love for her charge. Often, she would secret herself away from the light of the sun for a moment of solitude that might last centuries. The result was a permanent change to Onukuh's personal expression of self. Lambent skin tones faded into a pale nearly white shade.

Onukuh has been said to enjoy the adjudication of life on Juno, but she has no love for the individual creatures of the world, unlike her father Akkakuh. She will extinguish her own existence before she allows life to end on Juno, but at the same time she has allowed predation to flourish and for the powerful Uchafumlaji to expand their reach beyond their original environment. The history of Juno is littered with the apathy of Onukuh.

Unzulaja: The Night Serpent, The Slithering Dark

```
NB0218 – Report on the need for balance
PH 93,862, Day 206:
```

As Akkakuh created, and his creations lived longer, he found he had to rest. During this time the light of the star would fade from the sky and darkness would move across the face of Juno. So as Onukuh moved with the light and guarded the world of the day, Akkakuh believed a guardian of the night was also required.

But Akkakuh knew little of the night, for he was a being of light. He spent an hour contemplating the night as one of Juno's moons eclipsed him. From that meditation slithered Unzulaja. A serpent, with great black wings, and shining obsidian scales, emerged in the shadow of the moon. Along her head and down her back, spines flexed and twitched with a thin layer of Kuh connecting the spines to her flesh. As she came into being, she turned her eyeless head about, tasting the air for the light of the day.

Akkakuh looked upon his new child and immediately loved her, for that was Akkakuh's way. For long years the two would speak when the moon that gave Unzulaja life was full. Unzulaja would regale Akkakuh with stories of the life growing in the night while Akkakuh slept. In the light of that full moon Unzulaja would glow with purple light so Akkakuh could find her.

But between their conversations, Unzulaja found the Uchafumlaji. In secret, she nurtured their growth and encouraged their predatory nature. As the Uchafumlaji learned to hunt other sentient species of Juno, Akkakuh repeatedly warned Unzulaja to curtail the brutal nature of her favored species, but Unzulaja, with her great fangs and many rows of teeth, found the night should always be full of danger and hunger.

So, the rift between night and day grew, until Akkakuh and Unzulaja's relationship was defined only with hate.

The First Age of Juno

Time: Before First Contact. Two sentient species vie for dominance on the sun-drenched plains of the Western Continent of Juno. One lives in the light—the Kuhifadi—and dabbles in magic from great Akkakuh. The other—the Uchafumlaji—lives in darkness and deals in cunning and traps. Little do they know, they are not alone on this world, and there are more lands beyond what they can comprehend.

BFC (Before First Contact) 35,000: Kuhifadi begin working together to fight the powerful nocturnal creatures.

BFC 25,000: Uchafumlaji hunt Kuhifadi along with other diurnal creatures.

BFC 10,000: Larger Kuhifadi tribes created.

BFC 6,300: Uchafumlaji connect their tunnels into large underground cities.

BFC 6,000: Mages emerge from the Kuhifadi, inspired by Obarikaa.

BFC 5,863: Ngisikaa communal memory is developed, possibly direct from Kimmasi.

BFC 2,600: Kuhifadi gain the upper hand for the first time over Uchafumlaji in their constant wars.

BFC 1,200: Kuhifadi create permanent cities on stilts.

BFC 0: First contact with the Ngisikaa.

```
BT1272 - Report to Observation Supervisor
Names among the sentients of Juno.
BFC 32,564, Day 25:
```

Kuhifadi

A Kuhifadi will have a "baby name" given to them at birth. Once they gain adulthood, they take parts of one or multiple progenitor's names and add it to their own.

"Baby Name" syllables: Ku, Ta, Fu, Fa, Eh, Ha, La, Ma...

"Borrowed" syllables: Mwa, Ba, Ra, Hana, Di, Son, Una...

Full names: Kumwaba, Fuhanason, Tabadi, Mamwara...

Uchafumlaji

Uchafumlaji often need to identify themselves in darkness, in underground tunnels, and over long distances. Their language uses a type of clicking echolocation, and this appears in their names in both high-pitched and low-resounding utterances.

Syllables: Ji, Tcha, Kii, Ca, Uun, Laan, Foo, Zik, Woo, Qi, Gun, Doo, Vii, Wun, Chu...

Full names: Tchakiiuunfoo, Jiviikiiwun, Qijidoochu, Viicakiitchoon...

C.J. Hosack

The Line Between Light and Darkness

BFC 24,815

I stand at the edge with my toes on the line of darkness. One step over and I am in the forest. The elders forbid it. The forest is for Uchafumlaji only: those who dwell in the dark. But there...just there in between those first few trees are the ji berries. Pink and heavy in their juiciness. I can smell their sweet scent on the air. I lick my lips while my stomach grumbles. My gaze shifts down to my feet again. It's not that far, just a few steps and I'll be there. I could run right back out...unless I see a paka flower. The elders say it has been ten years and it is time for the paka to bloom again. I saw one once when I was little. They are dark petaled, rimed with a kind of glowing bright blue color, but when you bring them out into the sun—ah! What a light show! I want to see it again. Someone braved the forest then. Today I want to be the one to bring it into the light.

But that line...

It's creeping farther from me as the sun rises straight over my head. I take a step forward and I don't stop. My shaking hand snatches the berries and shoves them into my mouth—the sweet flavor exploding on my tongue. How something so sweet can come from the dark I do not know, but I fill my pouch with as many as I can carry. Through the branches I see a flash of glowing blue. Could it be? And so close to the forest's edge! I tremble all over with excitement. Forgetting everything, I step deeper into the darkness.

The brambles of the berry bushes scratch at me, but my eyes are focused on the blue. I almost trip over a root rising from the ground, but my gaze does not waver. I make it to the flower and gasp at its beauty, even in the dark. The light from the blue lines of the flower highlights the furry softness of the petals. The center glows a pale yellow like the sun. I think it's smiling at me. I smile back. Reaching up, I grasp the flower at the bottom of the stem. This will be a glorious day in the village when I return with a paka flower!

I pull it from the plant. It comes away easily, but the glowing stops. I am plunged into darkness. I turn around, but I don't see the path back the way I came. Panic floods me as the bushes rustle. Something is here with me. I swallow hard. Should I say something, or stay still? The rustling gets closer. There's a clicking noise coming from the undergrowth. I pull back my sleeve and lift up the Kuh on my arm, trying to see. Their glow is soft, but it glints off eyes.

"Ah!" I yell.

The eyes disappear.

"Turn the light down," a voice clicks.

"What?" I ask.

"Too bright," the voice says.

I pull my sleeve down. "Now *I* can't see."

I feel a presence beside me. Cold, but solid. As my eyes adjust to the darkness, I can see the creature is all white, almost glowing white, and taller than me.

"Who are you?" I ask.

"I am Qui of the Uchafumlaji."

I stumble backward, tripping and falling on my rump. One hand clutching the flower to my chest.

Scrambling I try to crawl away—to get up and run—but a cold hand grasps my arm. I open my mouth to scream, but clammy fingers close over my mouth. Half of one finger is missing; I can almost get around the fingers to scream.

"Shhhh," the Uchafumlaji says.

The bushes make a rushing noise like the wind blowing through the trees. A musical string of clicks sound. I think I recognize the sound of the name Qui in there somewhere.

"I'm here," Qui says. "I thought I smelled something. It was nothing."

The clicks from the bushes sound irritated.

"I know it's a privilege to be invited on this hunt so young, I'll be there," Qui says. "And no, my ideas are not silly. Someone in power believed in them or we wouldn't be here." The growl in Qui's throat at that last bit makes me tremble.

I don't know why Qui doesn't answer in the singsong clicking language, but I am grateful I can understand.

The rustling moves away, and Qui lets me go.

"It's dangerous for the Kuhifadi in the forest. Come, I'll take you to the light."

Qui leads me tripping and stumbling back toward what I'm hoping is the edge of the forest.

When the light begins to shine through the leaves, Qui stops.

I glance back into the dark forest, thinking of the hunting party. "Why are you helping me?"

"You shouldn't be here in the dark. You are yet young and small, and the hunters will make easy prey out of you." Leaves shift in the breeze making Qui's hand almost glow as it wraps around my hand and the flower it's holding. "In the light there is power. In the dark there is power. Where the two meet, magic happens."

The hand leaves mine with a tingle that I think must be magic.

"I have hope. I have hope that our peoples can make magic together," Qui whispers. "Keep that flower out of the light if you want to save the show for later."

I tuck the flower into my vest. I look up to offer my thanks, but Qui is gone.

* * *

My feet rush me back to the village as fast as they can carry me. I'm going to be late for the sun ceremony. Today is a special day when they will infuse the Kuh Amulet of Akkakuh with power from the sun. It's important that everyone attends. I've been practicing my singing for many cycles. I think about presenting my paka flower to the village during the ceremony. Everyone will be dazzled, and it will all be because of me but as I scramble up the ladder to our dwelling I realize if I show my berries and the flower to the elders, they will know I've been in the forest. There will be anger on the day of Akkakuh. Instead, I rush to my room and shove the pouch of berries and flower under my bed. I wash my hands and trade my shirt, vest, and knee length pants for a waba wrap, made of tree fibers beat so fine it is soft and see through—so thin it lets in the light, energizing all of my Kuh.

At the center of the village everyone is gathering into the circle. Fahana, the gatherer who birthed me, looks anxious.

"By the light, Ta. Why are you so late? You almost missed the ceremony!"

Fahana reaches a dark blue hand to me. I take it and we hurry to find our place in the circle. We are just in time—the log of a mallet is released against the giant bell. Its ring is pure and clear. My mind empties of everything as the village breathes to the rhythm of the bell's ring. The elders begin the song. At the center of our circle lies Akkakuh's Amulet, held fast by a clawed pole jutting from the ground. With our singing it starts to glow, the sun's light and rays bend to it. As the song swells, the light becomes brighter till it's blinding. I hold my hand up to my eyes. It's too much, even for the Kuhifadi who absorb the energy of the sun in our Kuh. The singing reaches a fevered pitch then a blinding light flashes over the entire village. My thin waba allows in all the power and energy. I feel like I can light the whole forest myself.

Everyone cheers in delight at the sight of Akkakuh's Amulet radiating light. It will be stored and used in times of trouble and darkness.

Musicians start to play and the circle dissolves into dancing. There will be much feasting and celebrating for the rest of the day in the light of the amulet. Fahana hugs me, but the look I'm getting tells me I'm going to be scolded later for almost being late to the ceremony.

"Thanks to the gatherer," I bow to Fahana then rush off to join my friends already dancing in the light. I jump and laugh and spin with my friends, wondering who I should invite to see the light show of my paka flower. There is clapping and singing. Food is brought to the tables. The amulet catches my eye and I joy in its light. It will give us power and keep us safe. I am reminded of how much I love the sun ceremony and wonder why I let myself get distracted and almost miss it. A friend takes my hand and twirls me in a circle.

A tray of food crashes. The person carrying it is lying on the ground. My friend next to me stumbles and falls out of the dance. Something bumps me and twists me around. The sound of the party turns from celebration to confusion. Someone cries out. Dark shapes move through the village toward the amulet.

"Stop them!" the eldest of the village cries, boney finger pointing at a blur of darkness. "The powers of Akkakuh must not be perverted by the dark."

I shake my head. I can't understand what is happening. Blackness envelopes the amulet and several dark shadows turn to flee through the crowd. The warriors of the village give chase. More people are knocked down as the shadows flee. Someone screams. A warrior in pursuit of the shadows breaks a Kuh releasing a flash of light and power. One of the shadows puffs away into ash on the breeze.

I lose sight of the shadows as the crowd rushes forward to watch. I wiggle my way to the front, but the warriors are already far across the field. I can't tell what's happening. My heart races as I wait, wondering if the shadows will return this way to hurt more people. There is a murmuring through the crowd and some are pointing to a blackness in the middle of the field just outside the village. When the warriors begin to return, they stop at the black shadow in the field. They pull away black cloth leaving a bright white heap in the grass. The warriors kick at it.

The crowd gasps. The word *Uchafumlaji* is whispered on everyone's lips.

"The sacred power will be used to power their dark machines," someone says.

The words *abomination* and *blasphemous* roll through the crowd.

The warriors return and report to the elders. The Uchafumlaji have fled with the amulet.

My head is spinning. I had seen Uchafumlaji in the forest not far from here. Were they the ones who had attacked and taken the amulet?

The sound of weeping floats through the chattering voices. The village weaver is crying at the side of the gatherer who recently gave birth to their child. There is blood all over, but no one is moving to heal them. It's impolite to stare, but my eyes won't leave the awful sight. I can't understand why no one is breaking a Kuh to heal the poor weaver's gatherer.

Fahana comes and takes me by the shoulders, leading me back to our dwelling. I don't want to go home, but I don't want to stay either. Once home I pace round and round in a circle. Fahana goes out for a while. I try to settle down for the evening, but I cannot. The darkness brings me fear and dread as it never has before.

When Fahana returns my questions spill out. The answers are grim. The weaver's gatherer is dead. Many villagers were injured by the shadows. I ask about what will be done with the Uchafumlaji lying in the field. Fahana says they were injured fleeing and that I need not worry because without their black covering, they will soon burn up in the sunlight. Justice is served, but the amulet is still gone. I feel its loss. A huge hole in my heart where the joy and power it brought used to fill.

"What will we do without the amulet's power to guide us and protect us?" I ask.

Fahana looks out the window toward the center of the village and the empty pole. Something dark passes over that blue face full of Kuh. It's always been a bright, glowing face, that face I've known so well since my birth. Even when I'm in trouble, the glow of light is always there. No answer comes, just a slow head shake. Even the tips of Fahana's ears seem to droop. I've never seen that before.

I tell Fahana I am glad the Uchafumlaji will die in the light.

Distressed, Fahana draws a bath for me and puts me in it, bathing me like when I was little, singing and stroking my back. Carefully cleaning each Kuh. They cover my body, my arms, my legs, my torso, my face. They are still glowing from the light of the amulet. Fahana cleans each one, carefully reminding me not to break any of them.

"But the warrior broke one in pursuit of the shadows," I say.

"Yes, and it hurt them badly and the Kuh will never regrow. It is gone forever," Fahana says.

I nod. I know this, but I've never seen one broken like that before. The memory of the shadow bursting into ash makes me shutter.

"Come Ta, it's time for bed." Fahana leads me back to my room.

The bath made me tired and sleepy. I suspect some of the fresh smelling herbs in the water may have helped with this. Fahana tucks me into bed, humming. I wonder if Fahana realizes it's the song of the amulet. I close my eyes trying to shut out the images of the day and drift off to sleep.

* * *

When the sun returns in the morning, my friends want to go see the Uchafumlaji in the field. No one has seen one up close before. The elders have warned us to stay away from it till the sun has finished its job, but we can't resist. We take our ball and head out into the field as if to play. It seems we are not the only ones with a similar idea. Another group of villagers is casually walking past the Uchafumlaji. A pathway through the grass has already been trampled down. The villagers kick at the Uchafumlaji. I can hear it groan.

When it's our turn to walk past my friends take the cue from the other villagers and each take a turn kicking the white form in the grass. The Uchafumlaji's moans are becoming weaker. When it's my turn I think of the weaver's gatherer and decide to go for the head. I pull back my foot and the Uchafumlaji covers their head with their hands. I notice one of the hands is missing half of a finger. My brain stops. My blood rushes in my ears. This is Qui, who helped me out of the forest. I was right, they were the Uchafumlaji who attacked. My friends are telling me to kick it hard, but I swallow. I'm so confused that someone who had shown me such kindness in the forest could have done such an awful thing to our village.

I notice now that Qui's eyes are almost swollen shut. Their lips are cracked and bleeding. There are blisters like Kuh all over Qui's body. I pull my kick so it barely touches Qui, but my kick pops a blister so Qui still cries out. My friends laugh, pulling me away to play ball, but all day my eyes keep drifting over to the white form lying in the grass. I wonder how long an Uchafumlaji can stand to be in the sun before they die. I chew the bottom of my lip.

Another group of villagers pass the Uchafumlaji and spit on Qui. Some heading out to work in the fields take a wide berth of the white body in the grass, not even deigning to look upon it. I grow increasingly uncomfortable as all motion from Qui stops. In my distraction the ball hits me in the head. I'm not feeling well so I tell my friends I'm going to find something to eat and leave them still playing in the field. I can't bear to walk past Qui, so I take the long way home around the village.

"Fahana?" I ask the gatherer.

"Hmmm?"

"Have you ever healed someone with one of your Kuh?"

Fahana shows me a broken Kuh on their arm. "Yes, once when you were a baby you were very ill. We thought we were going to lose you. The village healer could do nothing so..."

I gasp. "Does it hurt?"

"Yes, still does," Fahana says.

"I'm sorry," I say.

Fahana smiles, her dark blue face alight with affection. Fahana draws me into a hug.

"I would do it again right now. You are a joy Ta, and your life is precious."

That night my eyes keep drifting out my window toward the field. I can't see it from my window, but I wonder if Qui is dead already. Today was bright and sunny and hot and long. I wonder again how long an Uchafumlaji can live in the light before they die. As I toss and turn, I think of how Fahana had said my life was precious.

Before the sun comes up, I take the flower from under my bed and creep from my room. The light from my Kuh has faded, but I can still see well enough. I hold my arm out over the grass searching for the white lump. It is hard to do in the dim light of my Kuh. While I wander the field, I wonder why the shadows haven't returned. Why they don't come back for Qui.

At last, I catch a glimpse of white in the grass. I approach slowly. A breeze stirs the grass, but the body is still.

I'm too late.

I think about how I had felt, lost and alone in the dark. How I had foolishly let myself be led from the light farther and farther into the dark. I am certain now that if the other Uchafumlaji had found me they would have done to me what they did to the weaver's gatherer. Qui didn't know me but had offered me protection. And my payment for kindness had been a kick to the head.

I feel a tear roll down my cheek. I take the paka flower and place it on Qui. It will show its display to no one but Qui's still form as soon as the sun rises. I wish I could do more. I turn to go.

A ragged wet breath comes from the body behind me.

I freeze.

All I can see in my mind is the village. The image of it in chaos—people bleeding. I wonder if the villagers will hate me.

Justice is served. Fahana had said.

I swallow hard. Would it still be?

I turn to kneel next to the cold white body. Qui takes another difficult breath. I reach out my hand to Qui's chest. My nails are too long, they need to be cut and filed. For once, that's a good thing. I take a deep breath.

I break a Kuh. Light explodes from my hand, escaping everywhere, but I need it to go into Qui. I press the broken Kuh to Qui's chest, using my other hand to cup the light, to channel it into him. I feel the light leaving me. The pain is overwhelming. I've never hurt so much. I fall back into the grass clutching my hand, gasping. I can't breathe right. My breath is coming too quick and too shallow. My lips start to tingle. I am dizzily aware of Qui sitting up in the grass. Cold, clammy fingers take my hand. My hand is wet. The water soothes the hurt. I look up and Qui is weeping into my hand.

"Forgive me," Qui clicks.

"You're healed!" I cry, my own tears mingling with Qui's.

Qui reaches into the grass and pulls out a pouch. He kneels before me, head bowed to the ground, holding the pouch over his head toward me, in ultimate supplication.

"Take it," Qui says.

Gently I take the pouch. I open the strings holding it closed just a bit. Light from Akkakuh's Amulet explodes from the small opening, almost blinding me.

Quickly I close the pouch, clutching it to my chest. Joy floods my body.

"I am sorry. I didn't intend for anyone to get hurt. I thought...I believed in the magic of light and dark working together, but the hunters insisted on stealing it. That was wrong." Qui looks at me with sorrowful eyes.

The sky begins to lighten. I see the paka flower discarded in the grass. I pick it up and press it into Qui's hands.

"Go," I say.

Qui smiles. "I've never seen the sun display of the paka flower."

"Today you will." I smile. "Hurry now, before the sun or the villagers do more damage."

Qui bows again before me. "From this time forth the creatures of the dark will hunt your people no more. I will make certain of it."

Then Qui is gone into the fading darkness.

And I hurt, but it's a good hurt.

Hirolajak - Child of the Night, The Shadow

NB0218 – Report on the second generation of gods, the trickster
BFC 24,203, Day 13:

Observer BL2004 has once again begun to audibly narrate entries from the database bequeathed upon them by Kimmasi. I, NB0218, present this:

As the ongoing feud between Akkakuh and Unzulaja continued, Unzulaja found herself increasingly isolated in the night of Juno. Unzulaja attempted to do what their own creator had done and created a friend. Thus, was born Hirolajak, the shadow. Night's companion. Hirolajak was torn from the flesh of Unzulaja as the eclipse that birthed Unzulaja passed over Juno once again. His form was a biped with dark skin that drank in the light. A shadow that flitted with impossible speed even through the light of day. Though he had the general shape of the two sentient species of Juno, his head was that of the dominant night predator of the northern continent. His thin snout contained large fangs and rows of serrated teeth. His large ears, stuck straight up, and ended in tufts of dark fur.

Though the two became fast friends, Hirolajak did not share Unzulaja's disdain for the day and the attention of Akkakuh. Hirolajak scurried about the world seeing all there was to see and meeting all there were to meet. Both god and mortal, animal and plant came to know the presence of Hirolajak. For many he was a misfit or a nuisance. For many of the gods he was a figure of entertainment. Akkakuh came to love the tricks and jokes of Hirolajak. But for the sentients of Juno, he has come to be a creature of misfortune. Hirolajak has grown to love manipulating them into various comedic situations, rarely to their benefit. Indeed, among the Uchafumlaji, bad luck is often referred to as Hirolajak's Fun.

Ergalfadi - The Cloak of Death

```
NB0218 – Report on the need for endings
BFC 24,203, Day 42:
```

For a long while the creatures of Juno were immortal. Death was only present through predation and accidental injury. Akkakuh had never accounted for it when first creating the world, and life continued to flourish until the world was near to bursting. It became a time of horror, full of wars over scarce resources. Akkakuh and Unzulaja put aside their rivalry to come to a solution about what to do, but it was Onukuh who suggested the idea of an opposite to Akkakuh's life-giving perspective.

And thus, the Sun and Night pooled their powers to create Ergalfadi. When they first exerted their power on the world, they appeared as a yellowish-green mist that swept the planet and destroyed billions. War ended overnight as the world was decimated. The creatures of Juno had no understanding of the balance being created and simply saw it as an unknown genocide.

Over time, Ergalfadi's form came to resemble one of the Kuhifadi, but with their Kuh membranes formed around their head and body as if in a great hooded cloak. In one hand they hold a sickle that drips with golden blood.

Ergalfadi demanded that the price of their work be their possession of the life forces they took. Along their cloaked membrane jangle many silver bells, a bell for every life they have taken. They saw them as trophies. Akkakuh objected but was overruled by all the other gods. This decision opened a rift between Akkakuh and Onukuh, though it was the beginning of a strong friendship between Ergalfadi and the god of life.

Obakka - The Membranous

NB0218 – Report on proliferation of gods and the representation of the Kuh

BFC 24,203, Day 67:

Akkakuh, after the creation of Death, felt his grip on Juno slipping. He wanted to maintain his influence.

Hirolajak, forever eager to be involved with mischief, helped the sun god devise a plan. He had Akkakuh lie about his power diminishing. The lie prompted Unzulaja to make a play against her longtime rival, a play which backfired.

Akkakuh used the attempted coup by the shadow god to reassert himself and create a host of new gods that Onukuh, Hirolajak and Ergalfadi did not object to.

Obakka, the new god of the Kuh, was among them. As the guardian of Akkakuh's greatest creation, he became like a right hand and son to the sun god. He despises Unzulaja and Hirolajak, thinking the former is a monster, and the latter a foolish child.

He found it very difficult to converse with the sentients of Juno, for though his physical form was a shape they recognized, in general, he was constructed entirely of the membranous structure of his domain. And so, he did not have any definition or common features one might expect. To many, he was a featureless shade which increased the fear of the use of the Kuh in much of Kuhifadi culture. His existence also ensured the distrust of those who possessed the blessing of Akkakuh among the Uchafumlaji.

RG1212 - Report of a meteor strike in the ocean near Kuinuajuu
BFC 14,769, Day 273:

Following on the report by Chief Observer JL1372, I began an assessment of a significant instance of a meteor impact on the surface of Juno.

Initially, I find it notable the meteor struck the smallest landmass on a planet, commonly referred to as Kuinuajuu, primarily dominated by water. Further observation will be needed to determine if any magnetic field or attractive force drew the metallic asteroid to its resting place, or if it is to be credited to pure happenstance. As the Ngisikaa are the primary inhabitants of the island, I hypothesize that their development of culture through the sun crystals may have had something to do with drawing the meteor to them, although this is pure speculation.

We do know that because the Ngisikaa's unique method of attaining sentience is through the connection to their crystal homes, the meteor almost destroyed the local population when it cracked the island and destroyed much of the infrastructure the people had built over the last several centuries. This event caused a great depression in their culture, a dark age of sorts, as previously intelligent beings regressed after having their crystal homes—and therefore, their link to their ancestral knowledge—severed and destroyed. It is interesting to note that the event caused the Ngisikaa people to regress to a point where their "evolutionary path," so to speak, essentially matches that of the two other sentient species' in the world, bringing balance to the geopolitical power spectrum.

Speaking of the meteor itself, it does appear on the surface to be rather mundane—a typical mix of clay, nickel and iron—although my detailed scan of the object revealed some intriguing findings. Of note, the interior of the meteor exhibits the organic growth patterns noted in JL1372's original report.

There are portions of the outer surface of the meteor that have crumbled away and exposed the inner crystalline structure to the exotic stellar radiation. These inner structures appear to have grown out of the pits in the surface of the meteor, similar to the way in which vines will crawl through dark spaces to reach the sun.

The Ngisikaa appear drawn to the meteor. Many who survived have constructed new crystal formations around or even on the meteor itself. The collective that formed near the meteor exhibits the signs of increased intelligence common to those with a sufficiency of crystal memories, but they also show an increased rate of affliction of the "memory lock" members of that species can develop when exposed to too many crystal memories, even if their primary memory stores are rather small. To compensate for this, the community repository for that village is the largest known Ngisikaa repository that exists.

A final note for further study: the sub-structural patterns of the meteor's crystals are very similar to the patterns of memory crystals, even though the material of the substrate is different in elemental composition. Further study may reveal if the Ngisikaa could harness the meteor's structure to store memories in a "super library" of sorts, though how such an experiment could be designed, I won't speculate.

Daniel Eavenson

Fooon

BFC 5,165

Fooon was once again feeling hirself. Recovering from a loss of self was always a slow and foggy process. The memories that constituted the personhood of Fooon often found themselves congregating together in the common matrix of hir pod of other Ngisikaa, but it did require coagulation in a physical form before xie felt like themselves again.

Fooon took an accounting of themselves. Xie was younger than the last memory available. Hir new body stretched out hir tentacles, getting a feel for the flexing crystal still growing under the translucent flesh across hir form. Another of the pod signaled greeting with a rhythmic expression of appendages.

"Greetings. I am remembered as Fooon. May I inquire as to the current date?"

"Greetings, Fooon. I am Bilililili. By my nearest reckoning it is 15 years since the founding of our pod, and 698 since the emergence of our species memory collective from which our pod spawned."

"Hmmm, it has been nearly five years since my last emergence," Fooon said.

"Yes, I'm afraid that your last emergence was killed by one of the night predators. A large biped that was using tools. Witnesses said you had little time to react to the attack. Do you remember the last moments of your previous life?"

"No. And my existence during the interim period is blank."

"That is normal, Fooon. You did not exist. You were dead."

"And yet, I exist now. I remember a previous self."

"You are wondering why there is not complete continuity between this self and the previous iteration of your existence? It has not occurred to me to wonder about the gap previously. It is simply what has always happened since we began to store our memories."

The group paused. And considered.

Tentacles wafted through the air, sensing the air currents that passed through the pod. The gleam of the crystal memory structures played refracted rainbows of light across the group. Soon the rest of the pod joined as well, moving from the beach and the collection of seaweed and crabs they had gathered for the day.

Absently, several of the pod smoothed sand from the others as they resonated together through the memory matrix. The light from the crystals bounced between the gathered pod and back into the matrix. It pulsed and wavered through the air, almost becoming a physical thing. Their minds touched and searched for an answer to a question they had not considered since the founding of their shared memory.

What did it mean to be dead?

It lasted hours and the sun was far in the sky before Fooon gave an audible response.

"I believe that either my existence was removed for a period and then reinstated, or I am not who I believe myself to be. And my identity is only a belief that I hold based on the memories that have been associated within our matrix with the name Fooon."

"We concur," the pod responded in unison.

"We have determined the question but how can we decide the answer? We are the subject of the question, and

I have doubts we can reliably interrogate this question without impacting the answer. We risk bias."

A quiver of irritation shook Bilililili's front two feet. "Is bias so awful? It is merely the impact of our experiences. How else is the world to be interpreted except through such a filter?"

They considered this new question for another hour, and several of the pod returned to the beach and began to bury their catch in the sand so that it could rot to the proper taste.

Fooon came to a decision. "These are both excellent questions, but they cannot be answered together. I will endeavor to discover the meaning of death, and in the interim, think on the answer to Bilililili's search for a determination on the necessity for impartiality, I will search for a third party to arbitrate our inspection of this aspect of our existence."

The pod trilled in acceptance and broke apart, returning to the tending of the matrix and the necessities of the group.

Fooon searched for days. It was difficult, as xie could not travel far from the matrix without risking losing the cohesion of hir current self. The border of hir world was fuzzy. And it was easy to drift out to the extreme and begin to lose hirself before xie hurriedly returned to matrix. It was frustrating to see the other species of hir world free to wander as they wished while hir world could not spread beyond the connection to hir matrix. It was a thing so large now it could not be reliably moved without considerable trouble to the entire pod, and hir current existential search was hardly worthy of the expenditure of such resources.

But eventually Fooon was successful. Far down the beach a biped came out of the sea. It was thrown upon the sand with the force of the tide and left sputtering salt water as it crawled to the edge of the forest. Its skin was a sky blue and covered in growths of Kuh. Several leaked light from small tears. Torn and tattered material hung limply on the big biped as it got back to its feet and entered the forest.

Fooon had hidden hirself in the limbs of a nearby fruit tree. Xie had been using the shadows and hir transparent body to hunt the tree crabs of this coastal forest. Now xie hunted information from this strange outsider.

The blue biped had moved stealthily through the brush and sand until they reached the outskirts of the pod's clearing. They were watching the collection of crystals curiously, as the rest of the pod scurried about tending to the matrix. Fooon dropped soundlessly to the forest floor. The creature was focused on several of the pod coaxing new growth from the matrix. The tinkling of new crystal resonated around them.

Fooon reached out a trembling tentacle and touched the visitor tenderly on one of their Kuh growing from their shoulder.

The shriek from the biped sent the whole of the pod into immediate silence, their tentacles becoming rigid spikes of crystal ready to defend the matrix. The interloper, likewise, had produced a slim bladed shim of metal and was brandishing it about.

"Wait! We mean no harm!" But the creature seemed not to understand hir language. Shrill tones and trembling harmonics seemed to have the opposite effect of hir words. The creature turned to run but seeing that only Fooon was standing between them and their path through the jungle, they ran directly toward hir.

Fooon moved from instincts born not from mind or memory, but the flesh of a creature prone to predation. In a matter of moments, the newcomer was disabled, and their vital fluids were leaking into the sand. Fooon had also suffered several cuts, but none had penetrated beneath the crystal sub dermis. Already hir flesh was knitting together.

The creature whimpered on the ground as the rest of the pod scuttled over to Fooon and their fallen guest. Nervous words were exchanged between the pod as they questioned the best course of action. Over the minutes of their deliberation, the Kuhifadi began to moan and clutch at their wounds. Attempts to assist them were met with more violent swipes of the knife as hir victim tried to crawl away. The pod followed them for nearly an hour before they stopped moving, their eyes filled with tears and cries of obvious pain.

The pod responded with nervous movement and more conversation about how best to aid but an answer was not forthcoming, as xie knew little of the other races that populated hir world.

Hours later the visitor had propped themself against a tree and the pod had wandered back to the matrix and their daily work. The creature's movements had ceased and the sand around it was soaked in its blood, now black after so much time. Even the light from their Kuh had faded, and the coloring of the growths had become dark and sick looking. Fooon risked touching its wounds, and finding no movement or life, xie dragged the body into the forest to keep it from rotting near the matrix.

The corpse gave a shake and Fooon leaped back from it, colliding with a figure xie hadn't seen. A cold shiver ran through hir body and xie instinctively flinched back, trilling in surprise. Stepping from the shadows of the forest was another of the tall bipeds. They were cloaked in a long flowing hooded material that resembled the Kuh, but a dark miasma drifted around them. Their every step was a chorus of tinkling, but the sound was metallic, rather than the crystalline song of the matrix. The two songs clashed in disharmony. A long curving blade in the figure's hand dripped with a golden fluid. It swished back and forth in the air between them. Glints of silver twinkled under the cloak as the figure brushed passed Fooon and sliced at the air above the corpse with its blade.

A shimmer of light and the smell of magic—ozone mixed with summer rain—flooded the area. Fooon stood shocked, hir legs twitching and fidgeting, as a silver bell formed in the newcomer's hand and was quickly stashed beneath their cloak. They turned to walk away when they seemed to consider Fooon for the first time.

"Hello. It's odd for one of your kind to take notice of me."

Fooon shivered in response to the rasping breathy voice of the figure. "You speak our language?"

"I speak all language, for there is no barrier to death. Ergalfadi, at your pleasure."

"Greetings. I am Fooon. Was this one of your kind? We did not mean to kill it and hold no ill intent to your kind."

"No, this was simply a lost soul meeting its fate. And as always, I am here to collect. Have you never met one of the divine? Though I suppose your people have only Kimmasi who shares your form, and xie was never one to seek worship."

"The divine?" Hir voice quavered with delight and awe. "I have only a vague understanding of those that came before us. We have memory of only a few interactions and yes, most notably with the elder one called Kimmasi. Do you have an aspect of authority as Kimmasi is of memory?"

"Death and endings and the passage from here to the hereafter."

"Oh! You are the deity of death and demise. How fortuitous. I wonder if you might help me with a quandary."

"I cannot tarry long, but it seems that your interest has drawn me forth. What is it that fills your mind enough to seek the god of death?"

Fooon laid out the basics of the problem, and the experiences of hirself and hir pod. Ultimately, xie asked if the memories of death could be captured and kept in the matrix to create the complete narrative of Fooon's existence as Fooon.

"Hmmm, certainly your existence is more complex than the other species of this world. But perhaps not so much as you might think. Here, see." They laid out five silver bells on the sandy ground between them. "These are all the souls of beings that have called themselves Fooon. All of them were former members of your pod before they expired. This one"—they pointed to one more tarnished than the others—"had several different identities as xie drifted in and out of the crystal matrix that kept its memories. Often, xie forgot who xie had been and formed other concepts of hirself from memories stored by others, but xie died believing hirself to be an entity called Fooon. Hir struggles for this identity colored the memories to such an extent that it allowed for the reforming of this final identity after hir physical body was no more. This belief is what you now own, though to my eyes you are not the same creature. You are yourself, perhaps a new Fooon, but perhaps I am not able to properly judge, for death has no memory and souls are not the same as minds."

Fooon considered, but after a few moments the god turned to leave. Fooon quickly formulated hir question.

"But what is a soul? It's not something that I can detect myself, save for these forms of them that you keep."

Ergalfadi scooped up the bells and stored them back under their cloak. "Souls are the energy you generate. The imprint that you make upon the world as you progress through existence. It is what will pass on through the ether to what is beyond even my sight, for I am only the god of death and not of what comes after the souls leave my care. But they hold no memory in the way you store experience in your crystals. Souls are the imprints of a life upon the universe and a collection of self without the expression of identity."

Fooon reached out and Ergalfadi handed hir the soul.

"So, this is not me. I had no effect on this soul."

"But its creator left hir memories and you have used those as the basis of your identity. It had an effect on you. To say you are unrelated would be incorrect. But this

Fooon and yourself are not the same, though you remember being them. You are creating your own soul even now and will impress itself on the universe at the time of your passing."

Fooon considered. In that time Ergalfadi faded, likely continuing its business.

Eventually Fooon rejoined the pod and helped the others tend to the matrix. In the days that followed xie shared the memories of hir conversation with Ergalfadi and the nature of death. On the third day after the encounter with the god, Bilililili assembled the pod for a discussion. Fooon stood to the back, but Bilililili pulled them to the center.

"Fooon? Have you learned anything from your deliberation? Have you found a way to remember our deaths?"

"No. I do not believe that it's possible to retain those memories. I have been led to believe that most of that existence is as a small bell inside Ergalfadi's cloak. It is not so very valuable to us.

"I know now that I am not the Fooon that I remember being. Or at least I do not possess hir soul. What xie was after death was not entirely stored within our matrix. Only hir memories. If that is enough to be considered a continuous existence, it will perhaps take more consideration, but in this moment, I do not believe that it does."

The pod stood still, tentacles raised in approbation. After a suitable wait Bilililili turned to Fooon. "Then who do you believe that you are now?"

Fooon, twitching hir tentacles and legs in agitation, turned about three times before shouting hir name. But it was layered in harmonic resonances. Layers of sound that spoke of Fooon in multiple frequencies measured across the time of hir outburst.

The others shouted it back, and then a symphony of names rose from the pod. Harmonics layered hir whole history and the matrix of hir memories behind each name.

In the silence that followed, Fooon focused on this moment of discovery and self acceptance. "I believe that I am who I am now. And that the context of who I believed I was before, does not form the completeness of me. And when I die, the memory of me will add a layer to the conceptual births of our spawn that will continue the building of our pod. I am Fooon, and for now that is enough."

"Well spoken, Fooon," Bililili said.

Nate Battalion

Chulan's Honor

BFC 1,132

Jivikuun's claws bit into the packed soil ahead of him. He raked at the rocky wall, smelling the damp scent of fresh-thrown dirt, the bitter taste of rock chalk in the air, the faint odor of his partner Tajakii's sweat wafting from behind him.

"Ten more paces, then a break." Tajakii's high, small voice cut through the low grating sound of digging.

"Forty," Jivikuun grunted, a momentary silence filling the tunnel as he paused to shake dirt off his claws and roll his hunched, powerful shoulders back and forth in a quick stretch. "We've got hundreds more to go before we're close to breaking through."

Tajakii took the moment of pause to reach farther beneath his partner's feet with a hooked shovel, dragging the pile of dirt back and out of the way.

"Yes, but it's getting rocky," he said, brushing his own smaller claws through the accumulated loose dirt at their feet. "Harder on your claws, and it's been too long since we adjusted course, I need a listen."

Jivikuun grunted, waving his snout back and forth as he considered. He scratched idly at the wall, clumps of dirt falling from the surface mixed with smaller and larger stones.

"Fair enough," he said, turning back and setting his claws deep into the tunnel wall. "Ten paces more."

The two continued their work, digger and puller working in concert to move faster than if they'd both been digging side by side. Jivikuun was an ufriach, big, strong, with oversized claws at the ends of his sturdy arms. Tajakii was a chugundach, small and lithe, well-suited for his task supporting the dig, and trained for completing their mission when they reached their destination.

Ten paces went by in silence, only Jivikuun's snuffling grunts of effort blending with the steady scrape and shuffle of digging and clearing. Then, eleven paces, twelve.

"Hold." Tajakii gripped his partner's ankle, pulling it backward.

Jivikuun wobbled, set off balance, and threw out his hands to steady himself, sinking his claws into the tunnel walls on either side.

"Alright, alright! I'll take a break." He stomped his foot, shaking Tajakii's hand off his ankle and turning around. He set his back against the curve of the tunnel and slid down it, wiping the sweat from the top of his head and down the curve of his neck and back.

"I can't dig," Tajakii said, crouching down and pulling the strap of the water-skin on his back up over his head. "So if you pass out on me, I can't really finish the job by myself. Here."

Tajakii held the water-skin out for Jivikuun, who took it gently in his large hands. His claws weren't sharp enough to slice it, but he had to be careful not to squeeze too hard and puncture it. He lifted it to his lips to drink.

"I'll go back and get the packs," Tajakii said, turning around to bound back down the corridor. He took one leap and was yanked to a stop in midair as Jivikuun in turn grabbed his ankle. Tajakii crashed to the floor, rolling on his back with a growl for his partner.

"What the hell?"

"Listen the way first," Jivikuun growled back, splashing some of the water on his face.

"*Akkt!*" Tajakii clicked his tongue hard on the last sound, causing his partner to wince as the sharp sound echoed up and down the tunnel. "And if I do, you'll have buried yourself trying to dig without me when I come back. Sit down, rest."

He scrambled to his feet, long arms and legs scrabbling in the loose dirt underneath to get a solid foothold. Jivikuun reached for him again, but Tajakii threw himself back down the tunnel, chuckling as he escaped.

"Nah, you stay there," he called out over his shoulder as he disappeared into the darkness behind.

He jogged the hundred paces they'd come on the most recent push. At last, he caught sight of the glow-lamp sitting by their baggage, then the first whiff of the travel cakes Tchagunvii had packed for them when they had set out. Six meals had passed since they left the clan, but they still had plenty of food left, unless they got so far off track they never reached Clan Akaduuk's cavern.

Well, part of his job was to make sure they *did* reach their destination, and he had confidence in both his ability to find the cavern, and once there to convince Chief Akaduuk to join the coalition.

Stooping down, Tajakii put his arms through the straps of the packs. The first slipped over his shoulders and cinched tight against his chest, the second, larger pack resting high on his back. It was uncomfortable to carry while standing upright, but when he bent to walk on all fours, the pack rested at the perfect balance point on top of his shoulders.

A faint sound reached him, a soft rustling sound from back down the tunnel. He stilled for a moment, ears twitching as he turned to face the sound.

He cupped his hands at his mouth and shouted, "Stop digging!"

From down the tunnel, the sound stopped, a growl echoing back in the silence.

Tajakii grinned, clipping the glow-lamp to the top of the bag on his chest and setting off back down the tunnel. The weak light bobbed back and forth as the lamp swung to and fro on its hook. It had taken him longer than most to get used to the shifting light of pack-walking, but eventually he had gotten used to the rhythmic back-and-forth of the shadow, a fact he was very thankful for.

It took him only a hundred breaths or so to make the walk back to where Jivikuun was. His partner was sprawled against the side of the tunnel, raking his claws through the soft dirt and picking out stones. There was a little pile of them stacked next to him.

He looked up at Tajakii when the two were close enough to make each other out clearly in the near-total darkness of the tunnel.

"May we begin again, *my parent?*"

"I'm not your parent," Tajakii said, throwing the packs down and rummaging through them. "I'm just your dig mate." He pulled out two travel cakes and passed one over. "Let's have an early meal, then I'll listen the way."

"You act like you bore and raised me," Jivikuun grunted, taking the cake and crunching into it.

"Yeah, well, I don't really feel inclined to dig the rest of the way to Clan Akaduuk, dragging you unconscious behind me," Tajakii said. "A great impression I will make, casting our vision of peace and asking the chief to join our glorious and powerful coalition, all while carrying my dig partner slung across my back." He took a bite of his own ration. The dry cake crumbled away as he bit into it, so he held a hand up to catch the crumbs and tossed them in his mouth after.

"Would it kill Tchagunvii to bake these just a tiny bit less?"

"Yes," Jivikuun said, finishing his cake and getting to his feet. "I'm convinced he has a mine somewhere and he just digs them out of the walls."

"Sounds about right," Tajakii mumbled, cramming the last of his cake into his mouth and standing as well. He put his ear to the tunnel wall, first the end, then the sides, and finally the ground. They were silent for a long time as he listened.

"Are we too high?" Jivikuun broke the silence, squatting to be closer to his partner, who was listening at the floor.

"Sounds like it. Sounds like they—"

Tajakii fell silent, then popped up from where he was laying. "Back! Get back!" he hissed, pulling Jivikuun and dragging the packs back along the tunnel.

Jivikuun opened his mouth to say something, but then the tunnel floor gave out beneath them. The two grunted in surprise as the floor churned and softened under their feet. Then it fell, taking them both with it.

The thunderous roar of a tunnel collapse trailed off, replaced by the muffled sounds of alarmed voices.

Tajakii's eyes were closed, buried in the dirt, but he knew Jivikuun was nearby.

"I think we're there," Tajakii mumbled through his teeth. The clean scent of fresh dirt filled his nose.

"Shut the hell up," Jivikuun growled back.

The muffled voices changed pitch when the two of them began to move.

"Who's there? Who's there?" A heavily accented voice filtered through the dirt, closer than the others.

"We're here to talk," Tajakii shouted, working to swim through the loose mound toward the voice.

An unfriendly growl was his reply. "How many are you?"

"Enough to bury you if you want a fight," Jivikuun said from behind him. Tajakii felt pressure along one side as Jivikuun powered through the soil beside him.

"Bring it through then, we're ready," came the answering roar.

This is not starting out well, Tajakii thought.

"Wait!" He knew his voice would be muffled by the dirt and the sound of Jivikuun's digging, but he tried anyway. "Wait, we're not here to fight!" He struggled to free himself, muscling his arms back and forth to swim through the pile and out into wherever they'd landed. A dim, greenish glow caught his eye as it filtered through from below, and he reached out to pull their glow-lamp out with him.

He popped out into a tunnel, easily five times the size of the single-wide tunnel they'd been digging. Support beams lined the walls at intervals, with glow-lamps hanging from a few of the beams. Jivikuun stood two paces ahead of him, claws outstretched, facing off with a trio of ufriach a few paces down the tunnel. The three of them looked ready to pounce.

Tajakii rolled out of the dirt pile and jumped in front of his partner, waving the glow-lamp above his head. "I said we're here to talk! Just to talk!" he shouted, backing up until he forced Jivikuun to take a step back, away from the three strangers.

After a tense moment, the trio seemed to relax when no more people popped out of the collapsed tunnel to challenge them.

"Here to talk?" the one in the middle asked, taking a cautious step forward. "What about? Who to?"

"We're here to discuss a partnership, with your chief?" Tajakii mirrored the ufriach, stepping forward and holding his glow-lamp out to see him better. The gray snout pushed out over the lamp, shadowing their face. Jivikuun let out a menacing growl behind him.

"Partnership?" the stranger grunted. He sniffed at Tajakii. "Caving in our tunnels is a great way to start that off. I guess you can at least talk to the chief and *he* can send you away."

* * *

"We don't want your *partnership*." Clan Chief Akaduuk lounged on his couch, the pair of ambassadors standing at a safe distance across the cave, flanked by guards.

"Sir," Tajakii began, "the Kuhifadi are organizing themselves into larger communities with every passing day. As they build larger, more secure cities, we must evolve as well if we're to survive. What will you do when the surface-dwellers can all retreat behind their walls when you surface to hunt?"

"We will dig into their cities and slay them inside their walls. Walls mean nothing to us." Akaduuk leaned forward, the glint of the guttering fire at his feet crackling in his eye. "We will hunt them wherever they are, in the fields or in the towns; and we'll do it without some overlord clan that rules over us."

"Once again, we seek not to rule over any clan, but cooperation, organization. If we have a connected network of tunnels between clans, not only does that facilitate trade between ourselves, but—"

"What have we to trade you? What have you to trade us?" the chief thundered. "We all live in the same caverns, there is no special stone you have that we want."

"Food, clothing, amenities," Tajakii went on. "Your craftsmen have their specialties, as do ours. With the ability to trade, both sides would benefit!"

Chief Akaduuk was silent for a long moment staring at the flickering fire in front of him, long enough for hope to swell in Tajakii's breast.

At last, Akaduuk looked up from his contemplation.

"We do not need your people, your crafts, or your tunnels," he said, standing from his couch and walking across to the railing that overlooked the main cavern area.

"See, we have all we need here." He pointed with one long claw. "See there? My craftsmen are hard at work, able to perform *any* task I ask of them. See there? My warriors, able to defend us and hunt down *any* prey. See there? Our growing rows, bursting with all varieties of food. We don't need your network, and we never will."

Tajakii waited a moment before speaking to be sure Akaduuk was finished. He opened his mouth to continue and realized that under the heat of the chief's ire, he'd forgotten what he had been going to say.

Jivikuun stepped up in front of him to lean on the railing and look out over the cavern. "Will you need us when you're reduced to hunting small game for prey? When the sun-dwellers no longer fear us, how long until they take it into their heads that they should own the caverns too? What if the sun-dwellers—knowing we cannot harm them above—decide to come down here in force?"

Akaduuk stood tall, staring Jivikuun in the eye.

"If that ever happens, we'll show them what it means to be Uchafumlaji—to be darksiders. Now get out of my cavern," he growled, signaling to his guards.

* * *

Jivikuun and Tajakii stood back at the entrance to their tunnel, a gaping hole in the ceiling of the larger tunnel several paces long.

"Where did this tunnel lead?" Jivikuun asked the guards, who had brought them back after the chief finished talking with them.

"There's a lake a short way down from here," the guard replied.

"Do you have much trouble getting water here?" Tajakii said, but the guard ignored him.

"As soon as you get going back, we'll seal it up behind you." He held out a coil of rope to Jivikuun.

Jivikuun took it, the many climbing hooks tied at the split end of the rope tinkling together. He spun the rope in a circle a few times, then hurled it overhand up into the tunnel above. It took a few tries before he got enough of the hooks to catch on something. The two of them scaled the rope back into their narrow tunnel above, then pulled their packs up after them once the guards tied them to the rope.

* * *

"What a waste of time," Jivikuun grumbled as they plodded back down their tunnel. "When the Kuhifadi are all clustered in cities and their small towns are few and far between, Akaduuk's people won't have anything to hunt; they'll be reduced to farming, or hunting smaller prey, which is a waste of time too."

"We can't save everyone," Tajakii said, his head hanging low as he walked behind Jivikuun. "Chulan warned us not every clan would want to be a part of the future of our people. Some people are just stubborn."

"Still feels bad," Jivikuun replied. "Really, we should be digging the network there anyway, we shouldn't have to ask. They don't 'own' the caverns there, they just live there."

"We can't do that. If we start networking to clans that don't want to associate with us, that will just make them hate us more. Eventually, it would lead to a clan war, which is the opposite of what Chulan and our clan dreams of."

"Then we should shun them. They've made their decision; one of isolation and rebellion against their race. Should we find them on the surface, they become the hunted just as the Kuhifadi are."

Tajakii sighed. Many in the clan thought as his partner did. They considered any clans who refused to join the budding coalition as enemies, worthy of being shunned. There were even extremist proponents of attacking hermit clans and bringing them forcefully into the fold.

Chulan, their clan chief, always put down such talk.

"We dig the network to promote peace among our people and solidarity against the sun-walkers, not to seek rule over our brothers or to gain any advantage against them. Each clan must make a decision for itself what road to take. Some will choose to take their people a different way, and we must respect that if we wish to be respected in turn."

The only time Chulan had changed his mind had been when an ambassador team never returned from a mission. He sent others down their tunnel—expecting to find a cave-in—but the scouts followed the tunnel all the way to another clan's cavern, where they found the mutilated bodies of their ambassadors thrown on the ground at the tunnel mouth.

Chulan had led his warriors back down the tunnel. They found the clan chief and all his council and buried them alive, tying their hands and feet so they could not dig themselves free. They killed every person who had participated in the murder, and caved in the tunnel behind them on the way back home.

"Chulan will decide what happens next," Tajakii said, bowing his head to set his eyes on the swaying glow-lamp tied to his chest. "And be grateful you don't have to carry the weight of those decisions on your shoulders."

* * *

Clan Chief Chulan crouched in the gloom of the tunnel, peering out into the twilight. Even now, with that infernal sun sunken behind the mountains, he had to squint to see out. Sitting in the shade of the tunnel's mouth, he waited for his scout to return.

Down the mountain from his lookout tunnel lay a fertile valley. In its center, a city, floating on a lake. The Kuhifadi—the surface-dwellers—believed themselves to be safe from raids, safe from Chulan's predatory people. After all, with a lake beneath and all around, and walls above, where could an attack come from?

Chulan's clan had been ranging farther and farther afield for prey for years now, but it was time for a change. With more and more network tunnels finished and more clans connected to his own, the number of diggers and warriors available was going up each day.

In truth, Chulan's clan cavern was becoming a central hub of travel, expanding into a city to rival those of the surface-dwellers. It was a natural outgrowth of his people's efforts to connect the scattered and isolated Uchafumlaji clans, and one which some clans still saw as a threat to their autonomy.

No matter, Chulan thought, catching sight of the young chugundach scout he'd sent out overland. *If this plan succeeds, it will be undeniable proof that we are stronger together, regardless of our internal power struggles.*

He pushed his face out of the tunnel entrance into the wind sweeping up the mountain and scented the air, feeling the savage heat of the sun on his face. Surface air always felt jumbled. There were too many smells, all moving too quickly, and in too many directions. Not like cavern air, which breezed along at a reasonable pace, giving the nose time to pick out the details. In the horrible wind out here, he could barely pick out the approaching scout's scent, even though he was downwind of him.

The lithe warrior scrambled up the loose shale side of the mountain, careful to minimize the showers of pebbles that cascaded down behind him.

"Tajakii," Chulan greeted him, reaching out to pull him into the narrow tunnel. "What news?"

The chugundach dipped his head in respect. "All surface forces are ready. We don't really have much to do, you know. I think the clan chiefs are having a harder time stopping their warriors from revealing themselves than anything else."

"Point out their locations to me," Chulan said, waving down at the valley below. As Tajakii crept back to the lip of the tunnel to do so, Chulan thought he heard a dull scraping sound of someone approaching behind him. *Good,* he thought, *the timing is meshing well so far.*

"Clan T'eka's warriors are down there at the edge of the southern forest," Tajakii began, pointing out various locations below them. "Clan Viikun is in the shadow of that rock formation. Dar'edda there in that grove and Tadsugan closest to us, at the base of the mountain."

Chulan nodded, catching the scent of Jivikuun behind them in the tunnel. *Nice cavern air, slow and peaceful.* He turned to greet the newcomer. "Jivikuun, are we ready?"

"Yes, Chief, we're a go."

Chulan nodded to Tajakii. "Go, let everyone know we're beginning the assault."

The scout nodded and sprang from the cave, sliding down the mountain, not caring any more about disturbing the façade. Stone and shale slid down with him as he scrambled down—half crawling, half sliding—until he reached the tree line and disappeared.

Chulan turned to Jivikuun. "Have you told him yet?"

Jivikuun shook his head, watching his dig partner and lifelong friend until he vanished into the trees.

"I'm not going to tell him," Jivikuun said, his voice low. When Tajakii was gone, he turned away to lead Chulan back into the tunnels, down to where the real action would be, where the attack would truly begin.

"He believes in our mission, but he's just not willing to do what it takes to truly unify our people. I can live with that; I can shield him from what must be done."

"He'll find out eventually. He'll hate you," Chulan said, his voice low as well.

They walked in silence for a few minutes, until Chulan thought that there would be no reply forthcoming.

"I can live with that too," Jivikuun said, his voice husky with emotion. "But I don't think it will ever come to that. If he and I ever pass this way again, it will be a long time from now."

Abruptly, they arrived at their destination exiting the dark, narrow tunnels out into a larger shaft. The shaft ran at a steep angle, starting at a point just below the surface and extending down in a straight line about two hundred paces, where it angled to one side before finishing in a dead end.

"Hail, Chief," the team of twelve diggers greeted them. Chulan could see the shaft was complete. They were taking down the valuable glow-lamps they'd been using to light the dig and stashing them inside tunnels, then sealing the tunnels behind them. There were more diggers unseen behind every side tunnel, shoring them up for when the plan began.

"How thick is the bottom?" Chulan asked the lead digger.

"Only one pace thick," the digger replied. "We had to dig the angle to put it out at the top of the cavern instead of through the side where they might be able to stop the flow. The end will blow out with the pressure just fine."

"Good," Chulan said, looking back up to the top of the shaft, which had a thick lattice of support beams at the end holding the ceiling up. "Well, let's get it done." He and Jivikuun waited for the diggers to make final adjustments and they all retreated into a side tunnel that ran parallel to the shaft.

"Release the dam," the lead digger called up to someone unseen in the tunnel above them.

No answering shout came back, just the scraping sound of support beams being slid back out of the main tunnel.

A few moments passed, then a thundering rumble filled the tunnel from above. It grew until they could hear it roaring right on the other side of the tunnel wall. Tons of water smashed into the thin bottom of the shaft, punching right through and out into the cavern they had chosen to drain the lake into.

Clan Akaduuk had been offered peace many times. Gifts had been sent, and ambassadors. Year by year they had grown more sullen, more aggressive to Chulan's people. It was too late for them, Chulan could let them stand in the way of progress no longer. He didn't enjoy killing an entire clan, but just like that first avenging of his people he had ordered so long ago, this was necessary.

Now, he would solve two problems with a single solution. Not only would draining the lake show the prey they could never hide from the darksiders, it would also forever rid him and his people of the rebellious clan that had been a stone underfoot for years. It was almost a shame that so few would know of this triumph.

Chulan walked down to the bottom of the tunnel and pressed his ear to the floor. He could still hear the dull roar of the water as it drained out of the lake down into Clan Akaduuk's cavern, but it wasn't loud enough to block out the screaming. The people inside were in a panic. Likely, many would escape into side tunnels, but not the chief. Akaduuk would not survive, Chulan knew it in his bones.

The price of peace was high, and not everyone could stomach paying it, which is why he had hand-selected these diggers for the task. They would tell no one of what had transpired here. Survivors might tell stories, if they ever reached his clan, but that would be a problem for another day.

Chulan felt sorry for the loss of life; but in the end, it was necessary for the good of his people.

* * *

Tajakii slid down the mountain, heedless of the shale and stones falling beside him. It would soon be too late for their prey to do anything but cower in fear. He bounded through the stand of trees until he made out the crouching forms of Clan Tadsugan's warriors, obscured in a depression on the forest floor.

"Stand by to attack, they're starting the plan," he called out, turning as he ran to circle around to the rest of the hidden warriors—Clan Dar'edda, then Clan Viikun.

Finally, he reached Clan T'eka, the last group and the clan he was assigned to fight alongside. Chief T'eka nodded when Tajakii gave the order, turning back to peek out of the tree line at the lake town, floating safely away from them.

"If Chulan can pull this off, I'll be amazed," T'eka said in a low voice to Tajakii.

"It'll work," Tajakii replied. "Chulan is a brilliant leader, and honorable; worthy of being followed."

T'eka bobbed his head side to side. "*If* this works."

They sat in silence for a hundred breaths, waiting for something to happen.

"It's not—" T'eka began, but Tajakii broke in, pointing to the near edge of the lake.

"Look, those rocks were just below the water, I remember them from scouting the town."

"They're exposed now," T'eka noted. "The water *is* going down." He shook his head in amazement, then turned to his band of warriors. "The plan is working, prepare yourselves for the hunt."

After another hundred breaths, the water was notably lower. The lake banks were now exposed all the way around.

"Look, they've noticed," T'eka said, pointing at the walls.

Kuhifadi were clustering along the top of the walls on little wooden platforms built to hold sentinels. They were gesturing at the lake, clearly concerned with what they saw.

"But they don't know why it's happening yet," Tajakii noted. "The longer we wait, the easier the crossing will be and the less time they will have to react."

The chief nodded, but said nothing. There was a distinct glint of anticipation in his eye, a small grin baring his teeth as he watched the prey worry about why their lake was suddenly disappearing.

The bottom of the flattened lakebed appeared obscured through the water. On the other side of the town, Tajakii saw a group of warriors burst out of the underbrush, sprinting down the shallow slopes of the lake shore to splash into the water.

"Alright boys, that's the sign!" T'eka roared, standing up and leaping into a run. Tajakii and his warriors sprang into action a moment later, thundering down the lake shore and splashing into the ankle-deep water.

Their sudden appearance threw the prey atop the walls into a frenzy. Guards with weapons began throwing spears or slinging stones, others scrambled to get down from the walls, whether to hide or grab weapons Tajakii didn't know. It wouldn't matter.

Without the barrier of the lake, the hunters reached the walls in mere seconds, scrambling up the steep muddy banks of the island and sinking their claws into the wall. The people standing above—in their panic—ran out of weapons to hurl down on them by the time they actually could hit anything.

Tajakii set his claws into the walls and pulled himself up. He locked eyes with one at the top of the wall that was leaning over the edge.

The fear in its eyes drew him forward; faster and faster he climbed. The creature froze in terror, watching its death approaching, but could do nothing to stop it.

When Tajakii reached the top of the wall, he vaulted over it, the prey backing away and bringing up its weapon. A single sword could not stand against the hunter. Tajakii swatted it away and pounced, sinking his teeth into his prey. He felt the Kuh—soft membranes the sun-dwellers needed to survive the harsh sun—separate as he bit deep into the creature's throat. Sudden heat from the stored energy in the membranes being released washed over Tajakii as he bit deeper, a satisfying sensation of the kill. Its scream cut off as Tajakii ripped its throat out, salty blood spraying from its neck illuminated by a brief flash of light as more Kuh tore away, releasing all their stored energy.

Tajakii's prey slumped, gurgling its dying breaths. There would be time for the feast later. All around him, a similar scene played out as predator met prey.

Chulan has led us to this, Tajakii thought, letting his prey slump to the ground as he surveyed the scene, reveling in the victory of the hunt. He watched warriors from all clans sweeping over the walls, working together to herd and take down prey. After today, after this grand victory, no clan could resist Chulan's offer, not even Clan Akaduuk. They would finally bring Akaduuk into the fold, proving once and for all their honor and their sincerest wishes for peace.

He watched the victory unfold from his platform at the top of the walls, the salt smell of blood filling the air, the screams of prey, and the howls of victory.

Perhaps when they returned home, Tajakii would volunteer to bring the news directly to Akaduuk. Yes, he would, he decided. Their people must all be united.

With his own scream of victory, Tajakii leaped off the wall and joined the hunt.

BT1272 - Report to Observation Supervisor

Categorization of "The First Age" of Juno, including addendum to "names among the sentients of Juno."

BFC 1, Day 142:

On Kuhifadi:

Before the Kuhifadi had built a civilization in Juno, they were like the other diurnal animals, seeking shelter from the nocturnal predators, and finding their next source of food. The Kuhifadi were never fully dependent on the sun for nutrition, and instead looked for the most nutritious plants to sustain them. Rarely, they would even band together to fight back against the powerful nocturnal creatures. When they succeeded, the group was rewarded with days' worth of nutritious meat to supplement their diet.

Gradually, larger and larger bands of Kuhifadi grew, both from reproduction and from separate tribes grouping together. When this happened, they would share stories of hunts and strategies of how to channel the energy in their Kuh to best preserve the tribe's safety.

Only with the coming of the mages did the Kuhifadi truly rise above the smartest diurnal animals. Once the technique of locking a Kuh and releasing the energy was known, the information passed like a summer firestorm among the tribes. Any without the services of a mage—able to create spells many times more powerful than anything a regular Kuhifadi could do—were quickly wiped out or absorbed into the other tribes. With the mages came better defenses against the nocturnal predators, healing of life-threatening injuries, the ability to construct wondrous buildings, plants that produced bounties, and even more. For the first time, the Kuhifadi stopped their wandering ways and began to settle in cities.

On Mages:

The concept of the Kuhifadi mage comes from their method of reproduction. So the story goes: a Gatherer early in prehistory, after her child's death, tore another of her Kuh in grief and was surprised at the ray of light that shot forth. Though Kuh had been ruptured before in combat or by accident, it was always a chaotic occurrence. The deliberate mutilation acted as a focus for the early Gatherer to control the magic. Other genders grasped the idea and so the mages were born. This is also the source of rumors that mages never engage in procreation or sex for enjoyment.

Mages concentrate solar energy within their body and keep it from leaking by "locking" it in Kuh through a meditative process. They process the magic for a long time in their Kuh to build up their power, and non-locked Kuh can be used for the small magics that all Kuhifadi can do, but in order to practice large magic, a mage must ritually destroy the Kuh where energy has been stored, releasing all the power at once. The destroyed Kuh is incredibly sensitive to light thereafter, meaning the mage must cover themself to keep from being in constant pain from the sun.

Mages disassociate themselves from the other Kuhifadi by often adding Uchafumlaji elements to their names and dropping progenitor syllables, symbolizing their "rebirth."

Mage names: Kuzikcho, Tauunloo, Lakiivii, Mawun...

On Uchafumlaji:

Meanwhile the Uchafumlaji society has grown more in mechanical means than their Kuhifadi counterparts. One might say they have just as much capability in their traps and devices as the Kuhifadi do in using the exotic solar material.

The Uchafumlaji are greater explorers than the Kuhifadi, who prefer to stay in their new stilt-based cities. The underground predators have rapidly advanced their tunnels, now that many of the isolated tribes have discovered each other. Unfortunately, some tunnels are too deep for Observer sensors to probe, and it has been deemed too risky—even with cloaking technology—to enter their deeper warrens. Though the mages can be formidable with their manipulation of matter we know little of, the Uchafumlaji are the greatest risk to our secrecy in observing Juno.

Twice, a Kuhifadi mage has been recorded entering an Uchafumlaji tunnel, though the two species are normally bitter enemies. A combination of the magic stored in Kuh with the technological aptitude of the Uchafumlaji would be powerful indeed. This will be carefully watched in further years for other developments.

On Ngisikaa:

The Ngisikaa sense of self is a fragile one, stemming from a combination of memories lifting a non-sentient creature to one who can wonder about the universe. Their names are similarly as fragile, and one Ngisikaa may hold many names through hir life, depending on hir current set of memories. Non-sentient ngisikaa are never named, as any of them may as easily be chosen for uplift as not. Many Ngisikaa names have repeating or mathematical bases to them.

Full names: Nanana, Ii, Bebeebeeee, Foonoof, Reaer, Laliiiilal, Binalihaiidafinarija...

As the Ngisikaa develop (or possibly re-develop) their civilization on the island continent of Kuinuajuu, they find their identity strongly connected to their library of memories, to the point where they lose their self if they wander too far. Yet Observers note their elder librarians have been researching this effect, and training newly sentient Ngisikaa to develop their own personalities based around the memories they receive, rather than simply reliving the memories. This gives them not only a stronger identity, which lets them range farther, it also allows them to innovate in ways the Ngisikaa so far have not.

As all three species expand, progress, and chart more of their world, it is to be expected the isolated Ngisikaa will begin to integrate into the other cultures. Thus, with the embarkation of a Kuhifadi sailing ship across the inner ocean between the western continent and Kuinuajuu, I have chosen to demarcate this time as the end of the First Age of Juno.

We Observers wait, entranced, for what the future will hold...

The Second Age of Juno

Time: First Contact. It is an age of expansion, when the Kuhifadi and Uchafumlaji—in an uneasy truce—first find the tiny continent giving life to the Ngisikaa. With three sentients now working together, societal complexity increases, and certain small groups, like the Kuhifadi mages, find openings where they may wrest power.

FC (First Contact) 0: First contact between Kuhifadi sailors and the Ngisikaa. There is disagreement over the forms of gods.

FC 300: Last recorded sighting of a god, Dalkka. Other deities had previously cloaked themselves from sentients.

FC 450: Uchafumlaji tunneling breaks into a newly created, very small Ngisikaa settlement in the north of the large western continent. It is a harsh environment for Ngisikaa, and they are at first regarded as barely sentient tools by the Uchafumlaji.

FC 870–990: Mages grow in power, acting as powers behind ruling Kuhifadi.

FC 920–1340: Mages sneak into Uchafumlaji settlements to learn technology. Some are killed, some are accepted.

FC 1061: The Eastern Continent is discovered for the first time. There are strange and familiar plant and animal species, but no sentients, until now.

FC 1150: The worship of Unzulaja comes to Kuhifadi cities, often born by mages. Similarly, there is a cult of Akkakuh hidden in several Uchafumlaji warrens.

FC 1200: Many Kuhifadi let their abilities fade in favor of using the services of a mage.

FC 1325: Underground eruption, destroying a large Uchafumlaji city, Ngomechini, rumored to be from a mage rupturing all their Kuh at once.

FC 1450: Mages are looked down on by the Kuhifadi as a necessary unsightliness, but are praised by some Uchafumlaji as brilliant scientists.

FC 1525: There is limited trade between the Kuhifadi and Uchafumlaji for technology vs. magic. Both sides gain from this.

FC 1600: A few Ngisikaa are found in all major Kuhifadi and Uchafumlaji cities as historians and architects. It is unknown what the Ngisikaa think of this arrangement, but they do it willingly in exchange for Kuhifadi and Uchafumlaji leaving their memory storage locations alone.

Obarikaa - First Child of Magic

```
NB0218 — Report on the nature of magic on
Juno
FC 2, Day 34:
```

Observer BL2004 has begun to audibly narrate entries from the database bequeathed upon them by Kimmasi once more, though perhaps for the last time. I, NB0218, present this:

Obakka never believed that he alone could understand all uses and application of the Kuh. He thought that even Akkakuh, despite his great wisdom, had never truly explored the depths of his own creation. The Ngisikaa—though they did not possess Kuh of their own—had long observed and catalogued its use among the other species of Juno. So, Obakka found the smartest of the Ngisikaa and elevated them to godhood to help explore what the Kuh was truly capable of.

What resulted was a physical merging of the biology of the Ngisikaa and the Kuhifadi. While maintaining the crab-like lower body of a Ngisikaa, it shed the tentacles for the two-armed form of the Kuhifadi. Obakka named this elevated being Obarikaa and, as expected, the new god did indeed see what Kuh could truly do. She was Juno's first sorcerer and spread that knowledge amongst all sentients who walked in the light and could make use of the Kuh. The magical powers of the Kuhifadi were greatly expanded due to his teachings and experimentation.

But among the Uchafumlaji it only expanded their bitterness toward the gods and increased their worship of the night god, Unzulaja. In their estimation, the Night Serpent had been slighted by this new addition to the pantheon.

Dalkka - The Work of Creation

NB0218 – Report on the transition of gods FC 2, Day 86:

Life expanded on Juno after the massive purge during the birth of the death god, Ergalfadi. But Onukuh once again became dull and depressed in her duties. The god of life looked for some relief and beseeched Akkakuh for assistance after her long service and many good works. Onukuh had no problem maintaining life but found no joy in creating new forms of it.

And so, Akkakuh created Dalkka to take over that function for Onukuh. Dalkka took great joy in his work and caused a flourishing of new lifeforms on Juno. Though too zealous in his first attempts, which resulted in his many creations creating a period of calamity on Juno, the mentorship of Onukuh helped him find balance.

The form he took, however, cause quite a stir among the established sentients of Juno. Dalkka's body was made of the darkly colored crystals of the Ngisikaa, but with one head shaped in the likeness of the Uchafumlaji and another in the likeness of the Kuhifadi. Neither species were excited to see their likeness next to the other. Over time, vegetation and many Kuh membranes grew over Dalkka's form, perhaps in some subconscious reaction to the scorn of the younger species and their dislike of his appearance.

Hursagkaa - Love Among the Gods

NB0218 – Report on the need for love
FC 2, Day 182:

Hursagkaa was born from the union of Onukuh and Dalkka, who at one point took their friendship into love, and thus the god was born. Akkakuh was furious at the child's birth and declared that no god of Juno could exist without a function. It would be up to the two gods to determine what portion of their power they would give up. Onukuh took the burden, having long grown tired of Juno by this point, and designated the new child as a guardian and steward for the mortal acts that created new life.

Hursagkaa is fully aware of Akkakuh's disdain for their birth and returns the scorn. They do not openly side with Unzulaja, because of how dangerous the night god made the shadows for giving birth, but they hold no direct animosity towards her.

When taking on the responsibility of reproduction, Hursagkaa eschewed all concepts of gender, and became instead a blending of all. Creatures that observe them often see a reflection of themselves or a vision of their own desires for a mate. But for those who do not experience base attraction or no longer desire relations with others, Hursagkaa appears featureless and without any distinctive gender or sex. In all their incarnations, the appearance of two great rings is always present. Often the rings are attached to Hursagkaa in some way, though sometimes they are present in the background or appear as an uncanny impression of linking and intertwining.

This is the last decrypted section from the Kimmasi's Database. BL2004 abruptly returned to normal function and has no knowledge of their long ailment, but I, NB0218, hope to continue unlocking more of its secrets with BL2004.

Malcolm F. Cross

Elegy Of Light and Shadow

FC 345 (with fore- and afternote dated at CE 240)

Forenote:

Among the surviving texts from before the collapse, those held most sacred by all Kuhifadi who dwell on the Unawadji coast are undoubtedly the prophet Kurana's writings. One of the few facts we may corroborate of the prophet's life was that they were sent into exile by your distant forebear, Lord of Risen Light Kuhadi the Third. This we know from the surviving records of the ancient court, but the historical truth of Kurana is otherwise effectively unprovable. Only their writings survive, and even then, the academic opinion over the true authorship of *The Book of Radiant Water* has begun to lean towards the linguist's hypothesis that it was written by an imitator of Kurana's style at some point after 240 CE.

Kurana is not an especially uncommon name, and due to their exile, they were stripped of all titles of ancestry, meaning that it cannot be proven that the following document was truly authored by the prophet Kurana. Further, as it was extracted as an engram from the remnants of a shattered Ngisikaa memory-store-village, the provenance is extremely muddy. Yet as the most valuable finding of the entire expedition, I find it fit to be the first of our discovered wonders that we present to you.

As an aside, the wild non-sentient ngisikaa defending the store-remnants bore the madness-of-the-end, showing that they had not been given instruction by any sentients since the Final War, and I am pleased to report that their extermination was total and final, as is decreed in the vengeance-law.

My Lord of Dawn and Dusk, Bearer of Night's Lantern and Singer to the Sun with Akkakuh's Voice, with that said and all reassurance that I carry your laws to the edge of light and beyond, I must inform you that the vengeance-law against the Ngisikaa has greatly slowed our progress. Without the aid of our friends from the East, where Ngisikaa live in freedom, we would not have been able to retrieve these words. And perhaps, my Lord, the words themselves serve as a warning should we unthinkingly follow the ways of our ancestors.

The Letter:

Eniwara-Madi—first glint of pink-and-gold upon the dawn clouds that heralds the sun's lifting, my true warmth, my living miracle who carried our light into our little Eba—are the repairs on the old temple's foundations doing any better?

I think of that old, waterlogged wood and the way it sagged, and the night-coldness clinging to stone, and wonder if profaning our glowing dawns with such coldness might not be forgiven by Akkakuh if we could be certain the temple floors would not collapse again in our lifetimes.

Especially if it meant that your work could, at last, be over, and you could travel out to join us. These strange and rocky coasts where little grows would be far more pleasant for your flashing Kuh, and yet, despite their night-dark stone and coldness, there is still great beauty here.

The Ngisikaa are truly creatures of their own land—you have seen the carapaces Mamwadii brought back, but again I must tell you that living Ngisikaa are miracles of glittering light and crystal. Every one glimmers with its own inscrutable thoughts, and among their crystal-gardens it is as though the finest temple-glass has come to life...

I am delaying telling you our news, aren't I? Eni-Madi, I think of you reading these lines and telling me to put my pen with its florid inks aside and to simply write the black truth in black ink, in simple and clear words an architect can follow, and I imagine us laughing again.

I would rather think of that than tell you our news, but to keep you from worrying, we are fine. The tragedy is slight and...yes, yes, black truth in black ink.

Eba chose to cut one of their Kuh—a little cut, on the back of their left wrist. I don't think it has ruptured, I think it will heal, and they claim that if they are to one day be apprenticed to a mage and join one of the academies, they must learn what it is like, but...

I nearly wept. I did not weep, for that would have set a poor example, and it could have made our little Eba weep, and they were so happy with themself.

They were playing a game, you see. With the Ngisikaa child.

I have come with all my talent for language to this blasted isle (perhaps literally—Vasonuna thinks a great rock may have smashed the land and soil away to leave bare stone) to try and earn back some shred of my reputation and standing with the court, but it is for nothing. I cannot translate the Ngisikaa tongue, because the Ngisikaa do not speak.

They are intelligent, oh yes. They have personalities, they are clearly some kind of *people*, but Mamwadii and their traders have only managed to perform their previous trick of bartering fine mirrors for shed carapaces again.

But our little Eba...if they had not cut themself, if they had not risked destroying the power they hope to have as a mage before even gaining it, I would be proud. You would be proud. Perhaps we should be proud.

The game they play with their little friend seems to be something Ngisikaa play amongst themselves, at the edges of their crystal gardens. It is played with pieces of crystal cut and sheared into perfect prisms—Eni-Madi, these glass-squid use hidden beaks to harvest crystal, and if you could hire one it would make short work of your stonecutting.

Eba understands the rules better than I do. The game is about using the prisms to split light into its constituent colours, and using them to cast shadows and silhouettes and patterns. As the patterns build something very much like an image is formed, and each player takes turns arranging things...

The Ngisikaa can simply use their shimmering skin to reflect light into the prisms as they wish—they even glow brightly enough to cast light whenever they choose. A strong, pure white light—exactly like sunlight, not the muted glow and dancing colours of our Kuh.

I wasn't there, but Eba said that they had to have *perfect* white light in order to respond properly in the game with their little friend, and because it was dusk, they couldn't use their mirror. That is why they cut themself, so they could give the purest light to the game with their friend.

They say it doesn't hurt, but I know better.

The thing is, one of the larger Ngisikaa was watching the game. And after that it came up to Hanafu—one of Mamwadii's trading partners—and it arranged its tentacles so like how our little one folds their arms...

When Mamwadii showed it the silks, it opened its arms wide, and bowed the way Eba does when they make a particular move in the game, something about building on their little friend's image to make it stronger? I'm not sure.

Anyway. Eba explained it to Mamwadii, and they managed to trade six bales of silk for crystal-glass clearer and purer than anything I have ever seen, in or outside of the temple. The creature it traded with is now swathed in stretches of silk, adorning it like some manner of vest—the others have taken to calling it Ma-Mamwadii, second Mamwadii.

The curious thing is it now introduces itself as such. It doesn't speak, exactly, it...groans it, in a way. Eba's little friend seems to have a name too—*Iteeti*, which they say means three. I asked them if that meant the Ngisikaa have a language and they say they don't, because they don't need one.

So even if our little one has scarred themself, perhaps they have already earned their place in history with the game they play with their little friend.

I've certainly been useless here, although at least I could bandage our little one—but not as well as you could.

Hopefully you will receive this when Mamwadii returns with it, and have much to tell me in turn, in your simple black words, my love.

First Postscript:

More news, and Mamwadii hasn't left yet. Our little one is fine, just upset.

Ma-Mamwadii tried to sell Iteeti to Hanafu today. Hanafu accepted, and...well, it was all very confusing, but Ma-Mamwadii wanted to take Eba in exchange.

There weren't any threats, wasn't any violence, but I had to use the word I *think* Ma-Mamwadii understands as "precious" over and over again to get it to let go of Eba.

It scuttled away on its many crab-legs, looking—if anything—disgruntled...but I think it understood. Perhaps.

Eba was very frightened for Iteeti—a gang of larger Ngisikaa descended upon it, including Ma-Mamwadii...it seemed as though they wanted to tear the little creature apart, but they performed... I do not know how to describe it. A ritual. They brought one of the misty crystals—the ones swirling with light and energy—and pressed themselves to Iteeti until... Until Iteeti began to speak, after a fashion.

It called itself Ma-Mamwadii until Eba tearfully told it that it was Iteeti, and it resumed calling itself that—three piping whistles—but it seems different, now. It gestures the way Ma-Mamwadii does, using Eba's body language.

It is almost like Iteeti was a kind of pet, or perhaps cattle, and after the large ones were done with it, it became a child? Ma-Mamwadii called it "precious."

"It." As though they are all base creatures. They are people, but I know not how to divide them into gatherers and givers, farmers and smiths, poets and architects.

Eba's last game with Iteeti was a strange one. Eba says they traded cattle and people in their game, back and forth, as though Iteeti was trying to understand the difference. And after they finished their game and Iteeti went off to their village, Ma-Mamwadii came back with a group of smaller Ngisikaa and offered them to Mamwadii for six ounces of gold, each.

Mamwadii talked it—him? hir? —into accepting two ounces of gold each, and gave hir their fine hat.

Ma-Mamwadii now truly looks the part, but I don't understand how the Ngisikaa can treat their children like cattle...or how they could think we would treat our own that way.

Second Postscript:

I am sending Eba home. They cannot stay here. I am sorry, love, I know you are busy (always busy!), but it is not safe here for them.

It is safe for me, of course, because to return home would be imprisonment, and the danger has yet to come close enough to cast its shadow.

Eba will bring you this letter, and I look forward to knowing how much you will smile to see them.

They might refuse to tell you about the last game they played. If they do, I will explain it as best I can.

You remember (you will have read, a few minutes ago) about their cattle-trading game?

The game of light...the little pieces they use, the prisms. Some have symbols, and there is a set of rules by which one player can force the other to remove prisms with one symbol or another... I do not understand, and I have pled with Eba to write down what they understand of the rules. Please, make sure they send those back with Mamwadii.

These rules allow each prism to take on an aspect, and when it adds to the image of light and shadow, especially when a little stone is used to cast a silhouette, these aspects seem to have literal representations. Cattle, the sun, a boat, a man.

Eba and Iteeti made new pieces for the game. Kuhifadi, Uchafumlaji, and Ngisikaa.

It was very elegant—our child showed me the way the shadows cast by the Uchafumlaji were as night-creatures in their pits, hammering at their machines, all sinister edges blocking the light. And the Kuhifadi collected what light there was, casting it broadly and freely. And the Ngisikaa?

Iteeti allowed them to be taken as the Uchafumlaji and Kuhifadi saw fit. Allowed our people of night and day to exploit the Ngisikaa, to grow or shrink across the white field of stone they played their game on.

So many glittering colours, lines of red and green and blue light... Eba said it was like countries at war with each other. But it wasn't like playing a war game like moon-and-sun, it was like poetry.

Eba did not put it like that, but as I watched it was like a great and epic poem following the histories of nations and great people. There, the prism with its red cross, standing like a king and lord as it led its people. Here, the black stone blocking all light standing in the way of progress like some great monster. (Or perhaps like a poet overly critical of his betters.)

Eba and Iteeti played several games like that, all through the day, and I watched them. I tried to understand.

As Mamwadii loaded the seemingly stupid, non-sentient and animal-like Ngisikaa Ma-Mamwadii had given them, in the game I saw Ngisikaa being taken by the Kuhifadi and forced into servitude, acting like clerks or scribes, helping the Kuhifadi. Not cattle, *slaves*.

And yes, as we spread across the world, as we fought against the night and all that crawls in it, we grew strong.

We grew powerful. We became envied by the Uchafumlaji, more and more, until our light became something...worse.

It is not that Eba played the game meanly, or wrongly, they were simply...simply following the way the light had to play through the prisms. Following the logic of the game, step by step, as though it were one of your equations to determine the exact arch a bridge must have.

This much weight means the supports must be this thick, which means this many tons of earth must be shovelled away, and just like your mathematics, it was all inevitable.

Inevitable that the Ngisikaa were caught in servitude everywhere. And they were learning how to be people. People like us, that is. They are their own kind of people, but a people that don't think as we do. But in the game, they learned how.

They learned how to feel joy as we feel joy, they learned how to suffer as we suffer.

And all across the world, as represented by this silly play of light over stone, they suffered in a slavery we led them into. And after suffering a very long time, the Ngisikaa learned *anger*. A madness that reached from the first of dawn's light to its very end—a madness-to-the-end—and one by one the tiny crystal Ngisikaa gathered together and in their rage slew everyone.

Everyone. Uchafumlaji and Kuhifadi alike.

When Eba realized what was happening, they began to cry, and Iteeti watched them with curious dead eyes...only to stroke the back of their arm, where they cut themself, soothingly.

Iteeti made lights, complicated lights. Used one of the prisms that Eba said were meant to represent turns, and xie soothed our child by explaining that what had happened would not happen for many, *many* turns. That it might never happen, if Eba could teach others to understand Ngisikaa the way Eba can understand Iteeti.

But Eba cannot explain how they can read the glittering lights winding through their friend's tentacles, and when

Iteeti speaks, xie can barely use three or four words at a time—like a toddler.

This is no place for our Eba. They are unhappy here, they have hurt themself, and while they think of Iteeti as a friend, there are no other friends for them here. And after today, they're very frightened of Iteeti.

Well, not of Iteeti—of what that game showed them.

I'm frightened too, my love. Frightened, and inspired. I am no longer permitted to write the histories of our Lord of Dawn, but perhaps the history of the game our child played might help us understand what the Ngisikaa are, and what they want.

Eni, hold our child tight for me. Don't let them go, don't join Mamwadii on their return trip. Send as much parchment and ink as you can afford to, even if it is boring and black. I will return, eventually, and at worst we will see each other again when you leave the city to go to the solstice festival on the water—even exiles may attend that, and I promise you, both of you, I will bring a happy story to sing to you, not one of my depressing epics.

- Kurana

Afternote:

If *Elegy of Light and Shadow* is understood as holy prophecy, then we need not reconsider the place of Kurana's texts.

However, if the *Elegy* is merely a retelling of the third game spoken of here, where Eba and Iteeti are almost certainly masked as Child-of-Pink-and-Gold and Three-Glints, then we must reinterpret it as merely a possibility that Kurana feared coming to pass, not a direct prophecy of the Final War that came so close to destroying us all when the Ngisikaa rose up and struck us down.

As a prophecy that speaks of a future that already came to pass, we may ignore the *Elegy*. As a possible shape to events, we must recognize that while such an uprising has happened once, with much misfortune and misery, if we act in the same ways we have in the past, if we make the same moves in the game of empires we play, it is inevitable that we shall see the same results.

If you choose to continue the vengeance-law in your lands, it would speak to your wisdom—for we know the Ngisikaa live as their memories, and they still carry the memory of the atrocity of their uprising. But equally, you might turn your wisdom towards the contemplation of this possible-Kurana's words: the game was not a game of war, like moon-and-sun, but a game of histories, of possibilities. And when the game allowed for cooperation, as when Eba and Iteeti spoke to one another through it, it is a game that allows all to win together by standing as one, leaving no losers, and no one in suffering.

I beg that you find my efforts pleasing, Lord of Dusk and Dawn, wisest of us all, they who carries the sun's goodness and bears Akkakuh's light to all the people and into the dark of night.

- Kulaantcha-Tani, Wise Candle of the Lesser-Light at the school of First Morning Reeds, standing ever ready to serve the Lord of Dawn.

```
BT1272 – Report to Observation Supervisor
On naming of the continents of Juno
FC 1286, Day 266:
```

The large Western Continent is thought of as the birthplace of the Kuhifadi and the Uchafumlaji. It has been known, and will be known, by many names through time and by culture. Some of them are: Ardhi, Hapa, Kuchimbachini, Uchawi, Wanishi...

It stretches all the way from the polar ice caps and through the equator, allowing for an immense range of habitation for the Kuhifadi and Uchafumlaji, and now for the Ngisikaa as well. There are many features and cities along this continent—far too many to name—but below are recorded some of its greatest features and cities:

The Unawadji coast
The Great North Forest
Ngomechini (Mountain)
Masmechino (Uchafumlaji City)
Laanjiwe (Uchafumlaji City)
Kinambani (Uchafumlaji City)
Chulankumbu (Uchafumlaji City)
Dhiamani (Uchafumlaji City)
Uungunqi (Uchafumlaji City)
Juahaki (Kuhifadi City)
Mkubwa (Kuhifadi City)
Mwanga (Kuhifadi City)
Unaowaka (Kuhifadi City)

The Eastern Continent, though colonized later in Juno's development, provides many unique resources for the enterprising sentients that make their home there, and is often known as either Mahalilaana or Kusafirima. Though it is largely in the southern hemisphere and has limited biomes, the flora and fauna there have evolved from different biological pressures. Many are highly prized back on Ardhi.

The Smallest Continent, between the two, is where the first Ngisikaa was uplifted, and commonly bears the name Kuinuajuu. Bearing scars from multiple meteor impacts, and a largely tropical environment—especially toward the southern reaches—it is often used as a place of pilgrimage and reflection, and a repository of learning for the information the Ngisikaa have collected in their ancestral memory storage.

One of the most impressive features of this small continent is the remarkable suspension bridge connecting the larger main island with the small lower island. This feature—and the channel it crosses—is named the Gates of Hios.

Katie Cordy

Ashfall on Jade

FC 1325

Patumba dipped a long claw in the water, feeling the heat radiate upward. For a moment the steam around him seemed to fluctuate and shimmer, like the auroras he had once seen as a child. Disturbed, he grumbled, sounding and looking more like rock than the carefully carved cistern around him. The Uchafumlaji wiped the dripping claw against his thick trousers and remained crouching, despite the pain in his bum knee.

The steam was the same, its bizarre behavior a quick mirage from heat and exhaustion, surely. But the temperature he was not imagining. The water was supposed to be hot, but nowhere near scalding. Today, he was certain that if he had been foolish enough to dip a toe in, he would be crawling back to his partner Lesung with severe burns.

The hot springs were heated by the volcano Ngomechini, which loomed above the underground city he called home. The springs supplied the city's hot water while Tsonga River above provided the cold, fresh water. Small ripples interrupted the cistern's water, disrupting the water's normal flow from the pipes set deep in the hot springs. He pressed a hand against the trembling ground and frowned. Ngomechini would one day erupt again, yes, but the volcano had settled into a dormancy that would last for thousands of years. Generations of Uchafumlaji diggers had felt the volcano's deep slumber, knew this in their claws, in their stony scales, in the marrow of their bones. He had felt this himself for decades, had known until the last minute.

Now every bit of him screamed to run.

He stood and picked up his toolbox and lamp, willing his claws to be steady. Walking across the walkway within the echoing cistern, Patumba wished he had Lesung's hunter sense of smell. Surely, he was just imagining the scent of burnt matches? He unlocked the door to the lower hot spring pipes. The click of the key ricocheted across the cistern and he jumped before cursing at his uncharacteristic fright. There was nothing wrong. He was a worker, meant to take care of the maze of aqueducts and cisterns guiding water into the city of Masmechino. If there was something wrong with the system, he was supposed to fix it, not panic about impossible eruptions.

His lantern cast jagged shadows as he walked down a curving tunnel carved not by Uchafumlaji, but by ancient lava flows. The normal sleepy warmth of the hot springs had changed to a thick heat that pressed up against him as he continued downward, the discontented earth's rumblings periodically shaking through his boots. Patumba stood in front of the door set into the tunnel. He didn't need to put a hand against the door to feel the heat radiating off the wood. There was no need to check on the hot spring's pipes. He could hear them whistling from here, the scent of burnt matches choking as it released volcanic-scented steam into the room. He coughed as his lungs struggled against the invisible gas and turned around to head back up.

Every sign said that Ngomechini was going to erupt.

It wasn't possible. It wasn't. Yet another tremor pushed him forward. What could force a volcano to erupt millennia before generations of Uchafumlaji had foreseen? He thought of the unnatural way the air had shifted, refracted. Unless...it was the Kuhifadi? His people's prey and enemy could do abominable, unnatural acts with the power of the sun. What was a volcano if not the earth's equivalent of the sun? Could they truly twist any entire volcano to their evil machinations? To destroy his people, his city?

Patumba raced upward, his toolbox cracking against his leg, until he burst into the office where his fellow workers met to receive assignments, eat their midday meal, and gossip. The other diggers looked up, easily identifiable by their heavyset brows, broad shoulders, and claws longer than their forearms. So different from the grace and speed of hunters like Lesung. He had to get home, get home to his partner and their daughter.

"Ngomechini is going to erupt," he panted, leaning on the doorframe.

The younger workers tittered. "Sure, fossil," one muttered to his friend. "I'm sure the rubies are turning green too."

"I'm sure of it," Patumba said, clicking a claw loudly on a wood desk to emphasize his point. "Do you not feel it?"

They looked at each other slowly, rolling their eyes in an exaggerated manner.

"And what is causing it," one sneered. "A Kuhifadi mage? Been listening to too many children's stories?" He turned to his friends, raising his claws and making immature noises designed to frighten the very young. They laughed.

Patumba ground his teeth. It was incredibly unlikely—nearly impossible—but Kuhifadi attacks were in their emergency training, if these fools had even paid attention long enough.

"Had one too many shots of ashspit, oh wise one?" Another pretended to take a swig out of an imaginary bottle. "The volcanic almanac must be too blurry for you to read." They elbowed each other, each trying to outdo the other with their next joke.

Patumba glared at them, with their unstained clothes, their shiny tools, their cocky grins. Curse this lazy new generation and their disrespect. He wouldn't waste his breath trying to convince them. He didn't have time.

"Check the springs yourself," he spat, dropping his toolbox as loud as he could. The other workers jumped.

"Where are you going?" one asked as he stormed across the room.

"Home, to take my family to the surface." He didn't look back, letting fear and fury propel him into the city of Masmechino.

* * *

When he and Lesung had become partners, he had carved his lover a towering house decorated with obsidian mosaics. Here the two of them had spent decades entwining their claws, telling stories late into the night, hiding gemstones for the other to find later in their shoes, in a pocket, in the corner of a pillow.

Patumba pushed the front door open, calling, "Lesung? Les!"

He went upward, past the kitchen where they had laughed over countless meals, through the living room where they had decided to adopt Midi, and onto the roof where Lesung stood, hanging laundry.

They turned, startled. "Patumba? You're home so early."

He hugged them before they could speak another word, breathing in their familiar spicy scent. Lesung hugged them back, whispered, "My onyx, what happened? You reek of rotten eggs."

He let them pull back. They were shorter than him, a hunter, lithe and quick. Their claws were not meant for digging like his, but for designing traps and taking the lives of prey. Their emerald eyes sparkled with concern as they placed a hand on his chest. Stones below, he loved them, would love them until every mountain had eroded to sand.

"Lesung, Ngomechini is going to erupt. Soon." He pointed behind them, where the fan at the edge of the roof spun with unusual speed as the steam that propelled it became more powerful. Small dainty dresses and voluminous thick overalls waved on the clothesline, as if encouraging the two to run. "We have to escape."

Lesung froze. "No, that won't happen for millennia. It's been forecasted for generations." Seeing their partner's panic, they continued, "The diggers—you!—would have noticed the signs weeks ago, if not months ago. Look, the bells aren't ringing. Surely, if there was going to be an eruption, the council would have noticed, would warn us?"

Unless the signs were coming unnaturally fast. If he hadn't seen the shift in the air, would he have suspected the Kuhifadi at all? Would he just have shrugged it off as Ngomechini being a bit temperamental, like a sleeping child twitching during a nightmare?

"Please, Lesung, we don't have time. If I'm wrong, you can tease me until the end of my days. Please, we have to go, *now*."

Their breath quickened. Patumba knew they feared change, any break in routine. Meals were always taken at the kitchen table, never in the living room. Bedtimes were only extended for annual holidays. Lesung's entire closet consisted only of three comfortable colors. A threat to everything they knew? The possibility that it would all be destroyed? They were frozen, as if sculpted from marble.

He reached into his pocket, carefully pinching a small tree carved from jade. He had planned to hide the stone at the bottom of Lesung's favorite jar of tea, but now he pressed it into their palm. They stared at the token of love, ran a shaking claw around the minute leaves, and slipped it into their jacket's pocket, right over their heart.

"Okay," Lesung said, face set in determination. "I'll get supplies, you grab Midi."

* * *

Midi was not in her bed for her afternoon nap. Heart pounding, Patumba found her in the small cone-shaped tent he had sculpted when she came to live with them. It had been the only place she would stay in when her parents died until she had run out of tears and finally crawled into the arms of her parents' best friends.

Now, Midi looked at him not with the shadows of her past, but the twinklings of the future. Her grin sliced a chasm in his heart.

"Patty! Is it dinner time?" He always came home in the evenings. Patumba forced a smile and clucked her under the chin with a claw. The small child giggled. Did she notice how the earth beneath them trembled with increasing frequency?

"No, it's not dinner time yet. In fact...in fact, it is adventuring time. You know how Lessy goes to the surface to bring us food?"

"Yeah!" Midi grabbed the toys out of her tent, holding up small brass figurines. "They hunt the Kuhi!"

"The Kuhifadi, that's right." His stomach twisted at the thought of the skinny humanoids. "Well, we're going to go to the surface today."

"Oh!" She leaned forward, both excited and frightened. Her small claws closed around the Kuhifadi figure. "Now?"

"Yes, now!" It came out too sharp and she balked. "Yes, sapphire, now. I know it can be scary doing something new, but you're brave. As brave as Lessy."

"And as you, Patty?"

"And as me." Patumba picked her up, careful not to snag her dress on his claws. He hoped she didn't realize how terrified he actually was.

* * *

"We don't have time to warn the neighbors," Patumba said as he threw food into a bag. Every scale sung with nerves, already imagining the burning of magma. Lesung glared at him over their satchel of hunting supplies.

"We have to," they said. "If you're right, we can't leave them to die."

"Can Nkato come?" Midi said from her perch on the kitchen table.

"No." Patumba kissed the top of her head before grabbing the loaf of bread sitting behind her and shoving it in the bag. His hands shook so badly that he struggled to close the clasp. "We have to go now, Miditenj."

"But I'm hungry," Midi whined, picking up on her adopted parents' fear. "I don't want to go."

"We'll make roselichen cookies when we get back," Patumba lied.

"We can at least knock on doors and yell as we leave," Lesung began.

They were all thrown to the right, crockery flying from shelves and smashing to pieces. Patumba caught Midi as she fell to the floor and Lesung helped them both up. They gripped his arm so tight that their claws dug into his scales.

"I think," Patumba said to his partner, voice shaking, "that the neighbors know something's wrong."

* * *

Uchafumlaji streamed out of their houses, looking around. They pointed toward the silent bell towers, arguing on what was happening. Around them, the grey and black stone city glimmered with candlelight. The vast cavern above twinkled with the wealthy houses dripping from the ceiling.

Patumba pushed through his neighbors, clutching Midi close to his chest. Her claws poked his chest as she gripped his shirt. Behind him, Lesung cried that Ngomechini was going to erupt, that they all had to run.

He didn't care what his neighbors did. He had to get his family to the fastest path to the surface, to the south exit and to safety. Nothing else mattered.

The next earthquake shoved him into frightened strangers. In front of them, a whimsically carved stone bridge that connected the wealthy houses above them fell and destroyed the top story of a digger's house. Patumba untangled himself from the horrified group, checking that Lesung was right behind him as he pushed forward. Their emerald eyes shone with fear as the bells began to ring.

Uchafumlaji screamed and the crowd surged—a wild, terrified river. The currents pressed against Patumba, and he shielded Midi from strangers' claws raised in panic. He looked behind him. Lesung was nowhere to be seen.

"Lesung! Les!"

In his arms, Midi began to cry, a shrill wail that ruined any chance of him hearing Lesung in return. Casting around, Patumba ran up to a building and hopped onto its staircase railing. Grunting, he shoved his claws deep into the wall and used the leverage to pull himself and Midi up onto a high windowsill. He looked over the crowd.

The Uchafumlaji were a stone river, the grey, rounded heads all rushing toward the south exit. He'd had time to grab supplies. These families gathered their children and ran with nothing but the clothes on their backs. He searched among them for a light grey form, slightly smaller than average.

"Lessy!" Midi cried, pointing to his left. There they were, having seen their loved ones perched on the side of the building. Lesung darted through the mob, their grace never ceasing to astound Patumba even now. He climbed down, clutching the stone as another earthquake threatened to send him toppling. Lesung seized Patumba and Midi in a hug before pulling them back into the crowd.

The northern side of Masmechino burst like a dam, a wall of magma punching through the side of the city. Uchafumlaji around him had their mouths open, but he couldn't hear their screams any more than he could hear his own over the blast. The houses built into the ceiling cracked and fell like massive stalactites, tossing their inhabitants into the glowing orange tsunami. The Council Chambers disappeared under the wave; the bells silenced in the roar. Their government, gone. Midi's school, Lesung's favorite tea shop, the sculpture garden where Patumba had confessed his love to Lessy: gone. Red, burning rain fell as more geysers of magma burst from the streets, the explosions echoing deafeningly across the city. Seconds later, a burning wave of smoke and ash washed over the surviving crowd.

Patumba and his family spat ash, tears coursing down their scales from eyes stinging from smoke, grief, fear. Around them, the crowd wailed, pushing toward the south exit that now seemed impossibly distant. They had lost so much time losing each other. How would they ever get to safety?

The south exit disappeared in a boiling geyser of steam.

"No!" Patumba cried as he and Lesung jerked to a halt. The geyser roared, raining down hot mist even here, dozens of blocks away. They crouched, huddling together as the steam was overwhelmed by magma bursting through the newfound hole. Screams rushed toward them as the people once closest to safety drowned in liquid red rock.

"Stones below," Patumba cursed. He would give anything to open the cisterns and pour water onto the magma, hardening it. But there was not enough water, not enough time.

Water. The Tsonga River above them, curling around Ngomechini.

"Lesung!" He pulled his partner close so they could hear over the crowd and Midi. "The service tunnel for the river pipes! It leads to the surface!"

Lesung nodded, entwining their arm with Patumba as he barreled through the panicking crowd. His knee ached, the air increasingly difficult to breathe, and the heat burned his scales. Midi had finally gone silent, coughing into his neck as her tears soaked into his shirt.

"It's okay, sapphire. It's okay," he shouted to her above the roar. He didn't turn back at the sound of another eruption. He couldn't see more destruction, more lives lost. He focused on guiding them through the crowd before bursting into empty streets. If only he had thought of the western service tunnel earlier, a tunnel that he hadn't worked in more than a decade. They might have been on the surface by now. It was a tight tunnel, with no branches to multiple doors to the surface like the south exit. Once entered, there would be no turning back. But it was a chance. A chance at safety, at life. He could hear a few desperate families chasing them, hoping that he knew of some miracle exit.

Over the chasm and its bridge and they'd arrive at the service tunnel. His knee screamed and Patumba pushed it out of his mind, focusing on Lesung beside him, Midi against his chest, and the road in front of them. The empty houses penned them in, toys and shopping baskets discarded on the streets, candles burning and pies cooling on windowsills, all waiting for their owners to return and resume life. Shadows flickered—lengthened and shortened—as the magma cast red light over the city.

The bridge shuddered, cracked as they crossed, stone falling into the black chasm below. Lesung grabbed the railing for balance before pulling Patumba across. His head spun and he couldn't get his breath. His knee buckled and he stumbled, caught by his partner, before climbing the hill to the service tunnel.

Heat blasted the family as magma erupted from the chasm, destroying the bridge and the families crossing it. Glowing comets of liquid rock cascading down, missing Lesung by inches. Patumba pulled them close, trying to shield his small family as they dashed the last yards to the tunnel.

Patumba handed Midi to Lesung before ripping the entire locked door from its hinges, his claws digging deep gorges into the wood. He threw the door aside and took Midi from Lesung, motioning his partner forward. The magma flooded over the chasm, rising quickly toward the tunnel.

The service tunnel was pitch black, but Uchafumlaji had excellent vision, especially hunters like Lesung. Guided by scent and sight, his beloved led them unerringly through the dark, Patumba stumbling behind them. The roars of the magma grew louder, rocks and dust falling on them from the ceiling as the entire mountain shook. The tunnel began to brighten.

Patumba risked a glance behind. The magma was rising rapidly up the tunnel, casting them in red light. His knee wobbled, threatening to give out. How could they—how could he—outrun death? He hugged Midi to him, casting around desperately for any solution to a one-way tunnel.

He could dig, yes. But it was much slower to dig a new tunnel than to run down a preexisting one. There was nothing around them except for stone, magma, and, below them, the massive pipes that brought cold river water to the city. There was no escape.

Unless.

Patumba pulled on Lesung.

"Les, Les. Take Midi." He kissed the top of his daughter's head before settling her in Lesung's arms.

"Patumba—"

"No, diamond. Listen." Behind them, the magma grew closer, the air wavering from the heat. "I'm going to dig below us, right at that pillar. It'll collapse part of the tunnel and open a hole in the floor into the aqueduct. The river will slow the magma and you'll be able to escape."

"Patumba," they cried, grasping onto his arm. "Please, no!"

"Les! Les, please, I can't let you die. I can't let you die here. You're faster than me. Take Midi, take her and run and get to freedom. Please, Lesung."

"No! Not without you! I can't do this without you!"

"You can! You have to!" He pulled them close, holding his partner and daughter. Midi clutched to his shirt.

"Patty! Patty, it's so hot!" she bawled. "I want to go home!"

"I know, my sapphire, I know. I love you, Midi. I'll love you forever." He turned to his partner. "Go. I'll give you the time to escape." He put a claw under his partner's chin, tilting their head up as the tears steamed from their cheeks. "I love you. I love you more than there are grains of sand."

"I love you, too," Lesung choked out, kissing Patumba, their claws entwined. Then Patumba pushed them away, watched Midi stare at him over Lesung's shoulder as the hunter raced down the tunnel.

He turned toward the magma. The waves of ruby, garnet, and citrine rushed forward, the heat searing, burning his scales as it grew closer. Flexing his claws, Patumba ducked his head and tunneled down into the supporting pillar. The floor and pillar cracked—caved under his claws.

He thought one last time of his family, of singing during the midsummer festivals, of cuddling together in the winter, of laughter and joy and love.

Darkness, icy water, heat, endless burning.

* * *

Lesung burst out of the tunnel door set on the side of a cliff, crying into the surface air. Midi wailed, pounding her fists, clawing, crying, crying for Patty. Lesung collapsed onto their knees, holding Midi close as grief rocked their body.

A deafening boom interrupted them. Lesung looked up as the face of Ngomechini exploded, the resulting landslide washing away a burning forest half a mile away. The volcano itself looked as if some great Uchafumlaji had taken their claws and sliced half of the mountain's top away. The cliff protected the two survivors, diverting falling debris, shielding them from harm. The air was black, thick with ashfall. In front of them, the river rushed, grey and wild.

Patumba was gone. He was buried with their city, a mass grave of memories. Lesung shook, wanting to crumble, to join Patumba, their friends, their family, rather than live without them.

Midi curled her head under Lesung's chin, wailing, reminding them not all was lost. Lesung reached into their jacket pocket, pulling out a small jade figure, carved in the likeness of a tree. They held it up for Midi to see.

"Patty wanted us to be brave and to be safe. He'll always be with us, in our hearts. Do you understand?"

Midi nodded, wiping the ashfall off the jade tree. "Be brave."

Lesung pulled her close before standing and following the river downstream toward the nearest town. They hoped the Uchafumlaji there would take in any who escaped the destruction. Choking on their grief, Lesung and Midi started down the mountain. Away from Ngomechini, away from their home, and away from Patumba.

```
BT1272 — Report to Observation Supervisor
Categorization of "The Second Age" of Juno.
FC 1600, Day 27:
```

On Kuhifadi:

Their culture has become a proud one, steeped in ritual and tradition. Many modern Kuhifadi ignore or let their abilities fade in favor of the mages who train to be many times more powerful through shrouding their bodies and concentrating sun energy. There are many rumors about the sect, including celibacy, blinding, pale white skin, ritual mutilation, deviant behavior, and so on. Few of these characteristics have even been proven.

However, the mages allow such rumors to propagate, as it builds the mystery surrounding them, and further sets them apart from their fellows. With the rise of the Order of Obarikaa, the mages have become ever more secretive, working toward their own ends. Many of these are hidden even from us, for their most powerful shields of magic—formed from the exotic matter with which this species has grown to sentience—is impenetrable to Observers.

On Uchafumlaji:

In contrast, the Uchafumlaji societies have grown more egalitarian. They still hunt both Kuhifadi and Ngisikaa—for they are at heart predators—yet they also welcome both into their cities. Most clans have consolidated into large underground collectives, such as Laanjiwe, Chulankumbu, and Dhiamani. These are centers of progress and exquisite craft, rivalling and surpassing the wonders of the sadly destroyed Masmechino.

The Uchafumlaji are fully able to swallow their predatory instinct when trade is a priority. Or perhaps their instincts are merely converted from one to the other. Regardless, they are ruthless in extracting every bit of worth possible from their mechanisms when selling to Kuhifadi who greatly desire a way to ease their lives.

This is perhaps why the mages have started to make pilgrimages to the great Uchafumlaji cities, returning with knowledge of technology accentuating their magic.

On Ngisikaa:

The Ngisikaa have grasped this new age of exploration for them, building new memory storage locations in the north of Ardhi in the west, and in the newly colonized Eastern Continent. Much of their infrastructure is devoted to caring for their non-sentient counterparts, from which they raise new members of their species. Selection of a new memory storage location is a deeply considered question, brought before all Ngisikaa for each individual opinion.

There is much promise to this developing, three-pronged civilization. It remains to be seen what balance may be struck between the species of Juno.

The Third Age of Juno

Time: First Contact, the civilization of all three species continues to expand in complexity, though perhaps also in deception. Although this age of Juno is short, is it filled with much action and uncertainty. It is the time of mages, and of great technological advancement by the Uchafumlaji, and by great memories and movements of the Ngisikaa. Yet all may be for naught.

FC 1700–1825: Mages are in active communication all through the Kuhifadi empire, and underground in the Uchafumlaji collective.

FC 1747: Unknown to the other sentients, a shift in ocean currents has brought a boom of nutrients to the northern Ngisikaa settlement. There are more of the non-sentient creatures than the sentients can control, and the herd has split, some of them migrating southward toward more inhabited areas. They need a new memory storage location.

FC 1821: Several Kuhifadi leaders are assassinated in questionable ways at the same time. All evidence points to Uchafumlaji agents, though this is difficult to prove.

FC 1822: The most free-thinking Kuhifadi cities, Mkubwa, Mwanga, and Unaowaka, close their doors to Uchafumlaji visitors. More isolationist cities begin making plans of war. Protests of Uchafumlaji innocence are ignored.

FC 1827: Mages begin actively governing some cities through coercion or magic in what is now thought of as the beginning of the Darksider Revolt. There is much more coordination in their society than either Kuhifadi or Uchafumlaji knew.

FC 1828: Rumors rise of a major Uchafumlaji city in revolt. Half the inhabitants side with a faction of Kuhifadi mages, and the other half wants the mages exiled.

FC 1828: No one notices the quiet Ngisikaa exodus from the cities of the large western continent.

William C. Tracy

The Tour

FC 1747–1829

I am committing this day to an engram in the hope that I may persuade my mentor and the foremost memory keeper, Nanana, to reconsider.

Perhaps I should introduce myself then, for the one who will eventually absorb this memory and become one of the sentient Ngisikaa. That is how this is usually done, if my memories do not deceive me.

I am known as Tutoo among my village—the Ngisikaa who was almost not uplifted from the herd. The little one who now studies with Nanana hirself, and may one day take over hir position, when Nanana decides to give hir memories back to the great store.

But I lose my train of thought. It is not always easy to direct a memory engram for another. Most are simple daily recollections of what is it to *know*, to *be aware*, to be a *Ngisikaa*, and not a lowly animal ngisikaa. This one is for a particular purpose.

To wit: I have received an invitation in this, the latter half of 1747 FC, as determined by Uchafumlaji timekeepers. It was delivered to our small community by a ngisikaa who was previously kept by my cousin Hinafilanti in the Kuhifadi city of Unaowaka, far to the south. Xie would like me to visit and retrieve hir, to escort hir back to our village. Such an honor! As to why I was chosen, though I have never met hir, Hinafilanti chose the Ngisikaa who directed my uplift, Fuunbibi. As my uplifter was tragically killed by cranesharks eight years past, while wading near the shore, the duty of retrieving my uplifter's uplifter belongs to me.

This journey will add greatly to my knowledge of Juno, and more importantly, to my ability to command respect as one of the memory keepers, whenever I am so deemed knowledgeable enough to take part.

I would have no need to dictate this engram were all according to plan. Yet Nanana, who knows Hinafilanti from many years ago, refuses to see reason and let me leave. Xie says I am too young for the dangers of the world. Xie says, as an apprentice I must watch the herd of ngisikaa and find those ready for uplift. I argued there are plenty of other apprentices to watch those lumps, should any show a spark of reaching for sentience. Yet I am denied. I suspect bad memories between the two elders, but have no recourse. I must "mature before leaving the safety of the herd" and "accrue further years of study." I hope my journey shall be sanctified soon.

* * *

I had nearly forgotten the mechanism for deliberately encoding a memory engram, though I suppose I should get in practice. Keeper Nanana says they will be the primary way of recording my journey.

Ah, but once again, I am ahead of my own thoughts. It is me, Tutoo, once again, though this is the year reckoned as 1762 FC by the Uchafumlaji. Strange to think I may soon be among their number, after so long imagining that very situation while caring for the ngisikaa herd—contentedly munching their seaweed and marshcrabs near our memory depository. It may be smaller than the ancestral depository on Kuinuajuu, as our community was only founded sixteen hundred and forty-three years ago, but it shines as brightly as the one in the memories of my ancestors—those plucky adventurers who drove their herds across the sea on great rafts to reach the shores of Ardhi.

Yet I digress again. I resolve to stay on topic.

No, no, get back in the pen. You are not ready to go adventuring, little one.

Please disregard that last memory, if you experience it. You can see the herd is a little feisty today. We have had quite the infusion of newborns in the past few years, due to a richness of nutrients in the marshcrabs.

I was in fact attending to the latest hatching when Nanana found me and directed me to come with hir to the depository itself. There we partook in the original message delivered fifteen years ago by Hinafilanti. It was quite a surprise when Nanana told me I was to go on this journey! Not only not a refusal, as before, but a command for me to travel! Have I matured so much already? Or perhaps there has been a reconciliation by the elders.

I, of course, accepted at once. One can only count the trees in the forest, the stars in the sky, and the pebbles by the lakeshore so many times while herding ngisikaa before the urge to dump one's memories in the depository and walk out to sea becomes unbearable.

My mission is thus: Nanana says I am essential to experience the landscape of Ardhi, its cities, and its inhabitants. I am charged to record knowledge of the Uchafumlaji underground tunnels and their fabulous technology, the Kuhifadi cities on stilts gracing the southern plains, and the hidden Kuhifadi mages, who cross between the species, learning both magic and technology. At the end of my travels, far to the south in the Kuhifadi city of Unaowaka, I will meet with Hinafilanti, and escort the elder Ngisikaa back home, for xie has been long away from the herd and their memories are extremely valuable to our history.

Upon return, I will give all my new memories to the depository, so others of our kind may know how the continent has changed since the last intrepid adventurer left our village. Was that Li? Or perhaps Kuzikcho. I will have to check the memory depository.

Thus, my practice in creating these engrams. You see already I improve. You have not had to experience my shooing the new fry back into their pen, nor dealing with the belligerent herd alphas. I am certain you have experienced this daily routine ad nauseum, wherever you are in time and space.

I have been allowed to draft three of the herd for my travels, which I duly picked while attending to my chores one last time this afternoon. They will carry their food and mine, and allow for passage of a few trinkets to act as trade for those cities I encounter. I am told the Uchafumlaji are quite fond of ngisikaa legs both for their tasty marrow, and for the crystalline surface, which can be used in many of the creature's contraptions. I must say I am excited to see the large beings for myself. Our village had the help of an Uchafumlaji technologist many years ago—before I gained sentience—who installed the timing gates that control the herd's daily activities with a minimum of interference by the attending Ngisikaa.

I suppose I shall end this memory here. If you are following my entire narrative, the next time you experience me, I shall be on the road to adventure!

* * *

With all the excitement, it has been over four hundred days since I last recorded an engram for you, oh my future descendant.

It's me again, Tutoo! I suppose I should note that three and four are along with me, though alas, one is not.

Hm. Perhaps I need to back up. When last I left a memory for you, I was only leaving my little village, wasn't I? I have experienced much since then, passing through forests and plains, over rivers and through coves to restock our stores of seaweed and marshcrabs. I have marked the shift in stars to note my distance traveled, as well as the difference in holy Akkakuh's passage overhead. I look forward to the greater amounts of direct light during the days as I move to more southerly elevations. Already I feel hardier and more intelligent, taking in more of Akkakuh's light for both sustenance and thought.

But you don't care for this, do you? I imagine you have seen much more of the world than I have, living in the north in my little village. So, I will not bore you with experiences of the great forest of light I passed shortly after leaving, where each tree unfolded great flowers of Kuh each morning to soak in the rays, or the plains of vine-like balbuku, that store their excess energy in fruits the size of my whole body, sloshing with liquid light.

It was, in fact, in one of these fields that we lost one.

Ah. I have not yet explained. One, three, and four are my ngisikaa. I believe I mentioned before I was allowed to draft three of the herd to aid in my journey. As we do not name those who have not achieved sentience, I was left with a conundrum. I would need to address these three individually, at the very least, to know which supplies they carried and to direct them as I traveled. So, I settled on numbering them, for ease of reference.

You may be wondering if I my senses have failed me, by skipping numbers? They have not! For in our party are one, Tutoo, three, and four. I figured there were enough Tu's without adding to their number.

But as to our current plight, it was deep in a field of balbuku vines where we discovered the nest of nyodaji. One didn't even have time to squeal in surprise before the slithering nyodaji had surrounded it and were climbing up all eight legs to the trunk of its body. Three and four had skittered away, thankfully, and I was left trying to decide if I should smash a nearby balbuku fruit against the nyodaji in hopes to stun them.

My decision was taken away, as the slithering things coiled around one, biting it on its tentacles, eyes, and sensitive body. Light quickly leaked out as one fell to the ground and the nyodaji began feasting.

I was not keen on interrupting their meal—as three, four, and I were currently unharmed—though I could see the occasional baleful gaze from the feasting predators. I must admit, I scampered off soon after that, leaving one's body, as well as the supplies it had been carrying. A third of my food stores were gone, as were a few trinkets I had intended to sell.

Ah well, so go the strictures of adventure! I shall forage south toward the Uchafumlaji city of Laanjiwe, and I suppose Tu has now become one!

(That is a little joke, which I hope may translate over any language or cultural drift you, my descendant, might experience.)

* * *

Once again, I have been remiss in my engrams, though there has been nothing more than forests, meadows, rocks, and streams for the last half-year remainder of our journey to Laanjiwe. Even the predators seem scarce here, likely because of our proximity to a large Uchafumlaji settlement. That last is the main reason I record this engram, and I suspect there will be many more in the coming days.

I arrived at Laanjiwe's entrance cavern near twilight with three and four in tow. This entrance to the city was easily recognizable from the steady stream of Uchafumlaji—well wrapped against even the weak evening light—entering and exiting the cavern. Many were finely dressed, not only in the fabrics that covered their bodies, but in the glittering caps on the ufriachs' digging claws and the various instruments the chugundach trackers carried to help them catch game.

I soon found myself in darkness, craning my head to take in the massive creatures passing me by on all sides. These Uchafumlaji are over twice my height, though of course my species is built a bit more horizontal than they are. Inside, the wrappings disappeared, and I could see the gray pebbled flesh of the inhabitants clearly in the glow from my body. It is an unusual experience being the sole source of light (well, one of three) in these caverns. Uchafumlaji were squinting at me, and I made an effort to dim the light expended from my engrams. Three and four are not as bright as I am, as they are ngisikaa and have no engrams.

There were no challenges to my entry to Laanjiwe, and some Uchafumlaji even bowed toward me in respect. I penetrated deeper into the city, beginning to see residences, shops, inns, and places of craft. The number of beings here was daunting, many times the number of Ngisikaa in my little village, and even many times greater than the herd.

All at once, I was frozen by a large Uchafumlaji working at a forge, striking sparks while hammering with much strength at a tiny object. I signaled three and four to hold back—they were always the more responsive of my three ngisikaa anyway—and drew closer to see. The Uchafumlaji nodded to me and drew up to their full height, gesturing at their work. I stretched up on my legs to see what was on the anvil.

Before me was an intricate device, filled with tiny gears and levers, and little brass, iron, and steel cogs that whirled around each other. I was amazed at the force with which the Uchafumlaji had been hammering at the device.

"You speak my language?" the Uchafumlaji inquired in one of the commoner northern dialects.

"I do, if you can understand me," I said, modulating my chiming tones to pitches the creature could hear. I was rewarded with the blacksmith raising their eye ridges in surprise.

"I am called Uunqidoo. Then would you do me a great favor, honored Ngisikaa? I would ask our resident Ngisikaa, but xie is currently busy elsewhere."

"I am Tutoo," I said in response. "And I would be thrilled to help you." I tried to keep the excitement from trembling my joints and tentacles.

"Forgive me," Uunqidoo said. "Shall I invite your two comrades as well?"

I must admit I stared in confusion for some time, attempting to determine what Uunqidoo meant. Then I realized they assumed three and four might be Ngisikaa! I suppose it could be confusing to one not of my species.

"They are ngisikaa, and no matter," I finally said, after dismissing several less politic phrases. "What do you require of me?"

Uunqidoo bowed again, perhaps to hide their continuing confusion, then pointed to the contraption they were making.

"I have seen the analytical power of our resident Ngisikaa, Li, in the past. Would you be able to help me calculate the angular velocity of this oblong cam, as it spins elliptically around this conjunction of gears? It is essential for calculations of lunar eclipses."

The tales of the other species' difficulty with basic calculus seemed to be accurate.

I gave the number Uunqidoo needed immediately, but then pointed out the misalignment between two of the gears that would affect the calculation by three hours on the pertinent night.

Uunqidoo bowed again. "I am in your debt, honored Ngisikaa."

We exchanged a few more pleasantries, and Uunqidoo soon returned to their work, but not before presenting me with a handful of clipped metal bits. I tried to refuse, but they insisted, pressing the dull things on me. Eventually, I gave in, took them, and continued on to find Cousin Li, who had been living in Laanjiwe for many years now, and should be more familiar with the culture here.

* * *

Two engrams in two days! I shall attempt to keep to this schedule. I have met with Cousin Li, an older Ngisikaa missing one tentacle (a forge accident many years ago). Xie is quite busy, being, until now, the sole Ngisikaa in Laanjiwe. After a whirlwind of hellos, xie dragged me by several other workshops and forges in the city, helping with various calculations—the flow rate of an aqueduct, the upper limit of mass able to rest on a new tunnel's fortifications, the dimensions most pleasing to the eye for three cut gems, and the dimensions of several sets of gears for certain city functions. I confess I did not catch the names of all the Uchafumlaji ufriach and chugundach we helped, but we ended the day with even more of the metal chips, which Li tells me are used for barter with both the Uchafumlaji and the Kuhifadi.

Li has put me up in hir spare room, cluttered with odd unfinished projects. We have left three and four with the other beasts in the stables—with detailed instructions on how to care for them—along with a selection of seaweeds and marshcrabs. I fear Li has put the fear of Unzulaja into the poor youth tending the pack beasts with hir precise instructions on how long three and four must be outside each day to soak in light, and what their feeding schedule must be.

I am bedding down for the night, as Li has two nests better suited to folded Ngisikaa legs than the stone planks the Uchafumlaji rest on. We shall see what tomorrow brings!

* * *

I fear my streak has been broken once again. It is ten full days after my last engram. Li has kept me busier than I ever was tending a whole herd of ngisikaa. Word has gotten around in Laanjiwe that there are now double the Ngisikaa available for computation and calculation efforts. I do not know why these creatures cannot calculate such simple equations on their own. Li tells me it takes them far longer, and they must use writing utensils to keep track of numbers! So strange.

I have been asked by a chugundach named Tchajiji three times already to help with a new research project he is attempting. It is a new method of water regulation, to automate the underground gardens of Laanjiwe. Did you know, they even have a seaweed farm here, with marshcrabs nearly as tasty as the ones back home?

I admit I was drawn in by Tchajiji's excitement over his project and even offered a few paltry suggestions myself on how the holding chambers might better withstand pressure if changed to a spherical design rather than oblong. I intend to go back again tomorrow to help Tchajiji's partner Cajiuun, as they are head of the digging crews expanding the city's lower regions. They say they have some other problems I may be interested in.

* * *

Another four days have passed—it is hard to tell time here in the caverns of Laanjiwe, though the Uchafumlaji have special chambers with sunlight reflected from the surface far above by large mirrors. They only come into these chambers fully wrapped against the solar radiation, but Li and I must come here every few days, with three and four in tow, to recharge the energy of our engrams. I have spent nearly every waking moment with Cajiuun, and sometimes Tchajiji. Their insight and creativity are astounding, and they leap from one project to the next. They are very glad of having more Ngisikaa on hand to calculate for them, and Li has given me over to them entirely, in order to handle the rest of the town's problems by hirself. I must rest soon before I fall over sideways with my legs in the air, but I wanted to encode this engram—in case I forget—to say I may stay a short time in Laanjiwe before heading on the next leg of my travels. The Uchafumlaji here have devious minds to create such technology, though they labor over the numerical connections in nature such as the calculus of angles, speeds, and ratios. It is as if they cannot visualize a final product before it is physically built. I can see why Ngisikaa are welcomed among their kind.

* * *

A sad day to encode an engram, but also one filled with wonder for the next leg of my tour around Ardhi. I am resting out in the wilderness once more, a day's journey from Laanjiwe, with three and four by my side in the bright spring sunlight. Early this morning I waved goodbye with all ten of my tentacles to my dearest friends Tchajiji, Cajiuun, Wooviifoo, Gunkioon, and the rest, along with Cousin Li, naturally. Xie is quite perturbed I am leaving, as this means xie will be the sole Ngisikaa in the town again.

No, four, get back here. You're too fat already from marshcrabs. You need not go after every kuhbug and fern jelly.

My apologies. I am out of practice with these engrams.

I suppose I should step back for a moment, anyway. The year is 1783, by our calendar. The last nineteen years in Laanjiwe have been the best of my life, and I have learned so much of the world. I shall dump a selection of my daily memories into another engram, which may be crossed with this one by the following numerical sequence:

441513521485

Quite a clever joke in that number, I thought.

Ah, well, you will see what I mean after reviewing the daily memories. You may note a few stones I have placed around Laanjiwe in a humorous arrangement—ha ha!

Four has grown quite big feasting on the delicacies of the town, though three has kept its trim lines. That only means four is more equipped to carry the extra two boxes filled with the rafu I have accumulated over the years. I believe I have enough to pay for passage the rest of the way south! I have been warned the little metal bits may not hold as much value in Kuhifadi settlements, but then I have also heard rumors that relations between both species are improving, and that messengers are now traveling between cities lower down the continent. I hope I may see one of those above-ground cities soon.

* * *

Winter is approaching as I find the city of Kinambani. It will be good to get underground again. I have sent a young Uchafumlaji runner ahead to warn Cousin Nibeeni I will be arriving a week earlier than I anticipated. I decided to cut short my trek through the great lake region after nearly losing three twice to swift currents in the streams there. The marshcrabs are severely lacking in flavor as compared to those farther north, though four does not seem to mind. I shall put my impressions of that region in a separate engram...

* * *

I am quite glad I have remembered to make daily memories of the most interesting impressions in Kinambani, as I constantly forget to dictate engrams. As the year 1784 draws to a close, Cousin Nibeeni and I enjoy many of the celebrations the Uchafumlaji have created around the end of the year. Those in regions southern to Laanjiwe take their celebrations seriously!

* * *

It is 1792. Cousin Nibeeni has decided to make a pilgrimage back home, much to the consternation of the inhabitants of Kinambani, and I take that as my cue to continue my travels south before I am drafted into more calculations. While this city is interesting, it does not feature nearly as much innovation as Laanjiwe and many of the calculations Nibeeni and I were hired for were of the pedestrian kind—lengths and spans of new rooms, capacities of water reservoirs, and depth of foundations needed.

I have transferred many of my earlier engrams to Nibeeni to take with hir and I hope they enrich the depository sufficiently to satisfy old Keeper Nanana. Though that means I may not remember as much as I prefer of Kinambani and the wilderness around, it is vital the village has as clear an impression of the land around here. I begin to suspect another reason Keeper Nanana suddenly insisted I accept that invitation to go south past enriching the communal memory. I have heard reports through Nibeeni of an explosion in herd numbers over the last fifty years or so—enough that it may prove useful to know which parts of Ardhi can support splits in ngisikaa herd.

* * *

Chulankumbu is a wilder city than those I have visited so far, and the Uchafumlaji are not nearly as accommodating. Cousin Meaem and I spend most of our days together, and must even keep three and four with us! Either through misunderstanding or deliberate malice, the Uchafumlaji here refuse to differentiate between Ngisikaa and ngisikaa. Such indignity!

* * *

I only managed to extend my stay in Chulankumbu two years—enough to see all aspects of the city—and now winter in Dhiamani. This little underground paradise is a current of warm water after Chulankumbu. Cousin Nootnoot, though flighty, is an absolute joy, and we spend the days laughing and singing. I have discovered the Uchafumlaji cannot make resonances like we do, and are quite enamored of our

"Ngisikaa singing," by which they mean the words we say in a higher register. They ask us to give concerts! Though this is merely Nootnoot and I speaking nonsense to each other while keeping to words in our highest register. They reward us with generous amounts of rafu for these "concerts" and it is as easy as the calculations the Uchafumlaji cannot seem to do on their own without aid. Truly it is easy for a Ngisikaa to make hir living in the civilized world.

* * *

As the years pass here, I must admit I become anxious to see more of that other strange species, the Kuhifadi. I have passed many messages of the Uchafumlaji back to my village, but Keeper Nanana directed me to seek out the Kuhifadi cities and their mages as well as the underground strongholds of the Uchafumlaji.

When I happened to mention this to Nootnoot yesterday, xie gave a hearty laugh at my expense.

"Have you not seen the mages in Dhiamani, Cousin Tu?" Nootnoot asked of me.

"Where would I have seen them?" I inquired. Xie pointed out a passerby to me, and I waved my tentacles in surprise.

"You mean those small, wrapped Uchafumlaji? I always thought those were the mysterious breeding pairs the ufriach and chugundach joke about."

"Certainly not. Those are Kuhifadi mages, wrapped head to toe. They are a quiet bunch, keeping often to their lower caverns and workshops."

Today we traveled deep underground, into small passages an Uchafumlaji would have to duck through or enter on all fours. I had not been this deep in all my years away from the village.

Down here, the constant ringing of metal from the forges changes tone to a resonant, vibrant, chime. Nootnoot and I perked up as we heard sounds that nearly had language in it.

We saw a pair of Uchafumlaji around a forge, their pebbled gray heads a contrast with the smaller person between them, wrapped completely in rags and fabrics, as an Uchafumlaji must when outside. The two larger ones were striking a device on a table with precise hits from hammers tiny in their hands. Yet alternating with every strike from the hammers, the wrapped person put out a hand, and lighting shot from a bleeding wound on their arm. It was the only surface visible on their body, and it held light like the inside of an engram.

The person caught sight of us soon after we entered the room and gestured a stop to the Uchafumlaji. They approached with none of the deference I have come to expect from an Uchafumlaji, and bent down so their wrapped face was directly before mine. All that was visible were bright yellow eyes, surrounded by a tinge of blue.

"Greetings, honored Ngisikaa," they said. "I am Fubazik of the Order of Obarikaa. I have heard of your travels through the Uchafumlaji lands, and of your help in various cities. Would you like to see what we are making?"

At my excited acceptance—over the years, I have gotten much better at controlling the trembling of my legs in anticipation—they led me to the forge implements which was made of a highly polished metal of some kind. The Uchafumlaji called it "star forged."

The device resting on the anvil seemed similar to many of the devices I had seen in the underground cities, down to the very first one I had seen in Laanjiwe. It was all teeth, and gears, and mechanisms, and by now I could recognize where some of the parts had been manufactured. However, this device held differences. It glowed with an inner light, which I assume had been transferred to it by the mage.

"This is a new invention we have been working on," Fubazik said, gesturing to their unnamed compatriots. "With the additions I have made, it should require no recharging from the sun for years at a time, enabling it to be used in the tunnels connecting Uchafumlaji cities."

I had heard whispers of these tunnels, yet never seen one. I thought I had recorded every bit of the cities I had visited, though I realized now I had been greatly mistaken.

"And what does the contraption do?" I asked.

"That is thanks to Uchafumlaji ingenuity, and a bit from listening to you sing, honored Ngisikaa," Fubazik said. "It is able to engrave vibrations onto a barkwax roll. Our latest iteration enables a user to both engrave and play back the recorded words or sounds."

At the mage's request, I drew closer to the device, and saw that indeed within the collections of teeth and gears was a barkwax roll, with impressions indented on it in patterns. It took only a little calculation to determine the encryption from reality to recording, before I started humming an Uchafumlaji lullaby I had heard before.

"That's it exactly!" Fubazik exclaimed. "You are nearly a recording device yourself!"

"A simple pattern," I said dismissively, but I could not control the tremble as I reached out to feel the device with four of my tentacles. It was like a Ngisikaa engram!

We spent some time discussing how the mage was able to power the contraption through magic, and I learned quite a bit about how the Kuh operate—those membranes on the Kuhifadi which are so similar yet so different to my own body. I wonder if engrams can be converted to hold magic as the Kuh do?

Eventually, Fubazik invited me to travel farther south to the stilted city of Juahaki. It is here where the Order of Obarikaa have their citadel. Fubazik says the mages hear all of the happenings on Ardhi, and will be excited for my arrival. I am excited to meet them.

* * *

It is early in the year 1805, and today I finally entered the great city on stilts: Juahaki. I left three in the care of minders at the gate, having sold four back in Dhiamani. It seemed to like it there, and had become far too fat to travel, anyway. I had some trouble climbing the rope ladders used to enter the city, though soon got the hang of it, having to use most of my tentacles as well as my legs in a clumsy swarm up the rope. Three would have had no chance.

I converted most of my rafu to larger denominations and other currencies that would be better used among the mages. With all the conversions, I was left with a much smaller number of boxes to strap to three. I had sent back much of my earnings to my village in any case, as I had no need of all the wealth I had accumulated over the years.

Cousin Nootnoot departed around the same time as I did, to trek back to the village. Xie had been gone many years, and wanted to catch up with old friends, so xie volunteered to carry messages and memories from me as well. Xie also carried the designs I encoded for several fascinating devices which I hope may serve my village well.

Juahaki stands high above the central plains of Ardhi, shining in the sun. Ladders are packed with Kuhifadi coming and going. It is such a change to see people out in the sun who are not wrapped from head to toe tip! I have, of course, seen many Kuhifadi by now, passing into their lands from those the Uchafumlaji traditionally live in, and I never stop wondering at the way their Kuh operates. So similar to my own memory engrams, yet so different in purpose. I suppose it makes sense, as the Uchafumlaji have neither, yet have other benefits to their species.

However, this is the city of mages, and a significant portion of the Kuhifadi are wrapped just as Uchafumlaji would be. It is interesting that so many let the mages produce any small magic needed. I know that all Khadafi can do some magic, though only the mages are adept at it. I will need to look into that more while I am here.

I believe I caught sight of several of the larger species as well, though they slipped into dark shadows before I had a good look.

On the lower levels of the city—for just as the underground cities have multiple levels, so do these, though they are built upward on stilts—I encountered a group of Kuhifadi raising their upper limbs into the air and shouting in their odd tongue, which is so unlike the pitches of the Ngisikaa or the clicks, grunts, and hand signals of the Uchafumlaji. There was another Kuhifadi, draped with brightly colored cloths, speaking to the crowd. I had to dig deep into my engrams to revisit memories of this southern dialect, though the pronouncement slowly came into understanding. It seemed one of their popular leaders had recently died—or possibly been killed—and had left no one a memory of what happened. It struck me as quite an uncivilized way to go about succession plans. I suppose the Uchafumlaji have the same issue, but even if a Ngisikaa dies away from the village, there is always time to bring hir engrams home, assuming the body has not completely been destroyed.

I gave the matter no more thought as I clumsily climbed to the next platform of the city, where I found several Ngisikaa, for once. Most must have come from Kuinuajuu itself, in the middle of the endless ocean, for I knew none of them but Cousin Kalilak. Xie introduced me to the others, and we traded engrams of our homes. I trembled in awe at the sight of the ancestral home, with its ancient engram depository. Such history! Though the other Ngisikaa seemed nearly as impressed by my humble village, far to the north of Ardhi. We soon parted, and I went to Cousin Kalilak's dwelling—a marvelous structure near the edge of the third story, its walls open to the sky. If Kalilak's nervous and antsy manner is an indication, I think they might be drunk on an overabundance of light!

* * *

I made certain to encode this engram as soon as possible after exploring the city of Juahaki. It is a fabulous place, shining in the light from the cloudless sky over a vast plain of grass. One can nearly see all the way to the ocean from here.

Cousin Kalilak is a strange one, and I believe xie must have spent too long in the city of mages. Xie has been here since before I gained my sentience, but sees plots and dealings in every corner. Twice while out in the city, xie has pulled me aside to avoid a particular Kuhifadi. Once a mage, and once a leader of some sort. I have a suspicion Kalilak may owe them money?

Speaking of which, it is harder to find work here, and so I guard my remaining earnings carefully. Whereas, in the underground caverns, people were always looking for Ngisikaa to calculate their answers, here most things are done with magic, and no calculation is necessary. Only in those rare cases when artifice is used—and complex at that—are our services needed.

One such case came only a few days after I had settled in with Kalilak. I was told all the Ngisikaa in the city—five, it turned out, including me—were required on the top level of the city. This was reserved for the city leaders, the enlightened of the magisterium, and various official functions. Only one Ngisikaa from Kuinuajuu had ever been invited there before.

But the city was still growing, and the only way to grow a vertical city above ground was up. The leaders required their offices, the mages their research laboratories, and so it was deemed that the new floor would be placed underneath the top floor, to give more room for administrative offices, and places of business. I was already imagining how the Uchafumlaji might achieve such a feat, with great engines to crane platforms out of the way, powered by massive clockwork gears. The calculations would be simple, though the labor required would be great.

But here, the operation was much different. Thirty mages, swaddled in rich fabrics to denote their high station in the order of Obarikaa, stood on the highest level, one

Ngisikaa assigned to each group of six. As one, they slashed through their wrapping and the Kuh underneath, releasing light and a harmonic tone, upon which all of us Ngisikaa looked up in unison. It was eerily similar to the singing of the herd in their heights of passion.

Even my eyes were temporarily blinded by the swirl of light that settled on the top level of Juahaki. I spread my legs in a circle to best resist the swaying motion as the whole level began to lift. Workers had previously cut, unscrewed, burned, and disengaged any connections and the level lifted cleanly.

Then it didn't.

We all jerked sideways as a last remaining shop that had forgotten to detach its ceiling from the level above ripped free. I am certain fees and censures would roll forth from the administrative offices, where everything must have been bounced around into a whirl of chaos.

Yet this is exactly why my fellows and I were needed. Using the ultrasonic frequencies neither other species could hear, the calculations flowed between us, set at five points on the edge of the top city level. Only pitches that high would travel far enough to hear over the grinding, creaking, and squealing of the level lifting into the air.

We each spoke to our group of mages, directing them up or down, left or right, forward or back, to keep the level absolutely still as it traveled. No sense in breaking even more of the mages' trinkets.

We rose even higher into the air, until I thought I could see the whole continent spread before me, then floated to one side and began our careful descent. Four of the mages had already dropped from exhaustion, and another in my group was teetering.

Some minutes later, the top level of Juahaki set down on the new city level, completed on the ground next to the city. The mages rested as workers swarmed the construction, bolting them together, and we revived the ones who had fallen. I was put to work as a messenger for a time, communicating with my fellows as to the health of all five groups of mages.

Next, the operation was done in reverse, with each mage slashing a new line of Kuh and their accompanying Ngisikaa directing their flight until the two combined levels rested back on top of the seven below them.

Several more had collapsed from exhaustion during the second escapade, and I helped prop one from our group—a thin, short Kuhifadi—against a bulwark as their fellows got them water and food to refresh them.

It was one of the most massive undertakings I have been a part of. I will treasure the memory for years—that of literally flying through the air! Truly these mages are powerful.

* * *

One more engram for now. It has been several weeks since the new construction on Juahaki, but I am worried about Cousin Kalilak. Xie seems listless, and only picks at hir marshcrabs. I believe something is bothering hir concerning the Kuhifadi here. I have suggested that xie may want to return to our village in the north—perhaps the cooler air there will clear hir head. But Kalilak refuses, seeming even more suspicious of old Keeper Nanana than of the scheming mages here. I have dug through my memories, but can find nothing of Kalilak back home. I wonder if xie was involved in underhanded dealings and was forced to move down here?

Whatever the reason, I have decided to stay a while with hir, to ensure xie does not expire, alone in a city of thousands of people. At the same time, I plan to learn more of the mages, their power, and the control they seem to have over the Kuhifadi cities.

* * *

Today I leave Juahaki. With Cousin Kalilak's passing last summer in 1815, there is nothing and no one here for me to care for. Kalilak was a burden until the end, but I feel I did some good by staying with hir and perhaps reigning in some of hir more destructive tendencies. I and the other Ngisikaa in the city have absorbed the bulk of Kalilak's memories, dark and suspicious though many of them are. I keep my share far below the surface, where they can little affect the engrams that drive my purpose.

Nevertheless, I find myself traveling alone. Three disappeared sometime during my stay, and I am convinced Kalilak sold it off to pay some debt, though hir memories are unclear on that account. Another Ngisikaa may have absorbed those moments. No matter, for my funds are much reduced after my stay in the city of mages, and with marshcrabs in abundance from the monsoons which have been sweeping the plains, I barely need any rations with me as I travel. In retrospect, I believe I realized several years ago that this could be a haven for ngisikaa and a place to erect another of my species rare engram depositories. A shame the area is populated by Kuhifadi.

I put Juahaki at my back, and headed toward the trio of cities touted as the cradle of Kuhifadi enlightenment: Mkubwa, Mwanga, and Unaowaka. I hope their cultures lead to better than the underhanded dealings I saw during my time in Juahaki. The leaders of the city changed five times in ten years, in posts that are meant to last for eight years apiece before a call for accounting. Uchafumlaji were routinely blamed for assassinations, and even for somehow blackmailing city leaders, though only rarely did I catch sight of a tall, wrapped person sliding into shadows, and none for the last two years.

* * *

I shall have to rely on reports of Mkubwa's magnificence, as I have been denied entry to the city. After a year spent traveling the countryside and memorizing locations for the engram depository, I had been looking forward to talking with Kuhifadi again. But the guards at the gate were firm in their stance that non-Kuhifadi were not welcome in Mkubwa. Even the so-called "honored" Ngisikaa. Some nonsense about the pure thought of the Kuhifadi "elite."

* * *

Mwanga has been more welcoming that its sibling city of Mkubwa, though I receive furtive glances from Kuhifadi passing me in its streets. The newest election has raised a full contingent of mages from the Order of Obarikaa to rule Mwanga, something unheard of it its history. Groups of Kuhifadi regularly break off hushed conversations about the power of the mages as I scuttle by. I dearly wish there was another Ngisikaa in this city to confirm I am not becoming as paranoid as poor Cousin Kalilak.

I have, however, succeeded in my quest to learn more of the mages' power. Far more than my liking, in fact. I am regularly called to the side of one Ehsonqiji, a loathsome mage concerned only with their power. They quiz me on tasks the Ngisikaa perform and how quickly we can calculate. I believe they desire a way to convert some of their magic to my engrammatic memories, in order to programmatically store spells to be activated at a moment's notice.

* * *

My knees still tremble as I encode this engram. I have stanched most of the bleeding, awkwardly tying the tourniquet with my other nine tentacles. If only my funds had not been running dangerously low, if only I had never come to Mkubwa.

Ow, ow. Too tight. A little less, but then the blood flows, but tighter will...

I must apologize. My thoughts are scattered, and I must concentrate to record this engram so my future descendant may learn a valuable lesson.

Ehsonqiji bade me visit them late at night today—usually the realm of the Uchafumlaji, though the Kuhifadi mages admire the irony of working with their solar-powered Kuh when the sun is not in evidence. The mage is obsessed with the difference in our species. I have wondered the same often in my travels, though never so much to injure another. Yet Ehsonqiji wished to test their theory of transfer of Kuh energy. We had spoken of this many times in the past, often past my comfort levels as they questioned me on intricacies of how my crystalline skin grows, the force to pierce it, and how engrams exist in special sacks in my body.

Finally, they made their offer. Money. Lots of money, which I was sorely lacking. The funds would compensate for the loss of two of my tentacles: what Ehsonqiji calculated they need for their experiments. I refused, of course, but they pressed, wheedled, and threatened. Finally, seeing the latched door and the lack of aid, I broke and agreed, though only to a lower price. Only one tentacle. What is a piece of flesh but a physical thing? It is not my essence, and I will be less impaired than a Kuhifadi or Uchafumlaji would be by a similar loss.

But I am avoiding the reality you must have already seen when my attention slips in this engram. The amputation of one of my tentacles was quick, though not painless, and I admit I ran from the mage's presence as soon as I could. They were eyeing my other limbs with greed, despite our agreement.

* * *

I have managed to avoid Ehsonqiji's worst threats, but only by leaving under the cover of night with help from an Uchafumlaji spy I have been sending messages to. They are as displeased with the Kuhifadi's degeneration as I am, and so, in the year 1824, with no herd and only six remaining tentacles to my name—for Ehsonqiji did not stop their advances at just one—I am finally on my way to Unaowaka, to see Cousin Hinafilanti, the one who originally sent me an invitation so long ago. If I knew then what I did now, would I have left the old Ngisikaa to their own devices? I am uncertain. For though I have lost much, especially in the last years, I gained so much before that. I would have wondered my whole life what was out in the world. Now I know.

I departed the Uchafumlaji's company soon after leaving the city. They were bound back to their city, or so they wanted me to believe, but once they slipped and said "army," and I fear for the fate of the more northern Kuhifadi cities.

Now I move mainly at night, when Kuhifadi patrols are asleep. There are no predators in this area—the Kuhifadi took care of them long ago—but there are plenty of other dangers to watch for in this wilderness.

* * *

I have been given special passage into the city of Unaowaka, as only by dropping Cousin Hinafilanti's name was I not thrown into prison at the front gates. To think I should end up like this!

Cousin Hinafilanti hirself is a strange beast, dressed from tip to tentacle in fancy fabrics as the most influential Kuhifadi are. I put hir at an age with Keeper Nanana, or even older, perhaps three hundred and thirty years since xie gained sentience. Xie has been in Unaowaka since it was a single level, and only by this longevity, and whispering in the ears of generations of leaders, has xie maintained hir status.

Xie has found me excellent care for what remains of my two poor mangled tentacles, which had started to gangrene in the wilderness. They have also issued a stern warning to the mages in Unaowaka, and I am told Ehsonqiji will be well reprimanded, though I doubt the severity of the punishment. Their payment is long gone, spent in bribes, supplies, and medicine.

I have spent several weeks in Cousin Hinafilanti's penthouse, filling hir in on all of the goings-on of Ardhi. Xie has been the only Ngisikaa in Unaowaka for many years, and asks probing questions about the state of each city, the reach of the mages, and how the Uchafumlaji's crafts are progressing. Something is changing on Ardhi, and I do not know what it is, but I am at last beginning to tire of my tour, and longing for a simple life keeping ngisikaa hatchlings from climbing the marshcrab fence.

* * *

My few years in Unaowaka have been eye-opening, especially serving as the right-side tentacles for Cousin Hinafilanti. I have seen more plots and dealings than I thought possible passing through the upper echelons of Kuhifadi power. Most cities are run by the Order of Obarikaa these days, though many civil leaders are still the face of the administration. Hinafilanti has hir own share of plots, of course, though all aimed at the benefit of the Ngisikaa, attempting to reopen cities for our entry, and determining standard payments for our services. I believe xie even has some clout with the Uchafumlaji Circle of Chiefs, though how xie sends messages back and forth are still beyond me.

It is perhaps this far-reaching influence that made Cousin Hinafilanti come to my room in the dead of night two days ago, papers in three tentacles, and clothes and money in the others. They said I had until the first rays of the sun peeked over the horizon to pack whatever I needed to leave. I was to make no mention to anyone, and we would sneak out of the city like nyodaji through the grass.

I am encoding this engram, late in the year 1828, from somewhere on the road. Unaowaka is a blur in the distance.

Hinafilanti tells me we shall have to avoid the city of Chulankumbu, on the way back, for it is in open revolt with some inhabitants vouching that Kuhifadi mages are essential to their continued progress, and others wishing them death. Truly a strange time we live in.

* * *

Hinafilanti and I have wasted no time on our journey, but I must make mention of this. Yesterday we passed Juahaki, and I saw that it was in flames. As I watched, the highest level—where the enlightened of the Order of Obarikaa resided—crumpled to one side and slid off. I could hear the screams even from the next hill over.

It is time to return home, though every time I mention seeing the engram depository again, Hinafilanti makes some off-putting remark. Xie knows something of terrible importance, but will not share it with me. If xie will not tell me within the week, I will be forced to press hir for hir information.

* * *

Well, Cousin Hinafilanti has no need to tell me hir secret, as I can ask Keeper Nanana hirself!

We ran into the great mass of Ngisikaa driving ngisikaa yesterday afternoon—though I believe Hinafilanti has been aiming specifically for this meeting. How xie knew of this rendezvous location is beyond my understanding. As much as I have seen of Ardhi, I have been little involved in the politics of this world.

I have asked repeatedly why an entire continent's worth of our species is this far south, but I get no answer. Keeper Nanana has, however, thanked me for the extensive research I collected over the years, mapping the geography, culture, and politics of Ardhi. Xie says when the mass of our species reaches its destination, I will have the honor of the first engram placed in the new depository. This comforts me little, and indeed, I fear what this means for our civilization.

* * *

I encode this last engram—what must be the last engram—from the middle of an army.

Hinafilanti and Nanana are confident Mkubwa and Mwanga will fall before our might easily. I have been given a device, developed in secret and partially through my own memories. It is a thing of clockwork, with power from mages and somehow, uses the energy we Ngisikaa keep in our bodies.

The blasts it fires are terrifying, ripping through Kuhifadi and Uchafumlaji flesh as easily as a ngisikaa tears through seaweed. I hesitate, but fire the cursed thing—certainly a creation of Hirolajak—under the stern eye of the elder keepers. Hinafilanti has rejoined hir place among them and directs the army with terrible insight, based on hundreds of years of knowledge about the Kuhifadi and Uchafumlaji lands.

Our drive is to the plains around what once was the trio of enlightened Kuhifadi cities, but are now only a burned mass of wood, stone, and bone. An Uchafumlaji army appeared from nearly underneath Mwanga, causing the stilts it sits on to collapse in a catastrophe never seen before. They slaughtered the inhabitants, only to be hemmed in by the rear by ngisikaa, driven to a fury by days of starvation and sleeplessness. I tried to object over their treatment—what potential sentients would we lose? But Nanana would hear none of it.

I hear the Uchafumlaji advancing again. There is another army of Kuhifadi approaching from the south, and though most are refugees from the burned cities, there are mages among them, dealing powerful explosions and death at a moment's notice.

Is all this worth it for a new engram storage location? There are three I know of so far: the original one on Kuinuajuu, another far to the east on a different continent, and my home village. Why go to all this death and destruction for one more location to live?

Or did Hinafilanti see that the civilizations of Ardhi were already doomed, and choose to take advantage of that fact? I hope we may save as much knowledge as possible, for I cannot expect but a fraction of the Uchafumlaji and Kuhifadi enlightenment to survive this chaos.

And so, I give this plea to you, my future descendant. At least I hope you are there to relive these memories and I am not snuffed out without a thought:

See all of Juno you can. Learn of the people here. They are not bad, or wicked, even if they are misguided at times. I believe the sun will shine again on happy members of all species living in harmony, though it may be many years from now. If it takes the destruction of the Order of Obarikaa and the Uchafumlaji's cunning plans, then so be it.

But I must draw this to a close. Once again, I pick myself up, clockwork device held in four of my six remaining tentacles. The shadow of two armies draws over me, and I offer a prayer to Akkakuh and Kimmasi that I may live to see tomorrow.

BT1272 – Report to Observation Supervisor

Categorization of "The Third Age" of Juno, and events concerning the collapse of civilization.

FC 2153, Day 294:

First, a continued timeline, as events progressed very quickly over a single Juno year:

FC 1829: Kuhifadi in several major cities fight against the Order of Obarikaa: the mages guild. Two cities are burnt to the ground, refugees fleeing to surrounding cities.

FC 1829: An army of discontented Uchafumlaji tunnels into the center of Kuhifadi territory, erupting just as a Kuhifadi army, led by mages, marches to the nearest surface exit of the Uchafumlaji tunnel network.

FC 1829: At nearly the same time, the mass of migrating ngisikaa arrive from the northern memory storage location, led by a small clique of sentient Ngisikaa. The Ngisikaa have found a way to absorb much of the energy released by a rupture of the Kuh, rendering mages useless. They have also equipped themselves with finely tuned clockwork weapons, taken from memories of the Ngisikaa working for the Uchafumlaji. Both armies are overrun by the fragile creatures.

FC 1829: Civilization collapses, and records are extremely scarce. Even the tunnel network of the Uchafumlaji is compromised by agents of the Order of Obarikaa. Most memories stored by the Ngisikaa of this event are lost in the resulting battle.

FC 1829–2150?: The mages orchestrated revolutions even on the sparsely inhabited Eastern Continent, and because there was no influx of non-sentient ngisikaa in that place, they gain complete control. Communication is lost between the two continents for a long time, and even Observer records are incomplete.

On Kuhifadi:

From riches to rags, the Kuhifadi and their mages might have been considered the dominant culture of this age, though that was also their downfall. The mages now control vast swaths of the geography of the Western Continent, and nearly all of the Eastern. But control over dust and ruins is no empire. It will likely be many years before even the remaining mage enclaves can scrape together enough Kuhifadi to enact any new plans.

On Uchafumlaji:

With most of their cities collapsed, the Uchafumlaji's technology has largely been buried under the ground. Fragments survive, but without the infrastructure, the forges, the great aqueducts, cranes, and mills of their cities, any further iteration of existing technology is doomed to wear out eventually. It is a question whether those hunting pairs sent to search for remaining caverns can find enough pieces to put their domain together again.

On Ngisikaa:

The Ngisikaa are perhaps hardest hit of the three species, with the loss of many of their precious memories. Though the ancestral memory storage on Kuinuajuu is still whole, many of the citizens of that location were caught in battles and raids that occurred on the larger continents. Their experiences were lost, and with no record of what happened, the librarians of the ancestral storage must scramble to find what small scraps of knowledge may still exist out in the world.

Such times as these try the path of the Observers. For though we have witnessed many horrific events, we are bound merely to wait, and watch, and hope.

The Fourth Age of Juno

Time: Common Era. For two thousand years, or more, the species of Juno reeled from the disastrous Collapse. Only slowly did the sentients start to rebuild, not only their cities and infrastructure, but their very society. This time, however, it is free from many of the old traditions that bound the three species in enmity. It is an age of adventure, rediscovery, and finally, of reconciliation. We must hope this time, the end will be more stable.

CE (Common Era) 0 (= FC ???): During the Collapse, most non-sentient ngisikaa are driven back or killed when the Uchafumlaji see their chance to take out both light-living species. They underestimate the mages, who have been quietly building their strength in the shadows. Many Uchafumlaji are taken captive and forced to finally teach their technology to the Kuhifadi. This marks the official end of the time of the Darkside Revolt, and a long time passes while civilization recovers. There is not even an accurate accounting of days, and a new calendar is chosen, based on the founding of the first Kuhifadi city to overlook the new southern Ngisikaa memory storage location.

CE 80–200: In the early days of the new calendar, there are reports of a traveling utopia, which can pass over land or water, or even beneath the earth. In this city, Kuhifadi, Ngisikaa, and Uchafumlaji all live together, a central memory storage guarded by and acting as a conduit for the Kuhifadi's power, serving as a power core for augmented technology of the Uchafumlaji. There are several credible sightings of this city, known as Kusongangani. The city has never been successfully found.

N.L. Bates

Chasing Kusongangani

CE 81

It has been a long road, made longer by the string of ruined cities that stretches out behind us.

Some of them, we remember: from our own experiences, or from the engrams of the long-ago Ngisikaa whose memories uplifted us to sentience. Laanjiwe, with its once-impressive seaweed farms. Uungunqi, brimming with clockwork marvels. Juahaki, which used to tower over the continent on great stilts, gleaming in the sun. Others whose names are no longer remembered, not by us, nor the Uchafumlaji or Kuhifadi who have been left to pick through their ruins.

Perhaps other Ngisikaa remember, but so far, we have not been successful in finding others of our species, not since we went back to the ruins of the memory depository in the north. We have only ourself, and the single crystalline fragment of engram core we have managed to salvage. For all we know, we hold in our ten tentacles the last surviving fragment of centuries upon centuries of collected memory.

In this way, the Ngisikaa are no different than the other sentients of Juno. We too are left picking through the ruins of our former glory.

Perhaps the names of the dead cities we have visited are stored in the engram core we carry. But no, we will not steal from our people to sate our own morbid curiosity. In any case, the memories stored within even this small fragment of the northern depository would be more than a single Ngisikaa could hold. Sooner or later, the strain of holding so many memories would drive us mad.

It has been a long road in truth, but not long enough to make us desire such a fate.

This morning, we find ourself on the road with three other sentients, an Uchafumlaji and two Kuhifadi, who have fallen into step with us as we walk. This happens sometimes; the roads of Ardhi are long and hard these days, and many beings band together where they can. Other sentients sometimes spell danger, but they also promise company, and information.

"We're traveling south and east, for now," one of the Kuhifadi says. "To Kusongangani, we hope." According to the Kuhifadi, Kusongangani has not suffered the ravages of the Collapse in the same way as the rest of Ardhi; its roads are clean and well-maintained, its food supply plentiful. It shelters Kuhifadi, Uchafumlaji, and Ngisikaa, all three.

"We have never heard of such a city in the area," we muse. Or anywhere, really. Perhaps our memories are more incomplete than we realize.

"The city travels, friend Ngisikaa," the second Kuhifadi replies, resting their hand on the arm of their companion. "It's always found in different locations, but we've heard about it several times now, and from people we trust. There is good reason to believe it's still in the area!"

"A traveling city, eh?" the Uchafumlaji says, eye ridges raised in an expression too polite to be called disbelief. "That would be quite the sight."

"No more than anywhere else before the Collapse," the Kuhifadi replies, a trifle defensively.

The Uchafumlaji nods, conceding the point. "I have also heard there are Ngisikaa traveling toward the southern shore, some of them with crystals like the one you carry."

A wave of excitement rushes through us. "There are other Ngisikaa in the south? They are building a new memory depository?" For this is precisely our goal: to find a memory depository where we can deliver the engram core, and assist our people in rebuilding all the Ngisikaa have lost. Perhaps we could also gift to the depository some of the engrams we have housed in our person, and unburden ourself of some of the many memories we carry.

The Uchafumlaji inclines his head to us. “I could not confirm that, though it would be my assumption. But you'll certainly find other Ngisikaa, if you continue south.”

Some while later, the Uchafumlaji takes his leave to investigate what he suspects may be an entrance to some collapsed Uchafumlaji tunnels. Soon after, the Kuhifadi also go their own way, heading east to chase their traveling city.

Alone again, we resume our long trudge southward.

It is days before we run into more sentients: more Kuhifadi, sunning themselves on a large boulder. They are dressed, both of them, in loose-fitting leggings and shirts that almost match the blue of their skin, slitted in places to expose their Kuh to the sun. Deliberately so; their clothing is tailored, not torn. During a time when many beings wear tattered rags and haunted expressions, these Kuhifadi seem to have done well for themselves.

They amble into the road as we approach. We resent the time we will now have to spend observing social niceties, but they have positioned themselves so that we would have to step out of the road to avoid them, and to be so obvious would be incredibly rude. “Good morning to you both.”

“A good morning, indeed!” The first Kuhifadi is effusive, the second one silent. “Always good to see other faces along these little roads of ours. Always happy to make some pleasant conversation.” The second Kuhifadi shifts their feet as if bracing themself, and we feel the first stirrings of anxiety. “If you're passing through, though, we *will* need a little something in the way of tribute. Seeing as these are our roads and all.” And the Kuhifadi looks us up and down, with an appraising stare that utterly belies their friendly demeanor.

"A tribute?" We suppose we should not be surprised. These days, Ardhi is full of petty tyrants. "We have some rafu still. You are welcome to them." It is galling to accede to their demands, but the safety of the engram core is far more important than our money, or our ego.

The Kuhifadi exchange a glance. "Come now, friend," the first Kuhifadi says, in a tone that is not especially friendly. "We need a little something in exchange for our work, it's true. Helps us keep the roads safe." They lean forward. "But I'm sure we can come to some sort of arrangement."

Their studied smugness suggests they already have an arrangement in mind. We keep the irritation and unease both from our voice as we ask, "What is your proposal?"

The Kuhifadi gestures to their companion, a short and stocky being who stands head and shoulders above us, and says, "That crystal you're carrying looks mighty heavy. But Mwaraba here is a strong one. Practically a pack mule." The one called Mwaraba grunts. "Could be we could lighten your load a little. We'd be willing to do you that favor."

We must remain calm. Anger will not help us here.

"The crystal is an engram core," we tell the Kuhifadi. "A Ngisikaa memory crystal. It has no monetary value."

"No monetary value. Is that so." The Kuhifadi turns to their associate. "What do you think, Mwaraba?"

Mwaraba speaks up at last. "I think it seems awfully valuable to our Ngisikaa friend here."

This conversation is spiraling like an ocean current. "It is valuable to the Ngisikaa for the memories it holds, yes. But you cannot use it or sell it." The Kuhifadi should know this to be true, assuming they are not complete idiots. "It is worthless to you."

"On the contrary, friend." There is a definite edge to the Kuhifadi's voice. "It's worth your passage through here. Leave the crystal with us, and you'll never see us again."

"We cannot. The crystal does not belong to us—to me." Hopefully the stumble in our speech makes us sound no less certain of our words. It has been a long time since we have used that particular pronoun, but we have noticed that less collectively-minded sentients often respond more readily when we refer to ourself in the singular. "It belongs to all of us."

"To all of us, huh?" the first Kuhifadi responds, and we do not need to search our memories of Kuhifadi facial expressions to know their smirk is ugly. "Then you won't mind handing it over." And then, apparently without a shred of embarrassment at their own lack of propriety, they reach for the engram core.

We respond almost before realizing we have done so, channeling our rage and disgust into a wordless rebuke: a single strong, resonant chime.

Millennia of communication have taught the Ngisikaa what frequencies the other sentients of Juno can hear—what frequencies are pleasant to their ears. By extension, we have also learned what frequencies they find *un*pleasant. Both Kuhifadi stagger backward at our wordless outburst.

Perhaps the satisfaction we feel, watching the Kuhifadi clap their hands over their ears, does not become us. Even so, we let anger color our words as we modulate our speech back to tones the Kuhifadi can tolerate.

"The crystal belongs to the Ngisikaa people." One of the Kuhifadi recovers themself enough to stumble a little bit closer, and we raise our tone again just slightly. "It is not ours—not *mine*—to give away, and it is certainly not yours to take." Both Kuhifadi wince at the strident pitch of our voice. "But I will respect your conditions also, and find some other...destination." It probably would not be wise to admit that we simply plan to find another path to the depository, which in any case these Kuhifadi have no claim to. The *presumption* of them, to even pretend they do! But the Kuhifadi cannot be everywhere, so we will simply go somewhere they are not, and avoid any further unpleasantness. "Luck in...whatever it is that you do." We do not specify what *kind* of luck it is we wish them.

And then, before the Kuhifadi recover their senses enough to speak, we flick our left-side tentacles in a gesture that could be interpreted as being polite and turn back the way we came.

* * *

As soon as we are out of the Kuhifadi's sight, we turn east, walking until the plains give way to rocky foothills. Once we are far enough away, we will simply circle back around. Infuriating, yes, but the Kuhifadi have rattled us. Better to be cautious and arrive at our destination with the engram core unharmed. We bed down behind a rocky outcropping as the sun begins to set, and from there pass into fitful slumber.

We are not certain, at first, what awakens us.

The nights have been quiet, and this one is no exception. But then we hear it: the crunch of stone underfoot. At first, we think we have imagined it, but a few moments later, we hear the noise again.

Not our imagination, then; someone approaching. The interlocutors are taking pains to conceal their presence. The Kuhifadi, come to claim the engram core for themselves?

What cheek.

We look around. Even in darkness, the glow from our skin is enough to light the rocks we have sheltered under. It affords us a good view of our surroundings, but it also means the Kuhifadi will find us easily.

We can already see them, mere shadows in the darkness. We recognize the tall lanky one from this morning, followed by a stocky figure who is almost certainly Mwaraba, and then two, no, four more Kuhifadi besides.

We duck behind our boulder again as the Kuhifadi fan out among the rocks. Almost immediately, we hear one of the Kuhifadi call to their colleagues. Fortunately, we have already determined our escape route.

The Kuhifadi will catch up if we simply follow the winding road back toward the hilltop. But above us, the hills rise sharply, almost vertically, littered with small boulders and scrub brush that might form tentacle-holds for an enterprising sentient. Many of them are precariously placed, but there is a path to the top that will safely bear our weight. It might bear the Kuhifadi as well, but the Ngisikaa affinity for quick calculation is a facility that the other sentients of Juno mostly lack. They are likely to choose one of the easier-seeming paths, and the time they lose to falling rocks and tearing bushes should buy time enough for us to escape. We hope.

The Kuhifadi shout as we come into the open. We tune out their calls, scrabbling upward. We are not a fast climber, but our eight legs at least give us excellent stability.

Something metallic *tinks* against a rock near us. It occurs to us that the Kuhifadi may have weapons.

Pain explodes at the back of our head.

We feel ourself falling, feel the engram core sliding from our grasp. Flailing wildly, we throw our body against the engram core, smashing it against the rock face but at least stopping its fall, and catch ourself by latching onto one of the nearby bushes.

Head throbbing, fighting nausea, we resume our climb. But the Kuhifadi are close now, almost to the base of the hill.

"Watch your damn weapons!" The voice, too, we recognize from this morning. "Break the crystal and Lajikii will have all of us on a platter!"

We reach for another hold. Almost to the top now, but our injury makes us slow.

Below us, the Kuhifadi begin to climb. They do so with the exact lack of grace we had expected, but they are making better time than we had hoped. Too close. *Too close, too close, too close.* Our rising panic throbs in time with our aching head. Then our tentacles graze a particularly large, unsteady boulder.

We are not given to violence against other sentients. But we cannot let the Kuhifadi catch up. We give the boulder a shove, and are rewarded with the shouts and cries of the Kuhifadi below.

We run.

* * *

We run for almost two days without pause, until pain and lack of food and sleep have rendered us nearly insensate. We run until we arrive at what was once the city of Unaowaka, until our physical limitations catch up with us just outside what remains of the city's walls.

Unaowaka is surprisingly busy, and we allow ourself to be reassured by this fact. Surely the Kuhifadi thieves will not be so brash as to make another attempt with so many other sentients about. We can shelter, recover ourselves, and find another path forward.

We *will* reach the new depository. We must.

We could likely find accommodations within Unaowaka's crumbling walls, were we inclined to look. But we are too spent, too much in pain to bother. Most sentients of Juno, ourself included, have long ago abandoned any compunctions about bedding down in the street—where there are still streets at all.

We wake to find we have been abducted.

We reach with all ten tentacles for the engram core, reassured to feel its smooth surfaces still tucked beneath us. And we recognize the Uchafumlaji who sits a short distance away, watching us over the rims of his mud-spattered spectacles with an expression of mild concern. As we recover our senses, we realize we have not been abducted after all.

Someone—presumably our Uchafumlaji acquaintance—has stretched a blanket over top of both of us like a tent roof, secured with wooden posts, little more than sturdy sticks, driven into the ground on either side. "Good afternoon."

At least we know what time it is. "H-hello," we reply, too discombobulated for the moment to manage anything else.

He nods back. Even seated, he looms over us. "I'm glad to see you awake. Forgive me if I was being presumptuous, but I recognized you from the road, and you seemed in a bad way. Are you well?"

"There is nothing to forgive," we assure him, striving to regain some measure of composure. "We are well. We only needed rest." It is not entirely true, as the throb at the back of our head reminds us, but it will do for now. Belatedly, it occurs to us to introduce ourself. "We are Nalilililon."

His name is Tchalaanziqi, and he chuckles ruefully as he tells us that the tunnel entrance he was investigating turned out to be nothing more than a gully. "I hope you fared better than I did." But he sobers when we tell him of our encounter with the Kuhifadi. "It figures. Unzulaja knows there are enough of those types about—and I don't mean just among the Kuhifadi, of course. I hope they didn't separate you from all your coin?"

"No, we...chose to come back here instead." Without quite knowing why, we decide not to share with him the precise nature of the Kuhifadi's desire. We slide the engram core behind us as if to hide it from his sight, ridiculously, for Tchalaanziqi must have noticed it by now. We muse out loud to cover our awkwardness. "We will go east instead, and south from there."

"East, is it?" Tchalaanziqi muses in turn. "Like our Kuhifadi friends. They weren't wrong, you know. I keep hearing rumors of a settlement, even a city, in the area." He shakes his head. "I don't understand it. I was in the area but weeks ago, and there were no such rumors then."

"It could be the memory depository," we suggest. "Such a site could grow quite quickly, if there are sufficient donations of engrams—of memory crystals."

"Perhaps that is it," he agrees. "I *have* heard recently that a great many Ngisikaa are congregating off the coasts there."

Ah, but this is important news! Perhaps our kin have managed to salvage some engram cores from one of the old locations. Perhaps they are simply farther along in the construction of a new depository than we had realized. Or perhaps—wait. "Ngisikaa or ngisikaa?"

"Pardon?" His eye ridges furrow.

Ah. Other sentients do not always differentiate between the Ngisikaa and our non-sentient cousins. But likely these are ngisikaa, or we would have heard of such a gathering before now. We wave the distinction away. "No matter. This is good to know."

He opens his mouth to respond, but it is not words we hear.

It is a chord, or at least harmonics—all the same note, but multiple octaves, in bell-like tones. Our little shelter pulses with light, bright enough that Tchalaanziqi pushes his spectacles up over his eyes, bright enough to make us realize that we have not imagined it. Tchalaanziqi is speaking again now, with concern and perhaps a little bit of fear, but we cannot answer him, not when we must deal with this.

The engram core. Something is wrong with the engram core.

Did it get damaged during our escape from the Kuhifadi? Engram cores are sturdy things, but not, to our sorrow, indestructible. We run our tentacles along every inch of the gleaming crystal and feel no damage. Nor do our eyes spot any imperfections, not a single hairline crack, though we cannot deny that it is glowing when it should not be, engram cores only glow when they are active—

My fellow Ngisikaa stand all around me. Some of us, myself included, clutch Uchafumlaji-made clockwork weapons. Others have not been able to overcome their distaste for the things (and they are distasteful! But I have managed to convince myself that losing an entire memory depository to the ravages of war would be more so) and stand ready to aid in whatever other ways they can. To salvage what remains, if it comes down to that.

I hope they'll be safe. I hope we all will.

The crystalline engram cores all around us have dimmed, for the most part, to an ambient glimmer. Even as I look, the handful that had remained active go dormant. The very last light to wink out is one on my right side, as Nalililon (*ourself, we are seeing ourself*) places one last engram into the depository for safekeeping. I can only hope that the engram xie is encoding will be safe in truth. The glow around hir fades as Nalililon finishes hir task.

The glow fades, as does the memory, leaving me alone with a very bemused Tchalaanziqi. The Uchafumlaji has raised an arm to shade his eyes. Out on the street, I can see curious onlookers peering toward our makeshift tent.

We can see onlookers. We, for we are Nalililon and not Riaaaaaarl, that long-ago friend who encoded the engram we just witnessed. An engram that chose to play itself, of its own accord, with no direction from us.

Millennia of collected Ngisikaa knowledge say that is impossible.

Slowly, Tchalaanziqi lowers his arm.

"I, we, we are sorry," we stammer. It is admittedly an asinine response to whatever has just happened, on all possible levels, but at the moment all we can think is that Uchafumlaji are sensitive to sunlight, and we did not warn him. "We did not know—that was not—"

Tchalaanziqi, mercifully, waves us to silence. "It was unexpected. It's quite all right." We see him contemplate his next words, but in the end, he chooses not to ask. Perhaps he is being polite, or perhaps he sees we have no answers. "You're certain you are well?"

We stammer through an assurance that we are. We do not think Tchalaanziqi believes us—we are not certain *we* believe us!—but we do not know what else to say.

* * *

We leave Unaowaka just after dawn.

We do not feel nearly ready for the journey, but the engram core must take priority, and in any case, its sudden activation last night has drawn more attention than we are comfortable with. We had planned to lose ourself in the city until we had recovered enough to move on, but now every sentient here is one that might speak of the Ngisikaa carrying the engram core, if the Kuhifadi decide to follow.

Tchalaanziqi walks with us a ways, but our paths diverge again a short distance out of Unaowaka. Alone, we begin the long and miserable trek to the coast. We distract ourself from the ache in our legs and the throb in our head by reviewing our considerable knowledge of engram cores.

By the time we reach the ocean, we have concluded only that something is very, very wrong.

The cool waters are a balm, at least, and we take heart from knowing the Kuhifadi cannot follow us here. We let the current usher us toward the southern shores, staying close to the surface to make sure we do not miss the telltale glow of the new memory depository. We *will* find it, and the Ngisikaa who must be building it, and together we will correct whatever is malfunctioning within the engram core we carry.

We come across the ngisikaa herd, our little cousins, not long after leaving shore. They don't glow quite so brightly as the Ngisikaa, but their glimmer is distinctive, and they chime to each other as they go where currents and whimsy take them. We find we actually enjoy their vocalizations, nonsense though they are.

One, in particular, is feisty. It circles us often, vying for our attention with playful tentacles, and seems cautiously fascinated by the engram core. Reaching for sentience? Perhaps we should bring it with us.

That evening, carried on ocean currents, we dream of Riaaaaaaarl.

We dream we *are* Riaaaaaaarl, clutching a clockwork weapon, prepared to defend the depository from encroaching sentients. Kuhifadi, Uchafumlaji, armies, bandits; it doesn't matter. What matters is that the depository is protected—from heedless armies trampling crystals underfoot, from dozens of Kuhifadi mages whose burst Kuh releases more energy than we Ngisikaa can absorb, from underground Uchafumlaji tunnels that shudder and buckle and heave, until the engram cores around us are falling and so am I...

Something grabs for us in the chaos, and then it is not chaos at all, only a curious ngisikaa face. Even as we rouse ourself, it gets bored of waiting for us and reaches tentatively for the glowing crystal.

We gently swat its tentacles away. "Do not play with what you do not understand, little one." Of course, we do not understand either. Could the ngisikaa have triggered the engram core somehow? That should be impossible, of course; it is not a sentient creature. And this would not explain what we experienced back in Unaowaka.

And yet.

Little cousin trills at us. Perhaps it senses our distress.

The engram core activates twice more before we reach the southeast shore. The first time, we are half-asleep. We dream of ourself-as-Riaaaaaaarl searching through a maze of half-collapsed tunnels for an exit, for other Ngisikaa, for anything to help us carry the scant few engram cores we have managed to salvage to a safer location. We dream that we cannot carry all we have found, and cry out to the unhearing ruins as we contemplate which collections of our people's memories to leave behind.

We wake to little cousin's plaintive pealing nonsense, full of Riaaaaaaarl's frustration and despair.

We wonder why Riaaaaaaarl encoded this engram, if it is even real. An explanation, perhaps, of how xie came to leave this particular engram core behind?

Except that Riaaaaaaarl did not leave it behind, at least not right away. We discover this when the engram core lights up again, less than a day later.

This time, we are wide awake when it happens. We hear the same chiming we heard back in Unaowaka, and suddenly we are not in the ocean anymore. We-as-Riaaaaaaarl gaze out at a cityscape that we, Nalilililon, have never seen before, in engrams or anywhere else. Radiant Kuhifadi dwellings, stretching toward the sun, double as shady pavilions for Uchafumlaji who lounge in the shade below. The streets are well-kept and lit by a pale lilac glow that comes from dozens, if not hundreds, of carefully tended engram cores.

Little cousin's furious chatter jerks us back to the present.

The glowing of the engram core has attracted some of the other ngisikaa, and little cousin is telling them off with a possessiveness that we might find amusing in other circumstances. "You might make a good Ngisikaa one day, little cousin," we say to it. "Protecting engram cores is a good instinct." If only we understood how to protect this one.

Perhaps we should absorb some of its engrams into ourself. It might give us a better understanding of what is happening. Or, given that the core is already acting up, such an attempt may simply degrade it further, or saddle us with all the memories within and drive us mad.

"Assuming we are not mad already," we mutter. Little cousin chirps at us.

No, we will wait until we arrive at the new depository. There should be other Ngisikaa present when we attempt to correct the engram core's behavior, to ensure that someone is on hand to salvage the core if something does go wrong.

We gaze toward shore. The experience of Riaaaaaaarl's last engram is so strong, we almost imagine we still see pale pink gleams in the distance.

We blink, but the glimmers do not disappear.

We steady ourself against the rising tide of our own excitement. Perhaps it is only a trick of the light, or another unexpected activation. But when we glance at the engram core, it is dark and inert.

"Little cousin, do you see that?"

Little cousin vocalizes in reply; it has begun to respond when it hears our voice. Almost, for a moment, it seems to follow our gaze. But, seeing nothing of interest, it pulls one of the other ngisikaa into a playful tussle instead.

Of course it would not understand the significance of that lavender light; how could it? But we do. This time, we welcome the glow cast by an active engram core. It means Tchalaanziqi was right. The Ngisikaa are building a new memory depository here.

And we are close, if our eyes can already spot its light. Once we arrive at the depository, the other Ngisikaa who must be tending it will help us determine what is wrong with the engram core we carry. After we have corrected the problem and installed the core within the depository, perhaps we will journey out again, looking for more engram cores to salvage.

Or perhaps we will just rest, and care for the engram cores that have already been salvaged. We are looking forward to being in the company of other Ngisikaa again.

Soon.

* * *

Little cousin follows us when we leave the ngisikaa herd behind and make for the southern shore. Perhaps we should have dissuaded it, but we have grown fond of its company.

We decide that we will begin encoding engrams for it. It will take a little time for us to accumulate sufficient memories for donation and uplift—the process by which a ngisikaa becomes a Ngisikaa and its own person—but we feel it has earned its sentience.

But not yet. We will begin that process once our current task is complete. Little cousin is a joyful type, and we do not wish for its first memories to be of privation and distress.

We pause in the shallows to gather enough marshcrabs and seaweed to sustain us for the remaining journey. Little cousin thinks this is a great game, throwing stalks up in the air and draping itself with the fronds. We cannot help but laugh.

After the shelter of the ocean, traveling over land—even with the engram core wrapped in seaweed so it is concealed from the eyes of any passersby—feels woefully exposed. We follow a nearby river inland, simultaneously reassured and frustrated by the pale purple lights in the distance, which disappear during daylight before becoming visible again in the evening. The ocean is two days behind us, but the depository appears no closer now than when we began. Little cousin is cranky, being so far away from the ocean for probably the first time in its life, but at least the engram core does not activate again.

In the early hours of the morning, we are intercepted.

The approaching figure is bipedal and much too small to be an Uchafumlaji, though they are not clothed in the usual Kuhifadi way, but covered almost head to toe in tightly wrapped clothing. A mage, then, often not kindly regarded by even other Kuhifadi.

We, however, are more concerned by the color of their garments than the nature of them: a slate blue that we have seen before. This seems unlikely to be a coincidence.

"A fine morning to you, travelers," the Kuhifadi says. "Name's Lajikii." It takes us a moment to realize we have heard this name before—from the Kuhifadi that accosted us on the road to Unaowaka. The recognition dashes any hope we had that the Kuhifadi might simply pass us by. We mutter an introduction, which Lajikii acknowledges with a perfunctory wave of their hand. "What brings you to these parts?"

We resist the urge to tuck the seaweed-wrapped engram core farther out of sight. We must not call attention to it now.

"We have heard there are other Ngisikaa farther inland," we explain, trying not to let our voice reflect our nervousness—or our anger. "We plan to join our cousins there." If we do not mention the depository, perhaps Lajikii will have no reason to think we carry anything valuable.

Little cousin shuffles tentatively forward and, before we can stop it, pokes the Kuhifadi with a curious tentacle.

"You keep your limbs to yourself," Lajikii snaps. They reach a hand into their clothes. We glimpse the rough wooden hilt of a small weapon.

"Forgive our packbeast," we say quickly. "It is a ngisikaa, and not sentient." We tug little cousin back behind us, away from the Kuhifadi mage. It chirrups resentfully, but thankfully decides to acquiesce.

"Your packbeast, huh?" Lajikii turns back to us. Their anger is gone, replaced by a calculating expression that we like even less. "Don't look like it's packing much." Their eyes sweep us up and down. "You, on the other hand."

We realize, then, that we have made a mistake.

"We drafted it from the herd to assist with any tasks our cousins might need," we murmur, hoping against hope to divert the Kuhifadi's attention from the engram core. "Ngisikaa do this often."

Lajikii is not fooled. They gesture to the engram core. "And that?"

"Our food supplies." We must not sound desperate. "If we give them to our packbeast, it will only eat them."

"That so." Lajikii nods to themself, but we can tell they are not satisfied. "Looks awfully heavy for a bunch of seaweed."

We open our mouth, preparing to utter another stupid, doomed fabrication. But before we can speak, a chord rings out like a bell.

Octaves again, much like what we heard back in Unaowaka, but this time there is another note as well, a harmonic third. The trees around us blur and our vision frays at the edges as the engram core superimposes the contents of another memory upon us.

I see (*Riaaaaaaarl sees*) the ruins of the northern memory depository all around, crystals cracked and shattered, their light dull or dying. There are fissures in the earth where the Uchafumlaji tunnels have collapsed. Crystal dust crunches underfoot, and the bodies of Ngisikaa are everywhere, their skin just as dull as the broken engram cores.

No, no, no. Now is not the time!

The memory fades until all that is left is a pale pink glow, unmistakable even when muted by several layers of seaweed.

"If there's one thing I can't abide," Lajikii says, and there is a false conversational lilt to their voice that screams danger, "it's a liar."

We cannot hope to outrun a Kuhifadi overland. Perhaps if we run for the river...

But Lajikii must have seen our eyes flick in that direction, for they raise their voice. "Come on out, friends!"

Two more Kuhifadi step out from the trees, wearing the same severe gray-blue fabric. Like Lajikii, their bodies are completely swaddled in it. More mages.

Little cousin makes a plaintive noise.

"The engram core would do you no good!" we exclaim, unable to keep our frustration to ourself. "They are not something you can buy or sell. We will give you our rafu, it is worth more—"

"Here's the thing, friend. I don't give a shit about your money," Lajikii says. "My friends and I, we're looking for something. And that crystal of yours is going to bring it right to us."

We blink. "Engram cores are memory storage technology. They cannot be used to—to summon trinkets."

"Oh, no," Lajikii says, stepping toward us. "We're thinking much bigger than that. And your crystal is finally going to give us the juice to make it happen."

Their ignorance is appalling. "That is absurd."

"Last chance," Lajikii snaps.

We cannot give them the engram core. We *will* not.

We respond with a wordless shout in one of the frequencies we know the Kuhifadi detest. One of Lajikii's cronies raises a hand as if swatting a fly, but that is all. They must have taken steps to protect their hearing.

Then the engram core activates once more, almost as if responding to our cry.

We hear the chime again, and see through Riaaaaaaarl's eyes as xie dashes through the ruins of the northern depository. The horizon is still lit with a faint luminescence. Some of the engram cores must have survived. I run for them, moving so quickly that the world starts to pebble in my sight, until it almost appears that the broken engram cores are being replaced by structures I have never seen before...

"Kusongangani," Lajikii breathes, and it takes us a moment to realize that we have heard the word before, to realize that the Kuhifadi have seen the memory too.

Lajikii does not give us time to contemplate what this means. "Get hir! Get hir *now*!" And the Kuhifadi lunge forward in lockstep.

"Run!" we shout to little cousin, knowing it cannot understand us, and dash for the river.

But little cousin does not heed our advice. We hear indignant chittering behind us, and a shout from one of the Kuhifadi mages. "This thing won't leave me alone!"

"Just kill it, fool!" Lajikii shouts back, close behind us.

We are almost to the river, and know we should not slow. The engram core is more important. But we cannot help but glance behind us. Little cousin wrestles one of the unnamed Kuhifadi with animal ferocity. The other Kuhifadi steps in to free their companion.

That quick glimpse almost costs us dearly as we stumble. We throw our weight forward and roll, an ungainly mess of limbs and tentacles, and finally hit the water. Rocks bruise and scrape our skin, and our head throbs as the wound we received before Unaowaka bursts open. Behind us, little cousin cries out in wordless but unmistakable pain.

Flailing wildly, we manage to right ourself and push toward the center of the river. Lajikii wades out after us, radiating fury, but it is clear they will not be able to withstand the current. Little cousin totters toward the riverbank, keening softly.

The river is shallow enough to make swimming awkward, but the current is swift. Hopefully that will be enough to carry us out of the Kuhifadis' reach. We look regretfully over our shoulder, knowing there is nothing we can do to help little cousin, and see the three Kuhifadi draw their knives.

We briefly fear that the Kuhifadi will hurl the weapons at us or at little cousin. Instead, almost in unison, the three mages draw their blades down their arms, slashing through the Kuh hidden under their layers of clothing.

The engram core pulses in response—

"...energy the Kuhifadi store in their Kuh is exactly the same energy we Ngisikaa use to create engrams, and can be absorbed the same way." (*Is this our memory? Another's? We are not even certain.*) "The source of the energy is simply more diffuse—"

—and it does not matter whether it is our memory or not. We *remember*, and we have just enough time to prepare ourselves as the energy from the Kuhifadi's ruptured Kuh washes over us. We take it into us, not all of it, but enough that we do not discover how the Kuhifadi intended to direct it. They stagger, all three, stunned by the loss of the energy from their Kuh or the pain of their injuries.

We have only moments. We call out once to little cousin, more to assuage our guilt for leaving it behind than out of any expectation it might follow us. Then we swim for all we are worth, heading for the distant promise of the ocean, and the safety it might offer.

* * *

At first, the river carries us swiftly, and we hope we might reach the ocean before the Kuhifadi catch up. We do not doubt they are following. But as the river branches off into smaller creeks and streams, the main channel of the river becomes shallower until soon we are only walking, and any advantage of speed we might have had is lost.

We only realize how much more slowly we are moving when little cousin catches up, having followed us after all. It is still emitting its keening cry, though it quiets when it sees us, grabbing for us with its tentacles.

"Yes, we are here," we reassure it, shifting the engram core out of little cousin's grasp. It tugs at us, and we pat its face, trying to soothe it. "We are sorry you were hurt." It is clearly still distressed, but we do not know how to calm it, and the engram core is a much more pressing problem.

The core has not imposed any new memories on us, although it has yet to lose its amaranthine shine. We still do not have a solution for the way it continues to activate. But if we cannot keep it out of the Kuhifadis' hands, that will not matter.

Engram cores are as close to a sacred object as the Ngisikaa have. The Kuhifadi cannot be allowed to use this one for their own gain. If we cannot keep it out of their clutches, we will protect it by the only other method available to us: we will take the memories into ourself, and destroy the engram core entirely.

It is not a thought that any memory-tender would relish. Our aim is to preserve, not to destroy. But it seems that to succeed in the one, we may have to choose the other.

We resume our trek down the rocky riverbed, little cousin following behind. Faintly, we see the glint of sunlight on the ocean far ahead, but we do not have much hope that we will reach it before the Kuhifadi catch up.

We run until little cousin starts its plaintive keening again, and we are so exhausted we almost feel like we could join it. But over its griping, we hear Kuhifadi voices calling to each other in the distance, and know that we are out of time.

We pause to scan our surroundings, looking for somewhere to duck out of sight. It would not do for the

Kuhifadi to come upon us before we are finished. We should not need long.

Across the river we find a small pool, partially hidden by rocks and overgrown weeds. Hopefully that will be sufficient to conceal the glow of the engram core until we are finished.

Little cousin, close on our heels, makes a tremulous noise.

"No, no, do not cry, little one. Here." And we hastily begin unwrapping layers of seaweed, tossing gobs of it to little cousin. It offers a muted trill in response, and tucks into the seaweed with thankfully quiet enthusiasm.

We wrap two tentacles around the engram core, and think a silent apology to those Ngisikaa—Riaaaaaaarl, and who knows how many others—whose memories we are, in all likelihood, about to permanently destroy. The memories will be preserved within our own mind for a time, and it is possible the Ngisikaa may be able to recover them—and perhaps us—if we reach the memory depository before the madness of holding those memories overtakes us. But the Kuhifadi seem to have much of this area under their control, and we suspect that Lajikii will not allow us to pass through now, whether we still have the engram core or not.

The chord sounds again as we absorb the first engram into ourself, a full triad this time, in a booming knell that erases any hope we had of remaining hidden until the process is complete. Distantly, we hear the Kuhifadi yell. Our vision goes pink at the edges.

We are Riaaaaaaarl, and we are being pursued.

I think it is Uchafumlaji behind me, though I'm not entirely certain. They have become protective of what remains of their tunnels. I have long ago dropped the clockwork weapon I carried, much good the miserable thing did me in the end. I clutch the one engram core I have been able to salvage in four of my tentacles.

I had hoped the Uchafumlaji would give up pursuit once I clawed my way out of the collapsed tunnel and into the daylight, but I still hear footsteps pounding behind me. My only hope now is the lavender flickers of active engram cores in the distance. It makes no sense for them to be there; the depository is in ruins, I watched it fall myself. There should be nothing to see. But those flickers are all the hope I have, so I run for them.

We blink, and though the pink fringe around our vision does not entirely fade, we can see our surroundings again. Little cousin has looked up from its seaweed dinner, watching us uncertainly. The Kuhifadi emerge from the bushes somewhere upriver. One of them—Lajikii, we presume—points an imperious arm our way. The engram core pulses, growing ever brighter.

Little cousin makes a questioning noise, but we have no time for it now. We can only hope its caution remains stronger than its curiosity. We query the engram core again, this time attempting to pull multiple engrams at once. This would be a reckless action, if we expected either ourself or the engram core to survive. But neither of those is a concern, so we are free to move quickly.

The engram core pulses again, and we are—

ourself, encoding one last engram as we prepare for an army that might not come—

Riaaaaaaarl, squinting as I run toward structures that look almost like buildings, where there should be none—

other Ngisikaa, whose names we do not know, and the landscape changes around us until we are not even certain if we are seeing one memory or many—

ourself, staggering backward with the engram core balanced in our tentacles as the Kuhifadi close in. Lajikii leads the charge, tearing at branches and brambles that get in their way. Little cousin edges toward us, offering a querulous whimper. The surface of the river looks deep and dark, more like a tunnel than a waterway.

Another flash from the engram core, and we are—

Riaaaaaaarl, gaping at tall buildings that sprout out of the ground like great Kuh, when I suddenly realize that I can no longer hear footsteps behind me—

ourself, scuttling away from the charging Lajikii, as if we might still buy ourself enough time to finish destroying the engram core. But Lajikii is moving quickly, and the engram core holds many memories, and we are slow, too slow, so slow that we cannot even stop little cousin when it reaches out and wraps a tentacle around the crystalline core. Its body begins to glow even brighter.

Weird, membranous crowns seem to sprout like shadows from the trees around us, and we are—

Riaaaaaaarl, seeing what is unmistakably a memory depository in the middle distance, inexplicably tended by more beings than just Ngisikaa. A voice says, "Ho, friend!" and I feel a fresh burst of panic when I realize it is an Uchafumlaji that hails me; I thought I had shaken my pursuers but he is on me, but then he extends his empty hands and assures me I am safe—

ourself, raising our tentacles in a flimsy shield as Lajikii grasps their knife and cocks their arm back to throw. The engram core pulses in time with our despair as we realize how utterly we have failed. We could not protect this Ngisikaa treasure, we could not even destroy it, and now Lajikii will kill us and take it for themself. Lajikii stumbles after they throw, but it does not matter, the knife is already arching through the air, only the glint of its blade is dulled by the shadows of those trees that we do not remember being here

and then the knife
and Lajikii
impossibly
disappear.

* * *

We are surrounded by the soothing lavender glow of engram cores, staring up at a memory depository that should not be here. Only, we are not entirely certain where "here" is.

It is certainly not the river basin we were in only moments ago, somewhere on the southeast coast, being chased by thieving Kuhifadi determined to take from us the engram core that remains clutched firmly in our grasp. Their goals were nonsensical, they had thought to use it to call—

Wait. We do recognize this place.

We have seen it before, not with our own two eyes, but in engrams. Down here, on the ground, Uchafumlaji lounge in comfortable pavilions that mark the entrance to underground tunnels, shaded by reaching Kuhifadi buildings whose tops fan out like Kuh membranes. Streets wind away from us in all directions, and the path directly in front of us leads to what is clearly a memory depository, one larger and more complete than anything we had hoped to find.

And of course, none of it should be here.

Is this the madness? We did not expect it to come upon us so quickly. We did not expect that we would feel so...sane.

"Friend Nalilililon! That *is* you!"

We recognize hir voice immediately, of course; we have been living in hir head almost as much as we have lived in our own, of late. Dazed, we turn to face Riaaaaaaarl.

Riaaaaaaarl's expression is warm, welcoming, not what we would expect from a figment of incipient madness.

"I wondered if it might be you, given the engrams that the depository was replaying," Riaaaaaaarl continues. Hir conversational tone is unutterably jarring. "But we can never quite tell who the city will bring us until it does."

"The city," we echo blankly.

"Yes," Riaaaaaaarl says, gesturing all around us with hir tentacles. "Welcome to Kusongangani."

Kusongangani. The traveling city.

"Ah, but of course you are discombobulated," Riaaaaaaarl says, and we almost laugh at the understatement. "I think that is how most of us first experience Kusongangani, to be honest. It seems to come mainly to those who have a need for it. It's a fascinating thing, and some of us are studying the mechanism. But it means we are forever plucking newcomers from the most distressing situations!"

"Distressing situations. Yes," we murmur, to prove we are paying attention.

Riaaaaaaarl's expression softens, becoming concerned. "Ah, but...you are injured, and here I am prattling on. I will find someone to tend to your wounds. Here, let me at least relieve you of that engram core, and give you and your friend a moment to collect yourselves."

We blink at hir, uncertain what xie means. It is only once Riaaaaaaarl has prized the engram core from our grasp that we become conscious of little cousin standing at our shoulder, gazing wide-eyed at the city before us.

"We would welcome your help installing this in the depository, once you are ready," Riaaaaaaarl says, hir tone gentle. "I'll be back in a moment." And xie moves off down a street better tended than any we have seen in weeks or more of travel.

Perhaps we should follow, but for now we can only stare. We are glad that we have not failed, that we have not gone mad, that the engram core was not destroyed or stolen away to be used in Lajikii's unsavory schemes. But now that we find ourselves—unbelievably—successful, we don't quite know what to do.

Then little cousin says clearly, "Jaririiriiii." And, when we don't acknowledge it right away, it reaches out and tugs at us insistently. "Jaririiriiii."

"Yes, jaririiriiii," we agree absently. Part of us feels badly brushing it off, but our mind is whirling with everything Riaaaaaaarl has just told us, with the discovery of this impossible city. We need time to clear our thoughts. We will reconcile with little cousin in a moment.

"No," it says, clear frustration in its voice.

We turn to stare.

It gazes back with a studied stillness that seems very unlike the half-wild animal that followed us out of the ngisikaa herd. A very *silent* stillness, it occurs to us belatedly, as it has stopped its mournful keening. Until just now, we had not heard its voice since...since it laid its tentacles on the activated engram core.

Of course. We feel stupid for not realizing it sooner.

We look at little cousin. Its—*hir*—eyes are wide with expectation.

"Jaririiriiii," we echo, deliberately this time. "Is that your name, little cousin?"

"Yes. Yes!" And xie flings hir tentacles wide and dances about, too joyful to be awkward. "I am Jaririiriiii!"

Our weariness is no match for hir sheer delight at hir own awakening. "Well then, we cannot call you little cousin any longer, can we?"

"Oh, I don't mind." Xie turns to me, one tentacle resting on each leg and two folded in front, the very picture of playful exasperation. "But you haven't told me what to call *you*."

We really have become a boor, haven't we? "We are Nalilililon. And this"—we gesture out to the city around us—"is Kusongangani."

"Kusongangani," Jaririiriiii repeats, as if tasting the name. "I like it."

And so, we realize, do we.

"Well then, little cousin," we say. "Jaririiriiii. Allow us to be the first to welcome you home."

Reese Hogan

An Honest Life

CE 1201

My pal Tumwara once said folks are drawn to apocalyptic stories because...well, as I recall, it was something about the world feeling too far gone, and the need to wipe the slate clean and start all over again.

For Juno, I reckon that wiped slate was the Collapse, twelve hundred years ago. And for me, it's a brand-new captaincy, a new voyage, and a crew that's never met me. A clean slate. How fitting it should be on an expedition 'cross the world—an expedition which aims to discover what happened on the eastern continent after we lost contact during the Collapse, no less.

Tumwara came to see me off. They gave me a journal, and said, "Until we can find and reestablish the memory storage locations of the Ngisikaa again, it's on all of us to record new memories, Hahana. That includes you."

I protested that I ain't a writer. But Tumwara said, "Remember. A clean slate. You *can* be a writer this time around. If you want to."

Now sunlight beats down from a clear sky, filling the Kuh that cover my body with light and warmth. The ocean stretches out before me. Other ships in the fleet, of which my own *Ehhala* is but a bit piece, are scattered on either side. I want to sleep and fill my Kuh in the ocean breezes, like I used to, but I know this new crew thinks better of me. They see an upstanding captain—a writer, even!—who may be a bit untried, but who knows what they're about.

A clean slate. One where I reinvent myself with every word I write.

* * *

Land ahead!

So far, the eastern continent of Kusafirima is but a dead stretch of brown land. The ocean is choppy 'neath a cloudy sky. The sunlight absorbed by my crew's Kuh leaks unused magic from our bodies in a steady glow, making it clear how charged we've become under our sun these last few months.

The land, though, ain't even my biggest news. A few nights back, all the captains met on the parent-ship *Unauna*. The overseer of the expedition praised me for my navigation of the boundary currents during a stormy bout near Kuinuajuu's southern island. It felt like a swell sign for my new, more professional, career—at least 'til the overseer added, "Must come from sneaking around the inlets and fjords in northern Ardhi, eh, smuggler?"

My smile froze in place. I hadn't lied to get here, after all. I just hadn't supposed it'd be thrown in my face so casually.

A clean slate, I told myself. Not ashamed. Just reinvented.

"You got me," I said with a wink.

The overseer laughed. "Truth be told, I wouldn't mind you on one of the culturists' teams once we head inland," they said. "You have a good head under your Kuh, and probably some fresh perspective. What do you think? About going from smuggling to archaeologing?"

I grinned, more at ease than I'd been in weeks. "Reckon I'd be honored, helmer."

Their lip quirked at the sea rovers' term. "Captain Hahana, I don't think you've met Fujivii," they said, waving someone forward.

I glanced over, fixing to meet another sailor...and instead found myself looking at a Kuhifadi shrouded head to toe. Barely a scrap of blue skin or pointed ears showed, and no glow of solar energy leaked from within their robe.

A mage.

I must've stared. It was mages who helped bring about the Collapse twelve hundred years ago, even if it wasn't *all* mages. Mages from the guild known as the Order of Obarikaa are still legends used to scare Kuhifadi whelps, and I was no exception. In my profession—*former* profession—gray marketing with mages wasn't something I did. Ever.

How could they stand that constant barrier of fabric between themself and the sun? Was it true that meditation kept magic locked in their Kuh? Did they have ruptures 'cross their body, where they'd torn open their Kuh to use magic?

Yes, I stared. And then the mage approached me, and I put an arm 'cross my chest and bent at the waist, in respect to their position.

The overseer, with true double-crossing energy, chuckled and clapped me on the shoulder before leaving me alone with them.

"Captain Hahana," the mage said, from within the depths of their hood. "It was your ship that the Uchafumlaji called Jicalaan chartered last year for his journey north."

The shock of this casual comment was a hundred times worse than the overseer's one about my past.

I straightened slowly. "How can you know that, Honored One?"

The mage cocked their head. "Do you really think it coincidence that you were approved for this mission? A smuggler?"

My heart sank. Because I *had* thought that. Akkakuh help me, what a fool I was.

For that experience with the Uchafumlaji—more than the career itself—was the moment I was running from. I hadn't gotten into smuggling to transport those who'd once hunted down and eaten our kind, especially when I knew there were still those who didn't live by the pledge not to hunt us Kuhifadi. The only reason I'd taken Jicalaan's charter was because I was afraid to say no.

I don't know his story, though I strongly suspect he was a former indentured servant of the mages, escaping illegally. It seemed like a slippery slope for a smuggler already working the edges of the law—Uchafumlaji passing the word around, hiring me, always holding me hostage with the threat of being their prey if I didn't cooperate. I'll never forget Jicalaan staring at me through his reptilian predator's eyes, ignoring my stabs at conversation. He'd only spoken once the entire time—something muttered beneath his breath, about "fun." It chilled me to the bone. The solar energy within my Kuh was little comfort, seeing as how I'd never trained with it. That magic was the mages' domain. I didn't want nothing to do with either Uchafumlaji *or* mages.

Tumwara calls it narrow-minded. I call it *safe*.

After that voyage, I knew I had to leave the business while I still could. So, what under Akkakuh's light did Fujivii mean about it not being a *coincidence* that I was hired for this?

"That's behind me now," I told Fujivii. "And I'd thank you not to dredge it up again. I'm here honestly and aim to remain that way."

I could almost see the glint of eyes within their hood. "Not every voyage takes you as far as you'd like, Hahana. No matter how much you might wish it."

As it seemed the sort of thing Tumwara thought I should record, I've tried to do so here. But what's harder to put to words is my sense of dread afterward. I can only hope for the best. I live an honest life now. Even the mage and their cryptic threats shouldn't be able to change that.

* * *

Burnt patches gouge Kusafirima's terrain, as if fires burned here for decades on end. The air is still tinged with the scent of smoke, even after all this time. I'd thought the land to be desert, but now I wonder if it's an illusion; if it was once as alive as our own Ardhi 'cross the sea, but burned 'til most any trace of it was gone.

I heard folks' guesses as we debarked the ship, blackened slag crumbling under our feet. "Meteor." "Eruption." "Magic."

Aren't they nearly one and the same? I've heard tell of ancient Ngomechini—a volcanic eruption, yes, but supposedly caused by a mage releasing the energy from all their Kuh at once. This evidence of the Collapse has to be something similar.

My crew set to hauling supplies from the ship. I saw one of my sailors, Maraba, lean over to puke into the surf. I winced. I'd turned a blind eye to them sneaking drink the night before, but now I regretted it.

I looked around furtively, afraid someone would take it upon themself to discipline the poor wretch. I wasn't used to running with such a posh outfit. The captain of the ship next to mine looked severe enough to punish us both if they caught a whiff of it.

So I made a snap decision. I swung by Maraba's side and gripped their arm, then released the solar energy from one of the lesser-filled Kuh membranes on the back of my hand. Releasing Kuh wasn't commonly done by non-mages like myself, and the sacrifice of even the small magic showed right off in the dizziness that washed over me. But the energy successfully flowed over my fingers and into Maraba's belly, soothing their hangover.

Maraba looked up with a gasp. "Captain—"

"Don't mention it," I said.

"You didn't have to do that!" they said. "It was my fault—"

"I'm serious," I said in a low voice. "Don't mention it."

Maraba caught my embarrassed glance toward the other captain. A smirk played across their lips, as if we'd conspired in something illegal. It felt like a slide back from the honest life I wanted. A discomforting feeling. I have to do better than this.

* * *

Our first several days passed quiet-like, as we hiked inland and set up shelters on the blackened land each night, hoisted up on stilts to protect us from potential predators. The seventh day, however, those "potential predators" became all too real.

There are Uchafumlaji here.

They're shrouded as heavily as our own mage under the sun's rays, but are twice as large. The ones we've seen so far have been in the distance, always alone. I can't remember if they were pack hunters back in the day, before the accords passed that kept them from calling us prey.

Do these ones even know of the accords?

I've tried to remain professional, but these Uchafumlaji have me shaken. I swear I can feel the mage watching me, waiting for me to crack. I went two nights without sleep, too jittery to even write. The third night, I found Maraba, hoping a good sailor at my back would help relax me. No such luck. But Maraba had some Wanishin rum, which I lectured them for over a flask of the stuff. Let that go on my record.

* * *

I just saw how long it's been since I wrote. Dammit, I promised Tumwara better than this.

First off, the contact we'd hoped to make with the Uchafumlaji still ain't happened. When our mediators approach them, they disappear without a trace, no doubt into tunnels we can't see. Needless to say, I'm not sleeping any easier.

But we *did* finally find one today. A tunnel, that is. But not one in use. This was the ruins of one.

It's been over two months since we made landfall, and the flat desert wasteland has given way to mountain desert wasteland. True to their word, the overseer's placed me on an archaeological team, and we were the ones that stumbled upon a dark hole in the ground. The walls past the entrance were lined with curved discs, cracked with age, reflecting the sunlight away from the passage. I immediately knew we were looking at ancient Uchafumlaji technology.

A team of eight went in, including myself and Fujivii, the mage. Our leather wraps were knotted high around our thighs and shoulders, so the light from our Kuh membranes lit the space. A large chamber with pillars spread out underground. The walls were made with some marvel of engineering that wasn't quite stone and wasn't quite brick. Sections of ceiling had lost huge chunks of it to show volcanic rock beyond. Passages branched off every which way. Cracks ran along the ceiling, letting in roots and the smell of soil.

I must have been jumpy, because one of the culturists said, "Why under Akkakuh's light did the overseer send a spooked amateur down?"

Spooked indeed! I was about to haul them over the yardarm when Fujivii said, "They're here at my request."

Well, *that* killed my confidence real fast. The culturist who'd spoken paired us off. No surprise I was stuck with the mage after that. I silently swore I wouldn't be pulled into their scheming.

Fujivii took point, and it didn't take long to realize they were guiding us a certain direction, from the more developed chambers into deeper cruder ones. The material of the walls became natural earth, with signs of Uchafumlaji claws furrowed where they'd tunneled hundreds of years ago. I was about to ask Fujivii where they were taking us when we arrived in a squarish alcove.

This was where we found an unbelievably advanced piece of Uchafumlaji machinery. It was also where we found the body.

Decayed and withered, it had the thick rounded head and scaly skin of an Uchafumlaji. It lay on a long platform with the machine over its head. It made my stomach turn. I would have been less surprised to find a corpse of my own people here; this looked like experimentation on one of their own.

My voice shook as I said, "Where are we?"

"This is what I needed to talk to you about," Fujivii said. They walked 'round the machine to the other side. Against my will, I followed.

When I saw a steel box, my mouth went dry. I recognized that box. Or...no. The design on its lid was different from the one Jicalaan had carried on my ship. But similar enough. He hadn't let that box go the entire time I'd seen him. His eyes on mine as he'd stroked a clawed thumb over its surface. The way he'd muttered the word *fun*...

"You knew this was here," I whispered.

"Suspected," Fujivii admitted. "It's a dangerous thing the Uchafumlaji tampered with—dangerous to us all. I waited to speak with you because I only have a guess of what's inside, and it's top-secret enough that I didn't dare spread speculation—not even to the overseer. But if we open it and see what I think we will, then you'll see why you need to tell me everything about the Uchafumlaji on your ship."

I swallowed. "You're saying this ain't authorized by the overseer?"

"It is not," Fujivii said.

I blew out my breath. "I told you, Honored One. I'm here as an honest worker, with a clean slate. I was almost pulled in over my head once already. I don't want no part of illegal secrets. Not anymore."

"Captain Hahana, some things need more secrecy than legality allows," said the mage. "Just trust me on this."

But I couldn't. I couldn't trust a mage any more than I could trust an Uchafumlaji. Just like with Jicalaan, if I gave in this once, it could turn into a slippery slope I may never climb out from.

So I grabbed the steel box and said, "Apologies, Honored One, but it's the overseer I answer to. Not you. I'm bringing this to the culturists."

"Captain, no!" Fujivii shouted, putting a hand out. But I'd already picked it up.

Two things happened then. The box jolted as some kind of wires attaching from its base to the machine reached their limit. And the corpse on the platform jerked upright, its head smashing into the bottom of the machine.

I screamed and dropped the box, instinctively grabbing my belt knife. But some primal urge led me to slash open a Kuh on my forearm rather than plunging it into the body; magic against a reanimated corpse seemed a better bet than raw steel, in my panicked mind.

Pain erupted across my arm as my uncontrolled magic exploded across the room, with the raw power but none of the training or ritual of a mage. I reeled from the flash as the whole place shuddered, raining chunks of rock from the ceiling.

The corpse fell back to the platform the second I dropped the box. I saw now that it hadn't come to life at all; rather, there were wires jutting from its head, some severed and others still snaking up into the machine. The wires at the box's base must have still been attached to the body and pulled the head up when I'd grabbed it.

The box lay on the floor, contents spilled at my feet. It was white grit, its grains chunks of flat faces with sharp angles. Crystal. Crystal dust. Just like the revered Ngisikaa used in their memory storage locations.

My stomach lurched. The crystals of the Ngisikaa were sacred—they were the best method we had of recording history on Juno—and here was evidence that the Uchafumlaji had stolen one of those crystals and *destroyed* it. Had this crystal dust once held memories of what happened here during the Collapse?

Jicalaan had one of these boxes, I thought. *Right on my ship. And I never even challenged it...*

Then Fujivii pulled me from the chamber, running us back to the main room. We found the others, but it was clear by now we weren't gonna make it out. I held my injured arm to my side, dizzy and weak from using such large magic.

The same Kuhifadi who'd mocked me earlier saw the ruptured Kuh on my arm, along with the dagger still clutched in my other hand. Their lip curled as they pieced together what I'd done.

Then Fujivii grabbed a ceremonial knife of some kind, threw off their robe, and tore the blade through the Kuh down their left side. All the solar magic that had been ritually locked behind the membranes poured out in a flood of light.

The underground cave kept falling, but a shield of light now stood between us and the destruction, illuminating every rock above that would have crushed us. As the culturists huddled closer, Fujivii stood strong, pouring their magic into protecting us. I was struck by awe unlike any I've felt before. Not quite like basking in the light of Akkakuh himself, but more like breathing in the magical potential of us all, if we chose to follow the path of a mage.

In that moment, Fujivii was the light of the sun.

Afterward...after they'd signaled our position through our barrier...after we'd waited hours for rescue...after Fujivii's strength started waning, and we all stared at their ruptured Kuh and prayed our rescuers would hurry...after all that, Fujivii was no longer the light of the sun. They were carried to a first-aid tent, crying out in pain from the sun's light on their mutilated body, even as the rest of us breathed in relief to be free.

My one ruptured Kuh told the overseer and everyone else of my mistake. I'd almost killed our team and destroyed an entire city of history. I tried to tell them about the moving corpse and the wires jutting from its head—the indication of torture or worse. But the overseer had lost their patience with me. I was told I was an unreliable witness and had been seeing things in my hatred and paranoia of the Uchafumlaji that didn't exist. My ruptured Kuh was bandaged, and I was ordered back to my crew in disgrace.

I wanted to talk to Fujivii—to curse at them for causing this, to ask about the crystal dust I hadn't bothered mentioning after everything else I'd said was shot down—but the mage was in no shape to talk. So I turned back to this journal, because without these words, it might well not have happened at all.

* * *

I know I shouldn't put this in a journal of "important historical discoveries," but I slept with Maraba last night.

I badly wanted to tell someone—anyone—about Fujivii trying to use me, and about the destroyed memory crystal from some horrible Uchafumlaji experiment. Writing it in my journal ain't enough. But I don't want to endanger Maraba. When drink started loosening my tongue, it seemed safer to kiss them, and choke off my own thoughts and words instead. The way they ran their hands down the Kuh of my ribs damn near made everything worth it.

But this morning, I feel like a deadbeat rat bagger. I came on this mission to start a clean slate as more than a smuggler and scoundrel. Instead, my mental state has been questioned, and now I'm janking my crewmates.

* * *

At long last, we've found our first Kuhifadi ruins. The structures built on thick stilts have all but collapsed, their wooden remains half-buried under sand dunes and cacti. At one point, they'd been so much stabler than our mobile shelters that, decrepit or not, I mulled over sleeping in one for the night. The Uchafumlaji can't easily climb these buildings with their long-clawed hands.

The culturists set to work. I was not asked to help. I still haven't been allowed to speak with Fujivii, either. So I helped my crew set up the shelters. Afterward, I walked deep into the ruins.

Because I've come up with a plan.

If I can capture one of the wandering Uchafumlaji, then I can get answers about the wires in the corpse's head and the destroyed Ngisikaa crystal. And I can take that prisoner and confession to the overseer, so they can see I was right all along.

They'll have no choice but to trust me again.

I brought a ship's net from our supplies. I went to the opposite edge of the dilapidated city, far from the expedition. Then I climbed into one of the still-standing structures and waited for nightfall, when the nocturnal predators would roam.

Now I wait. My skin is wrapped tight 'neath black fabric to hide my glowing Kuh. The ruptured Kuh on my forearm burns beneath it like sin. My heart pounds as the light fades, the words I write getting harder and harder to see. I'm too far from camp to make it back before it's pitch black out, but I'm trying not to think about that.

I have to do this.

* * *

I'm lucky to be writing these words at all.

A few hours into the night, when my eyelids were growing heavy, I spotted him: a huge Uchafumlaji a couple dozen feet below my shelter, hood pushed back to show his leathery head and pointed snout in the moonlight. I cast the net before I could lose my nerve. I'd captured both largetooth spine turtles and horned lion sharks in my time, so my toss was plenty skilled, the folds of the weighted net coming down around him perfectly.

His head jerked up, more intelligence in his eyes than any lion shark. His clawed hand shot for the falling edge of the net. Akkakuh above, if he kept it from pinning him, I'd be done for! I reacted with part instinct, part resignation—I'd already ruptured one Kuh; what was another?—and I pulled my knife and slashed a Kuh on my wrist, blinding him with a burst of light.

A big mistake.

I was already unbalanced from throwing the net, and my rush to cut my Kuh didn't help none at all. The disorientation of using the magic hit me in a wave. I slammed against the ground twenty-five feet below before I even realized I'd fallen. I was so stunned that I couldn't feel the pain for several moments. Then it erupted 'cross my body, like I'd been hit by cannon fire.

Teeth clenched, I turned my head from where I lay, vision swimming, newly ruptured Kuh screaming with pain, nausea roiling my stomach. I was within arm's reach of the Uchafumlaji, if not for the net. Amazingly, the burst of magic had worked; he'd reeled back, his arm 'cross his eyes, giving the net time to anchor to the ground.

I'd actually done it. I'd caught him!

He lowered his arm. His gaze locked on mine, where I lay breathless on the ground. His eyes watered in the moonlight, with redness in the folds around them, as if my flash of light had burned his skin.

Despite that, his scaled lip quirked in amusement. He raised a clawed hand to his brow and tipped an imaginary hat.

"It was clever, I'll grant you that," he said in a deep rumbling voice.

I blinked, my breath shuddering.

His gaze roamed over my weakened form. "But you're not an exceptionally powerful mage, are you?"

"I'm not a mage," I managed in a whispered rasp.

The folds around his eyes raised slightly, then relaxed again. "Ah. Very good."

Before I could answer, he settled into a sitting position and pulled a gadget from his rumpled cloak. It started humming in his hand, and seconds later, he was slicing the fibers of the net, with something quicker and neater than any knife.

I went cold. This was something I'd always known about Uchafumlaji, but somehow failed to plan for: they were geniuses. We had magic; they had stuff like *that*. That's why mages had imprisoned so many Uchafumlaji for their knowledge after the Collapse. What had I been thinking? I wasn't trained in magic, and a single Kuhifadi had never been a match for an Uchafumlaji...

I tried to get an arm under me, fixing to get a running start before he escaped. But the world spun, and I collapsed with a gasp.

Dammit! Where was my knife? It wouldn've saved me, but would've been better than nothing. But my hands were empty, the knife that had slashed my Kuh nowhere to be seen.

"So there's no team waiting to descend on me?" the Uchafumlaji said. "No mage? No expedition overseer?"

I closed my eyes, lightheaded with fear. I never should've said I wasn't a mage. A slight fear of me may have held him back. Now, any moment, he'd free himself and rip my throat out...

"You act on your own, then," the Uchafumlaji said when I didn't answer. "How curious. Now why would you do that?"

The humming stopped. I forced my eyes open to see him pulling the ropes away from his body.

"You...you know of the accords..." I got out, almost begging.

He looked up with a long lazy blink. "And *you* know that attacking me nullifies them."

A strangled whimper escaped my throat.

He blew a breath from his nostrils. "Don't throw the 'accords' at me if you haven't bothered studying them, traveler. But I'll take mercy on you if you pass along a message for me."

I stared at him so long that he waved a hand in front of my face, seeing if I were still alive.

"Message," I repeated, too dumbfounded to say more.

"As you know..." The Uchafumlaji paused, studying me critically. "Maybe you don't. But as you *should* know, the mages in the Order of Obarikaa took many of us prisoner and forced us to teach them our technology. Those of us here on the eastern continent are the remaining descendants of the first free generation. But the last thing we want is to get carted back to Ardhi and forced into servitude all over again. Which means that *mage* you're traveling with is a threat to us all. So please pass along the word that the Order of Obarikaa is overthrown, and we're rebuilding now. The eastern continent starts anew, and we don't want you westerners to be part of it. We want you to leave. For good."

With those words, he stood and turned to go. I swallowed hard. A clean slate, he was saying. That's what he wanted. Like me.

But my own past had kept me from the clean slate I needed. If I went back to camp with no more than the Uchafumlaji's message to leave, I'd face more accusations of paranoia and worse. The overseer would never believe me; they'd think my mental health was spiraling further than ever.

I raised my voice. "That don't explain what you're doing with those destroyed Ngisikaa memory crystals. Or the wires in that Uchafumlaji corpse's brain."

The predator halted, his body going stiff. He turned just enough for one eye to pin me where I lay. "So you can talk," he said in a low growl. "And yet *that's* what you choose to say."

A thrill of fear shot through me. But it was *validating* fear; what I had seen was real, and important.

"Tell me what it is," I said. "Then, and *only* then, will I fork over your message. Good luck getting the mages to leave you be if I don't."

He turned to face me. "Are you the only one who saw it? This crystal? The wires?"

I pushed myself to my knees. The newly ruptured Kuh on my wrist sent pain shooting up my arm, but at least it supported me.

"No," I lied. "Wasn't just me."

He stepped forward. "You're here alone. No one sent you. Which means that you trying to capture me is a personal mission somehow. *Capture* me...not kill me." A muscle in his leathery jaw twitched. "You wanted a confession, didn't you? Or proof. It *was* just you. And it's still just you. Acting on your own."

Akkakuh help me. It was terrifying how smart he was.

"Well, it don't change my terms—" I said carefully.

"Oh yes," he interrupted. "It very much does." He let out a long sigh, but I could almost hear words in it: *Unzulaja. Ill-fated.*

...Fun.

No. I was imagining it. I had to be.

But I wasn't imagining his look of pity as he said, "I wasn't going to kill you, westerner. But unfortunately, I don't see that you've left me much choice."

He started forward, walking over the crumpled net. I scrambled to my feet, dizzy but upright, not daring to turn my back. Should I burst another Kuh? But how could I, without my knife?

My back hit the base of a stilt in the structure I'd ambushed him from with a hard *thunk*. My breath caught as I realized what the sound was—my journal, tucked in the waistband of the black wrap I wore.

"I have a journal!" I shouted, hands thrust out in defense.

The Uchafumlaji paused, his form towering over me.

"It's back at camp!" I said desperately. "If I disappear, the overseer will search my quarters and find it. And it has all the information about what I found. Everything!"

He pressed his clawed fingers to his forehead. "I'm almost insulted. My night vision is more than adequate enough to have seen the shape of a book in your clothes, and my hearing even keener when you backed into the post just now. It's another clever ruse, but ultimately useless. You don't, after all, look like a writer to me."

My mouth fell open. "Was that a jab at me? Right before killing me?"

"Is it the first one you've caught?" he said. Then, before I could stop him, he reached behind me and pulled the journal from my waistband.

I grabbed for it, but he held it out of reach. Then he held his other hand out, one finger raised in warning, before opening it to flip through. He shouldn't have been able to read it in the dark, but his predator's eyesight had no issues in the moonlight.

"You *did* write it," he said, surprised.

I glared at him.

"Conveniently, this will tell me exactly what you know," he said. "So allow me a second to analyze our position, if you will."

What followed was awkward, to say the least. I stood before him like a prisoner awaiting a delayed execution, with the added humiliation of my writing being read for the first time in my life.

"Your friend Tumwara is right," he said at one point. "You're abysmally narrow-minded."

His words stung. "And you're any different, not trusting mages?" I shot back.

He pointed at me, allowing me the hit. "You're a decent writer, though, for a former smuggler. Laying out whole scenes like this is quite the extra mile for a captain's log."

"I wanted a detailed account," I muttered.

He went quiet and kept reading. I reckon I could have sailed to Ardhi and back by the time he lowered the book again.

"So, you've only ever met this one Uchafumlaji, this Jicalaan," he said. "And your mage knew about him the second they met you. Clearly, your mage was watching

Jicalaan, even back then. My paranoia in not trusting your mages is justified."

I nodded warily.

"Your mage is still watching you," he went on. "Which means your...disappearance...would not go unnoticed. That makes this harder. We want you all to *leave*, not have your mage's curiosity further piqued."

I swallowed, nodding again.

He held the journal out with a sigh. "You're only out here, trying to capture me, because you want to regain honor with your overseer. The crystal dust and corpse are of less concern to you, from what I can tell. So if I can help you with the former, maybe you can forget the latter. Yes?"

My hand shook as I took the journal back. "I'm listening..."

"Your expedition is hoping to discover what happened on the eastern continent. If you were to stumble upon the memory location of the Ngisikaa—and find it destroyed—then your overseer and mage alike will know there's nothing more to be found here. They'll go back home and write Kusafirima's history off as lost forever. And if *you're* the one who leads them to this memory location, you gain their respect back. Best of all, you don't have to say a thing about me or the crystal dust or any of it. I'll give you a direction and it will be up to you to convince your overseer without mentioning me. And in return, I'll let you live. We all win. Do we have a deal?"

A destroyed memory storage location? Had the Uchafumlaji destroyed it, or had the Collapse? Was it related to what I'd seen in the underground Uchafumlaji city?

I shouldn't have been fretting over it, with my life handed back to me. I couldn't help it, though. I wanted answers.

But I knew I needed to take what he was offering and get away, while I still could.

"Deal," I said.

He gave me the location. Then he walked away. I never even got his name. And once more, I turned to my journal as the only place to share this.

I can't kick the strange idea that it had been nice not being alone with the thoughts in here, if only for a while.

* * *

I approached the overseer at sunrise. Grudgingly, they allowed me into their shelter. Fujivii the mage lay on a portable litter inside. The newly ruptured Kuh membranes on their body were hidden under gauze, but their face—for the first time I'd seen—was uncovered. My gaze lingered on the ruin of their left cheek, where a cluster of Kuh should've been. I think I'd known deep down that Kuh didn't grow back after rupturing. Never much cared before. But now...

Fujivii's gaze drifted to the wrist I'd wrapped the night before, to hide my second ruptured Kuh. I folded my arms over my chest, covering it.

"We should turn northeast, helmer," I told the overseer.

They frowned, abandoning their packing to turn to me. "What? Why?"

"*If* the Ngisikaa ever had a memory storage location here, they would've needed more moisture, a cooler climate, and more green," I said. "That's north, not south, like we're headed."

"We didn't necessarily expect to find a storage location," said the overseer with narrowed eyes.

"But why throw away the chance?" I asked. "I daresay I sailed past their home continent of Kuinuajuu dozens of times, and when the wind shifted last night and brought me a similar scent from up north, it all came clear. Call it a sea rover's hunch."

The overseer started to shake their head, but Fujivii said, "I recommend we trust them, overseer."

It wasn't all said and done that fast. I was sent out for the discussion that followed, and no one came to get me afterward. But when we did finally start moving again, almost half a day later, we headed northeast.

The mage's role in it leaves an uneasy feeling in my stomach. I need to talk to them, as soon as possible.

* * *

I've finally—*finally*—had a chance to talk with Fujivii.

They're on their feet now, still heavily shrouded against the sunlight, and moving gingerly as if their ruptured Kuh pain them something fierce. I caught up with them a few days into our trek, and said abruptly, "You saw what was in the box in the underground city. You knew it was there. You led me to it."

Fujivii turned their head, their face all but invisible behind the hood again. "Now that you've seen the remnants of the memory crystal too, and recognize the danger, are you ready to tell me about Jicalaan?"

I remembered Fujivii saying they hadn't wanted to spread gossip about what was in the box without proof. "What do you want to know?" I asked. "I never saw what was in his box."

"I want to know where he disembarked your ship," said Fujivii. "We lost track of you both north of Mwanga."

I hesitated. After my meeting with the strange Uchafumlaji a few days earlier, it felt like a fast turnaround to throw one of his own to the mages after he'd let me live. "Tell me what you think the crystal dust's purpose is first, Honored One."

To my surprise, they answered right away. "The Ngisikaa are the memory keepers of the entire planet of Juno. It is the mages' concern that the Uchafumlaji here have been breaking crystals and seeding them with false memories featuring them as the heroes and victors of the Collapse."

My breath caught. "And you think Jicalaan was trying to spread this altered memory dust 'round the world?"

"Perhaps," said Fujivii. "Or perhaps seeking a permanent memory storage location to contaminate."

It couldn't be true. Could it? The Uchafumlaji I talked to had said they just wanted to be left alone! But...what if that was why? So no one discovered what they were doing?

Maybe I shouldn't have cut a deal so quickly. I should've pushed harder, dug for the real truth.

I could tell the mage about him. They could help me find him again. With their protection at my back, I'd be safe. Except, for some reason, I *believed* the Uchafumlaji's fear, when he'd talked of the mage: *The last thing we want is to get carted back to Ardhi and forced into servitude all over again. Which means that mage you're traveling with is a threat to us all.*

I didn't think Fujivii would do that. But honestly? There's something very unsettling about them. They know more about me than they should, and they pushed me to tamper with ancient artifacts behind the culturists' backs. I've never trusted mages, and with good reason. The Darksider Revolt is a big part of our history books, when the mages rose to incredible power. It killed hundreds on all three species' sides—the Kuhifadi, the Uchafumlaji, and the memory-hoarding Ngisikaa—ending in the Collapse that erased huge chunks of civilization and history.

"About the Uchafumlaji..." I began hesitantly.

"Say it, Hahana," said Fujivii, a tad impatiently.

"Was part of your mission here to get more indentured servants?" I asked. "Is that why you've been trying to hunt them down?"

There was a pause before Fujivii answered. "I'd actually hoped to reestablish relations. But there's a lot of work to be done, as evidenced by the fact that they won't even let us approach them. Plus, the ones here are wilder than the ones back home. I'm not sure how communication will go, even if we manage to speak with them."

Wilder? The one I'd almost captured hadn't seemed "wild" at all. In fact, he'd made me feel damn near primitive in comparison.

"Now tell me where Jicalaan disembarked your ship," Fujivii said.

Was it wrong that I named a random port in the distant north, far from where I'd actually left him? The mage hadn't directly answered my question, after all, so why should I answer theirs? And after my strange prisoner had let me live—and even let me keep my journal, no less!—the least I could do was get his take on this "false memories" business before siccing the mage on his countryman.

He may think me narrow-minded, but this talk with Fujivii told me I wasn't the only one.

* * *

I've been looking for my Uchafumlaji again.

Just walks after dark, away from camp, hoping he'll find me. If he really does think our team will find the destroyed memory location then head back home, he should know it may not be so easy. Once he realizes that, maybe he'll tell me the truth about what I saw, to clear their names.

But no dice. With our deal made, it's as if he's vanished for good.

My casual lover, Maraba, asked if I've been sneaking out at night to practice magic. I was so startled, I spilled my mug of rum. They laughed, and said that between the new wrap on my wrist and the times they'd seen me with the mage, well...

Long story short, we ended up way outside camp, long after dark, on Maraba's word that I'd "protect them if anything happened," and that "a little danger will liven up this dreary journey."

Maraba, it turns out, is a terrible influence on a clean slate.

* * *

Looking back, there were signs something was off. Maraba and I ended up farther and farther from camp as we traveled from the dry mountains into greener land, sometimes not returning 'til just before dawn, and no one ever gave us guff. The mage stopped hounding me. And—perhaps most telling—we never saw sign of my Uchafumlaji.

But one morning, we were crossing a muddy stream and passed some flotsam caught on a log. A bundle of rope. Barely anyone glanced at this ancient trash, but I did a double take when I saw it was a ruined net, fibers sliced so clean they'd barely unraveled. I paused. A scrap of parchment was attached, trailing in the dirty water. I could just make out blurry handwritten words: *Hang back. Alone.*

I grabbed a knife from my belt and slashed my pack's strap. The bag fell into the shallow creek, spilling supplies. I cursed.

A few folks started helping gather the strewn clothes and food. "I got it!" I snapped, as rudely as possible. "Just keep on!"

That chased them off real quick. Maraba alone hesitated, but I said, "Tell the overseer I'll catch up," then they nodded and disappeared, too.

I started wrangling my wet things and tossing them on the bank, shaking mud from my hands.

"Couldn't you have just said 'nature calls' instead of destroying your bag?" asked a voice dryly from the nearby bushes.

I huffed. "Didn't think of that."

"Of course not."

I could just see the Uchafumlaji's massive reptilian form through the bush's leaves. His eyes were pinned on mine. Despite everything, I shivered.

"I need to talk to you," I said, crouching to grab my dropped knife from between two slippery rocks.

"As do I," the Uchafumlaji said. "That life partner of yours is a spy for the mage."

I fumbled the knife I'd just picked up. It clanged on a rock before sinking back into the murk. "W-What? Life partner? Spy?"

"It's no coincidence they accompany you every single night," he said. "They're hoping to overhear your conversation with me and report it."

"How could you know that?" I asked.

"You'll sleep better if I don't go into details, westerner."

I looked up sharply, the knife forgotten.

He waved a hand dismissively. "The good news is it means you clearly haven't broken our deal by telling your mage anything. Otherwise, they wouldn't have needed to approach your life partner to spy for them. The bad news, of course, is that a life partner you can't trust makes for a devastating future."

I shook my head, dazed. "Okay...this ain't the point, but Maraba's not my *life partner,* so you can stop calling them that."

I caught a frown on the face beneath the cowl, then the Uchafumlaji stepped out from behind the bush. He was about ten feet away, up on the bank, his head-to-toe cloak even thicker than the mage's.

"But you've had many physical encounters together," he said, puzzled. "That sends a strong message, at least among the Uchafumlaji. Of course, when these partnerships were useful in taking down prey, it only made sense to become a lifelong couple and know every nuance of how the other hunts. I thought perhaps the Kuhifadi had a similar sort of permanent symbiotic relationship."

My mouth twisted. Sure. Why *not* stand around casually discussing their best practices for hunting down my kind?

"Didn't you read my journal?" I asked. "Maraba and I...it's just a fling. Don't the Uchafumlaji have flings?"

His brow furrowed at the word, but he caught up quickly. "It's not unheard of. But between the aboveground partnerships and belowground reproduction, it's rare to complicate things with tertiary...flings, as you say."

"You're missing out," I said pointedly.

He drew in a breath, exasperated. "I don't feel you fully appreciate the depth of a partnership's commitment to one another. But that is, as you say, beside the point. The *point* is for you to stop looking for me. And guard that journal of yours with your life, if you don't want it falling into your mage's hands. You may even consider burning it—though, to be perfectly honest, it would be a shame. It's a good history of good intentions, if nothing else."

I gave a slight laugh.

"Now what did you need to tell me?" he asked.

My smile fell. "The mage knows about the crystal dust," I said. "They think the Uchafumlaji intend to use it to spread false memories. I thought you should know."

The predator's eyes flicked in the direction my party had disappeared. "Oh. I see."

"Is it true?" I asked.

"Of course not," he growled. "But what you saw in that underground chamber isn't for the Kuhifadi to know. It's sacred and personal technology. And...and sad. If Kuhifadi knew of these cultural secrets, it would shame us all." His voice dropped lower. "I'd thought all instances of it had been erased."

It wasn't only the underground city I thought of then; it was Jicalaan, and the way he'd stared through me as he'd huddled around his box. Had he seen me as an enemy, who might take this precious secret? Had I been one wrong word away from being bumped off forever?

"I am called Cazikji," the Uchafumlaji said. "And I believe I saw in your journal that you're called Hahana."

I nodded reluctantly.

"You know better than to trust mages," said Cazikji, "even if you meddle in magical arts yourself. You kept the confidence of the Uchafumlaji who chartered your ship, despite being deathly afraid of him. You are an outlaw—"

"Hey, now," I interrupted. "*Former* outlaw."

He shook his head. "You still live by their code. You know how to keep a secret, because to do otherwise is unthinkable to you. *And* you convinced your overseer to turn northeast, despite being out of favor. You have influenced this mission, Captain Hahana, without feeling the need to betray someone's trust to do it. And it is that I appeal to now. I wish to tell you the truth about this crystal dust, so you can help me find a way forward without this knowledge being either widespread or used against us."

I stepped back with a splash, almost dizzy with what he was saying. "P-Please don't ask that of me. I'm here to start an honest life, not to be burdened with more secrets."

"Your 'honest life' is only honorable if those in authority also have good intentions," he said. "If that Uchafumlaji who chartered your ship was running from a life of indentured servitude, was it 'honest' of you not to turn him in, just in case? What about healing your life partner's hangover so they wouldn't be flogged for excessive intoxication? Wouldn't 'honesty' have been telling your overseer?"

I stared at him, stunned.

"You *are* living an honest life," he said. "Which is why I want to tell you."

Slowly, I pulled my waterlogged bag from the stream, then hauled it up to the bank beside him. Part of me still wanted to run. But the other part held my breath, fearing this moment might disappear.

I lowered myself to the grassy bank. Cazikji sat down beside me, his beady eyes on the direction my party had disappeared.

"The dust you saw in the box was indeed the remnants of a Ngisikaa memory crystal," he said. "The Uchafumlaji found some of their broken memory crystals after the Collapse. The machine and box you saw were a technological attempt to preserve our people's memories once the Ngisikaa no longer could. What followed was an excruciating and doomed process from the start. It didn't work. It caused pain—not to the dead, but to the living. Seeing their loved ones' bodies used for these experiments. The tests on those who volunteered as living subjects went no better. I don't even like to think about those times."

"So...they dug wires into corpses' heads?" I asked. "To extract memories?"

"Yes."

"But it didn't work."

"No. Many of the attempts were on the life partners I told you about. Partnerships that focused now on study and research, rather than hunting. The experiments were either on ones who'd died, or ones who were living but died during the experiment. And their living partners...it drove them mad. It was like Hirolajak had ripped out a portion of their souls."

Something sparked in my memory when Cazikji spoke that word. One of their gods? Where had I heard it before?

"The Uchafumlaji that hired you," said Cazikji. "You say he had a box like that, perhaps containing some of the crystal dust. If he took it with him, it could only be because his own life partner was involved in these experiments. He must've taken the box and fled. These experiments are of great shame to my people. We know how sacred the Ngisikaa memory crystals are. For one of our own to have taken that dust...he must have been in great pain to run from the Uchafumlaji with the evidence of what we'd done. He would've faced great punishment if he'd been caught."

My mouth fell open. The way Jicalaan had stared at me, almost *through* me. I'd assumed it was predatory...but what if he hadn't been seeing me because he was looking at someone else entirely? Someone he'd lost?

"But why 'fun'?" I whispered. "That's what he muttered as he stared at me. 'Fun'..." Then I looked up in sudden realization. "Hirolajak! The word you just said. That's what it was. Hirolajak's..."

"...Fun," Cazikji finished, nodding. "An Uchafumlaji expression. It means uncommonly bad luck. Hirolajak is a shadow creature of great misfortune. We call him the Shadow of the Night."

So this encounter, a year later and half a world away from my time with Jicalaan, was how I finally learned the truth: Jicalaan had been deep in grief. He'd been on the lam from his own people with contraband he'd be persecuted for having, but was literally all he had left of his lifelong partner. What had happened to him? I'd sailed him up north to Mkubwa and never heard from him again. Maybe his escape had been successful, and I'd been a crucial part of it.

I was suddenly fiercely glad I hadn't told Fujivii where he'd gone.

"You're smiling," Cazikji said curiously.

"I'm thinking if he'd just told me he was smuggling illegal goods, it would've saved me a lot of heartache," I said.

We laughed.

Then Cazikji said, "So can I trust you with *this* illegal good? The secret of our failed experiments?"

I didn't even have to think before nodding. Because Cazikji was right. There was a place for honesty, and there was a place for the right thing to do. And though I hadn't much thought on it before, they weren't always the same thing.

* * *

When I arrived back, I told Fujivii to call off their spy. "I've talked with the Uchafumlaji," I said, "and what we saw in the underground lab was only the remains of Ngisikaa memory crystals that the mages in the Order of Obarikaa themselves destroyed. The Uchafumlaji considered the memory dust a sacred symbol of their oppressors' cruelty—a reminder of what they were capable of."

Fujivii was furious at me for not bringing my Uchafumlaji straight to them. I thought they'd arrest me, but instead, we continued on. A distance formed between me and the others as they caught on to the mage's anger. The overseer alone started walking with me, holding mostly one-sided conversations about relations between the Kuhifadi and Uchafumlaji. I don't remember when I realized that he was seeing me as a liaison for the next time I was approached. It made me laugh at first. Then I started listening—because it may yet come up.

But Cazikji seems to have disappeared entirely this time. I've written his story in my journal, but I may still burn it as he suggested; for now, I never let it leave my sight. Maraba apologized, but we haven't been together again. Cazikji was right about that, too: a partner you can't trust wouldn't make for much of a future.

* * *

We've finally discovered the memory storage location. To call it destroyed crystals is an understatement. What must have once been an immense storage location is now a sand dune of crystal dust, its grains jagged and blinding in the sunlight.

We assumed it had been long abandoned. But we were wrong.

Two Ngisikaa were behind the dune. The sun glinted off their glass-like skin in much the same way as the crystalline dust. Their round bodies were suspended above the ground on segmented chitinous legs. Their heads bulged back over their bodies, big yellow eyes low on their brows, and beneath that, a mass of prehensile tentacles. Their bodies glowed with solar energy, brighter and infinitely more faceted than our Kuh.

If I haven't seen many Uchafumlaji in my years, I've seen even less Ngisikaa. Artwork and depictions only; never one in the flesh. Sentient Ngisikaa have such small comfort zones for their storage locations that people who've seen them either sought them out or hired them for their memories and calculating abilities.

These ones, however...

They were sorting the crystal dust into piles, their tentacles constantly moving. Strings of words were barely audible beneath the tinkling of the glassy dust, as if their speech was as unbroken as their work.

"They are sentient Ngisikaa," Fujivii said quietly, "or at least they once were. But after the crystals were destroyed, they had nowhere to store the vast amount of memories during the Collapse except within their own bodies, and their minds broke. They're too addled to communicate now. We could try bringing them back with us to Ardhi. But I suspect they're too far gone."

Fujivii was right. The Ngisikaa had been neglecting their base needs in favor of sorting these shards of memory, and when Fujivii tried to guide them away, they became agitated. It was decided that we'd remain until their bodies failed entirely.

I sat on a crystal dune one evening, my journal in my lap, and watched over the dying Ngisikaa. It was there that Fujivii found me.

They greeted me with only three words: "I believe you."

I looked up in surprise. Fujivii sat down on the dune beside me.

"What happened here was not the doing of the Uchafumlaji," they said. "They merely collected what they could in the wake of the Collapse as an artifact. I apologize both for thinking otherwise, and for pulling you into it."

"Thank you, Honored One," I said quietly.

"But the real tragedy is now we'll never know the truth about what happened on Kusafirima, with all these memories destroyed," they said with a sigh.

I bit my lower lip. "Would they really have answered anything, anyway?"

Fujivii cocked their head. "How do you mean, Captain Hahana?"

"Well..." I struggled to explain. "*Memories* aren't *facts*. Not exactly. They're versions of facts. How are the memory storage crystals any different? Whose memories were they?

The Uchafumlaji enslaved by the Order of Obarikaa? The mages who took control during the Darksider Revolt? The Ngisikaa, who weren't nearly numerous enough to see it all happen? Those are different stories. Different facts."

Fujivii turned, their eyes locking on mine. "You're claiming a simple accounting of events alone isn't enough for a memory."

"The Uchafumlaji who chartered my ship—Jicalaan—was a memory of a specific thing," I said. "A predator who watched me hungrily the entire voyage and wished he was still allowed to eat me. That was a *fact* to me. But now...I know that the memory was false. What I experienced wasn't even true. How do we know we could trust the memories the Ngisikaa would have given us any more than I can trust my own?"

The way Fujivii studied me told me they knew there'd been plenty I hadn't shared. But all they said was, "You've changed, Hahana. These aren't things you would have said when I first met you."

I smiled wryly. "Part of a clean slate, maybe."

Fujivii smiled as well. "Discovery comes in many ways, and it never brings you where you think it will. Did you expect to befriend an Uchafumlaji? Did you expect to become a writer? Did you expect to show a talent for learning the ways of a mage?"

I almost choked. "A mage?"

Fujivii reached down and touched the scar on my wrist, where my ruptured Kuh had never grown back. "Do you think your average sailor does this?"

"If needed, I imagine so..." I said hesitantly.

But Fujivii just shook their head with that same small smile.

I took a deep breath, flustered by their suggestion. "Well...I need to focus first on our mission here. The Uchafumlaji. If I'm to be their liaison, as the overseer seems to want, I should tell you that they wish to rebuild

Kusafirima on their own, without our help. They want us to go back home."

A throat cleared behind us, then a deep voice said, "With your help, Hahana, I believe that's open to negotiation."

In the last rays of the setting sun, Cazikji sat down beside us. As he and Fujivii fell into tentative conversation, I turned back to my journal and documented it all, but I'm struggling to put this final feeling I have into words—the feeling of warmth and success. A more trusted position. Possibilities for a better future. An Uchafumlaji friend. A memory that brings me happiness instead of fear.

Maybe I'll just tell Tumwara this, when next I see them:

The clean slate was never about a new start. It was about discovering and reframing what was already there.

Cedan Bourne

Bait

CE 1255

Excerpt from "The Shadow Cycle" (Uchafumlaji Myth)

Hirolajak, god of shadows, the child of night, was hungry. His stomach rumbled like sand moving through gravel.

He was always hungry.

Being born of Unzulaja, he lacked the Kuh and could not feast directly on the light of the sun.

He longed to eat meat, so he wandered, looking for creatures he could catch and eat.

After some time, he came upon an Uchafumlaji cave. "What great fortune!" he said. "Uchafumlaji are eaters of meat. I will steal from them instead of catching my own."

He crept inside and found a small Uchafumlaji sitting down for a meal. He waited until they were distracted, slipped their bowl away and dumped the contents into his mouth.

He was outraged to discover that the bowl contained only air.

Hirolajak's stomach rumbled like thunder on a summer night.

The Uchafumlaji lifted their head at the noise. Their eyes grew wide at the sight of Hirolajak. "Hello shadow."

"Child."

"You have my bowl."

"It was empty."

"We have only a small amount of meat left. We must save it in case we fail at the hunt."

"You should be out hunting now, to get more."

The Uchafumlaji's stomach rumbled—they were hungry too. "The sun is too bright, and we cannot hunt until the sun goes down."

"You could make a clever device to catch prey instead of hunting it."

The Uchafumlaji frowned. "What kind of device catches prey?"

"One I'm about to invent. Fetch me three straight sticks as thick as your toes and a large heavy rock."

The Uchafumlaji brought Hirolajak what he asked for. Hirolajak used his claws to make clever notches in the sticks and arranged them into a standing right triangle with long extensions off the vertices. He placed the heavy rock on top of one of these extensions. "Now, you place the meat you have left here as bait." He pointed at the horizontal stick's extension. "When prey takes the bait, it will displace the stick and..." Hirolajak bumped the stick, causing the heavy rock to come crashing down.

The Uchafumlaji jumped up and down, clapping their hands. "Shadow, you are clever! What is your invention called?"

"I shall call this a 'Trap.'"

"I must show everyone. We will be able to capture food during the day!"

The Uchafumlaji showed the trap to the rest of the tribe and the elders agreed to use the last of their meat as bait. They set up the trap and moved away to wait for prey to set off the trap.

Hirolajak snuck back and stole the bait from the trap without setting it off. Laughing, he ate the meat.

CE 1255, Kusafirima (The Eastern Continent)

Zikwoowun mumbled to himself, too preoccupied to notice his surroundings—the dust on every flat surface and the grit under his boots. "We'll use this bridge as a...bridge. No."

He liked to rehearse things to say, in case he was presented with an opportunity to appear clever. He was sometimes jealous of his sibling Cauunwun, who, to his observation, had no desire to sound clever. "We'll build this bridge together... Let us use this project as a... No."

Zikwoowun had his hood pulled up, shading his eyes from the bright sun. The Ngisikaa were day creatures, and Cauunwun had agreed they would approach in the light as supplicants. Before the Collapse, the Uchafumlaji had darkened glass which they used to block out the sunlight—the knowledge had been lost. Maybe the Ngisikaa still knew how to make it. He would ask them after he asked the question he and Cauunwun were sent here to ask.

After questions there would be time to see the city and its engineering marvels in proper darkness. The city was a reflection of the knowledge held within the memory storage.

"...a bridge to the future? Yes. Together we will bridge our shared past into a shared... Let's build a bridge together—"

A rock fell from somewhere and caused a small avalanche. Zikwoowun jumped but couldn't locate the source of the disturbance. He thought he heard padding footsteps, but he wasn't used to locating things by sound above ground. He closed his eyes and was able to identify the footsteps as his sibling.

He opened his eyes in time to see him rounding the corner. "There you are."

Cauunwun was tilted forward in his perpetual scamper, cloaked as Zikwoowun was against the sunlight. "Unzulaja's tears, Zik! Can you believe it?"

Zikwoowun raised an eye ridge. "Believe what? That we made it? No—"

Cauunwun took hold of him, one arm on each of his shoulders and turned him in a slow arc.

Zikwoowun's mouth fell open.

The western tip of the Eastern Continent was wild, blasted, parts of it were outright destroyed, but the memory storage of the Ngisikaa was a refuge where all were welcome. A living city and a temple of knowledge.

At least, it had been.

The city was a ruin. Judging from the dust and debris, it had been destroyed some time ago, but not long enough ago for nature to start reclaiming it in earnest.

Zikwoowun closed his mouth and opened it again. Not sure how to make the words. He pointed instead.

Cauunwun answered the question Zikwoowun couldn't find the words to ask. "I don't know, Zik."

Zikwoowun realized the rockfall and the footsteps were the only noises he'd heard his entire walk. "The whole city's dead."

"Now we're going to have—"

"Shh."

Cauunwun blinked but stopped speaking.

Zikwoowun closed his eyes again. Another set up footsteps. Soft and distant. Moving away from them. He snapped his eyes open. "Someone else is still here. This way."

They moved deeper into the ruins. Zikwoowun paused frequently to listen and adjust course. They got close enough that Cauunwun could hear the footsteps as well. Whomever they were chasing was cautious but unaware they were being tracked.

Cauunwun used the hand sign of the hunt. *Quarry ahead. Over the bridge.*

Zikwoowun looked up. *Bridge?*

Despite the destruction of the city, the bridge—a real life example of the problem they had been sent to solve—stood in, if not pristine condition, then in working order. Two massive structures like gates stood at either side. Cables ran from these to the bridge deck itself, allowing it to span a gap no ordinary bridge would.

It wasn't magic. It was better than magic. It was engineering.

Zikwoowun moved out onto the bridge. He needed to get a closer look.

Cauunwun slipped past him, scouting ahead.

Every time the Uchafumlaji of his tribe made a bridge like this it fell down. What kept this one up?

Cauunwun made a clicking sound to get Zikwoowun's attention and held up his hand. *Stop.*

What?

Cauunwun pointed. It was difficult to make out in the bright sun but a thin blue person with blonde hair, loose fitting pants and no shirt stood at the other end of the bridge. *Kuhifadi.*

Zikwoowun froze. Maybe they hadn't been spotted.

The Kuhifadi made a sharp slashing motion with their hand across their upper arm. Zikwoowun had only read about it, but he was sure the Kuhifadi had ruptured a Kuh—they were unleashing their magic.

The wind grew still.

The sky darkened.

There was a rushing sound right before the wind returned.

The bridge began to sway.

"Trap!" Cauunwun placed a hand flat on Zikwoowun's chest and shoved.

Zikwoowun stumbled backward, tumbling ass over snout.

"Run Zik!"

Zikwoowun ran back the way they had come. Cauunwun ran the other way. Further onto the bridge, toward the Kuhifadi.

* * *

Another cable snapped. Cauunwun shifted his path instinctually, almost imperceptibly. The cable missed by a hair's width. His new path took him close to the other side of the bridge. He jumped and kicked his foot off the rail.

The bridge undulated, rolling like the ocean.

The ground was now well below his feet. Cauunwun was forced to roll on his landing. The wave came up to meet him and he transferred its upward force into forward momentum.

Cauunwun smiled. He was having the time of his life.

Another cable snapped behind him. Another. They snapped in rapid succession. Dust and rock burst out of the seams of individual slabs on the bridge. The wave form of bouncing bridge went from serpentine to angular.

Cauunwun lengthened his stride, hopping from slab to slab, barely maintaining upward momentum as each slab tumbled away under his feet.

Cauunwun was past the far gate. Almost there.

The Kuhifadi had their back turned, walking away along the road on this side.

Cauunwun dove, leaping over the last few slabs before they fell. He crashed into the Kuhifadi, wrapping his arms around them, turning, and throwing them to the ground.

He stood over them. "Next time make sure your prey is in the trap before you spring it."

* * *

Zikwoowun didn't mind the taste of dirt—especially fresh loamy dirt with a hint of moss, or the clay near where his family had their home.

Dust, on the other hand, he could do without. He spat but couldn't get the taste out of his mouth. Dust was dirt without a soul. The slippery desiccant oozed down his throat, attempting to make him as dry as it was.

He walked through the chasm, past the ruin of the bridge—such a waste! To get to Cauunwun and the captured Kuhifadi.

Cauunwun had tied them up, but from their bearing you wouldn't have thought them the prisoner. They sat, cross legged, body tilted to gather the last of the sun's rays.

Zikwoowun folded himself to the ground and closed his eyes. When he had started his trek across the chasm, he'd been furious. Rage had given way to exhaustion, or maybe, depression.

He recoiled from a pain in his nose, swatting reflexively. His eyes snapped open, and he glared at his sibling. Cauunwun had flicked him in the nose with a foreclaw. Something he had been doing to Zikwoowun since they were children.

He opened his mouth to complain but Cauunwun held up a hand to silence him.

We don't have time. Cauunwun was referring to his mood. Hunt signs weren't as nuanced as speech, but this was a well-worn path in their conversation.

Fine, he signed. *Now what?*

Need a plan.

He laughed without sound, then coughed. *Lost. Following your lead.*

Cauunwun moved to the Kuhifadi. He loomed over them, blocking the sunlight. "Do you speak Hapacha?"

The Kuhifadi blinked but didn't speak.

"What language do you speak? Uchawiku? Kusamar?

The Kuhifadi blinked again.

Cauunwun caught Zikwoowun's eye. *Kill them?*

For what?

Trying to kill us.

An escape attempt.

They don't belong here.

Neither do we.

Cauunwun looked into the distance. *The bridge. They destroyed the bridge.*

Zikwoowun didn't want to look inside himself, afraid he would see his heart collapsing. They had come to ask the Ngisikaa about that bridge, how it still stood, how to build one. He closed his eyes. *Not enough.*

Probably killed the Ngisikaa.

Zikwoowun studied the Kuhifadi. They seemed detached, uninterested in anything outside their own head. He could imagine them coldly killing. He spoke in Ardhanian, an old language often used in inter-species trade. "Why did you kill all of the Ngisikaa?"

The Kuhifadi surged to their feet, eyes blazing,

Cauunwun casually grabbed their bound hands and pulled them back to the ground. He chuckled and spoke in Hapacha, which they spoke at home. "Clever Zik. That was as good as them admitting they speak Ardhanian."

It hadn't been Zikwoowun's intention, but he accepted the compliment.

Knowing they had been outed, the Kuhifadi spoke. "I am not a murderer." Their Ardhanian was accented, but understandable.

Cauunwun scratched patterns in the dirt with his feet. "Sounds like something a murderer would say."

Now what?

We stick to the plan. Cauunwun switched back to Hapacha, watching the Kuhifadi for any reactions. "We knew there might be no answers here. Next, we travel across the ocean to Kuinuajuu and ask the Ngisikaa there."

The Kuhifadi's eyes flicked when they heard the name Kuinuajuu—the oldest Ngisikaa memory storage—but gave no other reaction.

Zikwoowun scuffed his feet in the dirt. The journey here had taken them six weeks. He didn't want to wait another two or three weeks before getting an answer.

Cauunwun placed his hand on Zikwoowun's shoulder. "With our ship, we can shortcut through the Gates of Hios."

Zikwoowun brightened. He'd always wanted to see the great fallen bridge that used to connect the mainland and southern islands of Kuinuajuu, and it would save them half a week. But if the little ship that brought them to the Eastern Continent had been any larger, it wouldn't be able to pass over the ruins of the bridge now lying at the bottom of the channel. Thoughts of one fallen bridge brought him back to thoughts of another. He swallowed a bitter taste in his mouth and his eyes flicked to their captive. He signed, *What of them?*

Kill...and eat them?

Zikwoowun blanched. Uchafumlaji weren't supposed to eat Kuhifadi anymore. *No.*

A joke.

Not funny.

Bring them?

Cauunwun tapped a claw against his teeth—a tell for when he was formulating a plan. *Yes.* The Wun's would bring the Kuhifadi to the Ngisikaa as a gift and they could mete out their own justice.

* * *

Cauunwun tied the Kuhifadi to the mast of their little ship, the *Siskin*, which wasn't much more than a boat with delusions of grandeur. It had a draft just large enough to be safe out on the ocean, a single half height cabin, a mainsail, and a jib. "Mages were dangerous."

"I don't know," Zikwoowun said. "They don't dress like a mage. Mages wear wrappings all over."

"Their arm is wrapped."

"One tiny wrap? That's not how mages work."

"They used magic to drop the bridge."

"Could've been a trap instead of magic."

Cauunwun frowned.

The Kuhifadi stayed tied to the mast.

They had done some light hunting in the woods and had caught enough dranits for a little fresh meat. Cauunwun broke down the carcasses and Zikwoowun cooked the meat with a small fire. They were still well provisioned, but the variety was nice. They could also catch fish if it came to that.

Cauunwun sat on the foredeck munching on a dranit, his tongue navigating around all the little bones, enjoying the breeze and the salt air. The Kuhifadi leaned against the mast, studying him.

He turned to face them, chewing thoughtfully. "Do you have a name?"

They continued staring.

"We could always make up a name for you if you won't tell us... Blue? Fish bait? Hm, no... Ballast?

No response.

"You're staring at my lunch. Are you hungry Ballast?"

They blinked.

"I know you can understand me. Serpent's teats, I know you can speak. You already gave that one away, so the silent treatment isn't going to do it." Cauunwun stood. "Let's try again." He held out a dranit leg. "Hungry?"

The Kuhifadi studied him for a moment longer before giving in. "Water."

"See, not so hard." He took another bite and chewed thoughtfully, showing no signs of getting up to get water for the prisoner.

A soft-sided canteen flopped onto the deck, its sides wobbling like a fish suffocating in the air. Cauunwun traced its arc back to where Zikwoowun was standing.

"Cauunwun." Zikwoowun's voice was low and growl-like. "We don't taunt or torture prisoners."

The Kuhifadi's arms were tied behind his back around the mast. They used their legs to bring the canteen closer to themselves.

Zikwoowun climbed down off what passed for a bridge on the small ship. They lifted the canteen and pulled the stopper. The Kuhifadi opened their mouth, and he poured water in, careful to not spill any. He took a drink himself before replacing the stopper. He set the canteen down again and helped himself to a hunk of dranit. "I've always wondered: do Kuhifadi eat, or are you all just...sun eaters?"

The Kuhifadi tried to maintain their stoic mien, but several unreadable emotions passed over their face.

Zikwoowun held out the meat. The Kuhifadi turned their face away.

"Suit yourself."

The Kuhifadi slumped. "We do eat."

"Great—"

"But I don't eat meat."

Zikwoowun shrugged. "No problem! We can catch some fish for you."

"That's not what I meant... Maybe I used the wrong word?"

"Take as much time as you need"

"I don't eat animals. Only plants."

"Oooh. Okay. Plants."

"I'm sure we have something that is plants."

"Thank you."

"We have gnois! That's plants."

"Traditional Uchafumlaji gnois has fermented fish in it."

"I had no idea. Honest. I'm sure we can come up with something."

The Kuhifadi was seized by a coughing fit. After it passed, Zikwoowun gently got them more water.

"Thank you...?"

"Zikwoowun."

"Thank you, Zikwoowun."

"You're welcome...?"

"Ix."

"You're welcome, Ix." Zikwoowun turned and shouted, "Cauunwun!"

Cauunwun was staring off into the distance behind them. He didn't turn at his name.

Zikwoowun shouted again, "Cauuuuuunwun! Hey!"

Cauunwun snapped his head back to look at Zikwoowun. "What?"

"Do we have any food that's just plants? They only eat plants."

"Probably." Cauunwun turned and looked behind the ship again.

"What are you looking at?"

"Did you notice the ship behind us?"

"No. What ship?"

Cauunwun pointed. "The black spot on the horizon. I noticed them shortly after we made sail. Here." Cauunwun handed over the ship's glass.

The ship jumped into focus. If Zikwoowun was judging the scale right, it was easily three times the size of the *Siskin*. Seen through the glass, the sides were iridescent blue and green. "Pretty ship. Wonder how they made the colors meld like that."

"They've been with us for hours."

"And?"

"I think we're being followed, and I doubt they're friendly."

* * *

Ix held very still.

Unawaba and their crew were still after them.

Ix couldn't end up in their hands.

They would catch up soon. The Uchafumlaji had a fine little ship, and it was taking Ix where they wanted to go, but it was no match for the *Xerian*, which had more sails and mages aboard.

Ix could augment the speed of the Uchafumlaji ship but with their hands tied they would be unable to rupture a Kuh.

Probably unable to rupture a Kuh.

There was a boat hook in brackets over on the rail. That would be sharp enough to rupture a Kuh.

Normally it would be possible for them to magic their way out of the bonds without rupturing a Kuh but Ix had been using energy to convert sunlight into nutrition. They needed a plausible escape plan that would work with very little magic.

Up to this point Ix had no need to escape, so hadn't tested their bonds in any way. They did so now, flexing and twisting to see if there was any play in them: there was not. The mean little Uchafumlaji—the one called Cauunwun—was skilled at rope craft.

Ix's legs weren't bound.

The Uchafumlaji had both stripped off their boots when they boarded the ship, but they had left Ix's on their feet. Unlacing one of the boots was within Ix's available energy budget. They tucked their foot up and back as far as it would go, and with a tiny amount of magic threaded the lace from the boot through their wrist restraints and to the other boot. The lace secured to each boot, they pumped their legs up and down, using the friction of the lace as a makeshift saw. With only minor magical encouragement the wrist restraints parted fiber by fiber.

The pain in Ix's suddenly unbound arms was sharp and hot, like thorns wrapped around the nerve in their elbow joint. They were weirdly grateful for the rope that was still around their torso, which stopped their arms from going wide and giving away that they were no longer bound at the wrist. As much as Ix wanted to hurry, they waited, taking long slow breaths and waiting for the pain to ebb.

They risked a glance over their shoulder. The Uchafumlaji were still debating. From the sound of it the *Xerian* was done pacing them and was now gaining.

Ix ducked out of the remaining restraints and reached out toward the boat hook.

The thorns that stabbed their elbow were now in their ass. Ix hadn't known it was possible for someone's butt to fall asleep, but there they were, biting into their lower lip so they didn't cry out in surprised pain.

Ix pushed through and was able to reach the boat hook's wooden handle. They gently lifted it from its brackets and pulled it to their chest.

The goal was stealth, not pyrotechnics, so they needed to create a small puncture in the Kuh. The magic would leak out, powering the enchantment over a long period of time.

They would need to use the tip of the boat hook to make a small hole, not a tear.

Except the boat hook didn't have a tip. The ends of both points were rounded, something Ix hadn't seen. Maybe all boat hooks were made like this, or maybe this one was defective in some way. Ix wasn't a sailor, they didn't know.

They returned the boat hook to its brackets.

The Uchafumlaji debate seemed over. The smaller one moved quickly around the sails, pulling ropes and changing angles. Ix assumed it was an attempt to get more speed out of the little ship.

Ix needed to hurry. If the little Uchafumlaji looked down, they would notice Ix wasn't restrained.

Ix couldn't resist scratching their leg, a luxury after being tied up.

Scratch?

Ix could use their power to grow one of their fingernails long enough to puncture a Kuh. They concentrated.

Nothing.

Ix slumped back against the mast.

They were out of energy. They needed food.

The piece of dranit meat was still sitting where Zikwoowun, the larger Uchafumlaji, had left it.

Ix considered it. Principles upheld would be cold comfort if Unawaba captured them.

Ix reached out for the meat.

There was the clang of metal on wood: a grapple.

Ix was too late. Unawaba had overtaken them.

* * *

The grapple had gouged into the wood of the rail near the prisoner.

Something was odd about the Kuhifadi, but Zikwoowun brushed the thought aside. The ship was about to be boarded.

Zikwoowun doubted he could pull the grapple free, so he left it. The rope attached to the grapple was the weak link and he focused his efforts there. It parted with a ringing shot as his digging claw slashed through it.

Cauunwun was still dancing along the rigging lines. He was a better sailor than Zikwoowun but getting enough speed to outrun this predatory ship seemed unlikely.

Zikwoowun wondered if it would be better to fight the pirates when they boarded or to surrender.

More grapples latched onto the rail. Zikwoowun moved to clip those as well. He felt a hand on his shoulder.

"I can help."

Zikwoowun jumped, his claws ready to strike. The Kuhifadi had escaped and was standing behind him. He shrugged their hand off his shoulder and crouched, ready to defend himself.

The Kuhifadi held up both hands. "Ix, remember?"

"You escaped."

"They are reeling us closer. They will board soon. I can help."

Zikwoowun stood back up to his full height. "How?"

"I had planned something subtle, but we're past that." Ix drew a line with their finger across the Kuh on their upper arm. "Slash here."

"What? No." Zikwoowun studied Ix. He didn't know much about mages, but he knew trusting them wasn't a good idea. They could be working with the pirates for all he knew.

Ix held his gaze.

Zikwoowun held up a hand and repeated himself. "No."

"Please. We need to escape."

"This is a trick. You're working for them."

The *Siskin* lurched and changed course drastically as the grapple lines took weight.

Ix shook his head slowly, still not breaking eye contact. "I'm not." They tapped their Kuh again. "Please. It's our only chance."

Zikwoowun broke away from Ix's stare, glanced over at the pirate ship. It was probably a mistake, but he couldn't think of any other options. He muttered a prayer, called himself a fool, and did as asked.

Orange light flowed out of the ruptured Kuh like illuminated pollen before coalescing into a curl of liquid lightning. It shot out as a beam, slicing through the grapple lines. The *Siskin* jumped forward, propelled on a wave of light.

There was no feeling of motion. No rushing wind. No sound of snapping sails or creaking rigging. A bubble of light encapsulated the whole ship.

The pirate ship disappeared over the horizon.

Ix lowered their hands. The light dissipated and the ship coasted to a gentle drift.

The deck vibrated under their feet when Cauunwun dropped from the rigging with knives in both hands.

* * *

Ix had allowed Zikwoowun to rebind their restraints so Cauunwun put away his knives and got the ship moving under sail power again.

The three of them sat in a rough triangle on the main deck.

Ix looked relaxed, the captain of the ship, despite their restraints.

Zikwoowun looked nervous, but he always looked nervous.

Cauunwun was also nervous, but tight muscles make for limited mobility, something he wished to avoid if he had to kill a mage. He signed at Zikwoowun. *I talk. You observe.*

Okay.

"You could have magicked your way out of your restraints at any time. You could have avoided capture—"

Ix made a gesture Cauunwun didn't understand.

He ignored it. "Why?"

"Why what?"

"Why did you allow us to capture you?"

"Your capture was genuine. I didn't expect you to make it over the bridge."

Cauunwun wasn't sure he believed them.

Ix looked at his navel. "May I look over your stores? I'd like some food if there is any I can eat."

"I'm not comfortable with you moving around." *We should kill them.*

"Perhaps one of you can accompany me?"

"I can take them," Zikwoowun said. *How does one kill a mage?*

"No." Cauunwun tapped a claw against his teeth. *They will fall asleep.* "I'll take them." His gaze wandered out onto their wake. There was speck on the horizon that could only be the pirate ship. "Ergalfadi's bells, they're persistent."

"What?" Zikwoowun stood.

"Look."

"We used flamboyant magic and they're still chasing? Suicidal. No one attacks a ship with a mage on it."

"Unless they have their own mage."

"Explains how they caught us in the first place."

Cauunwun looked down at the Kuhifadi, nominally tied to the mast. "Time for another miracle."

* * *

Zikwoowun did the asking. Cauunwun didn't think Ix liked him very much. Probably something to do with all the naked hostility.

Ix looked tired, but undefeated. "Bring me a knife."

"Hold on," Cauunwun said. "What makes you think we're going to give you a weapon?"

Ix's mouth twisted into a sardonic smile. "I thought you were smart, but I may have been mistaken."

"Cau, either we trust them, or we don't. They want to get away from the pirates as much as we do, otherwise they wouldn't have helped the first time. Right?"

Ix nodded.

Cauunwun produced a knife from somewhere. He flipped it so he held it by the blade, and with a flick of his wrist the knife was stuck point first into the mast a small distance above Ix's head. Cauunwun stormed back to the rail where he could see the pirate ship, which was noticeably closer.

Zikwoowun grasped the knife with one hand and jerked, but only pulled himself closer to the mast; the knife stayed fixed. He took hold of the knife with both hands and with his foot against the mast was able to lever it free. "I guess I should untie you."

"I don't need to be untied if it will make... Cauunwun?"

"Yes."

"More comfortable."

"Okay, uh, how will you do the magic?"

Ix made eye contact. "I'll need your help."

"Oh. Okay. How? Um."

"Sit."

Zikwoowun lowered himself next to Ix.

"Now find the Kuh on my upper arm."

Zikwoowun had to adjust the rope and unwrap the binding on Ix's arm to expose the membrane. It shimmered in the sunlight, opalescent, like a soap bubble. "Okay... Now I cut it?"

"Not this time. Cutting would let too much power out at once. We don't want to do anything dramatic. Poke a small hole in the Kuh with the tip of the knife."

Zikwoowun smiled. "You're like a kid's present, only instead of candy you're filled with magic."

"Exactly like that, only nothing at all like that."

Zikwoowun held the knife poised above the exposed Kuh. "Ready?"

"Yes."

He gently pierced the Kuh with the tip of the knife. Glowing flecks like embers on a stirred fire puffed out the hole. Minutes passed as he waited for something else to happen, but Ix looked like they were taking a nap.

Ix opened their eyes. "It's started."

"What are you doing?"

Ix flicked their chin in the direction of the pirate ship.

Cauunwun's sharp intake of breath raised Zikwoowun's curiosity even higher, a feat he wouldn't have thought possible. He climbed up near him.

Zikwoowun knew the pirate ship must be closer, but he couldn't make it out at all. A thick mist rose out of the water. "We'll lose the ship in the mist."

"Flying Ngisikaa gonads." Cauunwun dashed away.

Ix blanched. "Was that a good expletive or a bad expletive?"

"Sounded like a bad one." Zikwoowun trailed after his sibling. "What's the problem?"

Cauunwun had retrieved the glass and sextant. "Zik, change course. Quickly. While I can still make out the moon and the horizon. We're heading for the Gates of Hios, and they have a narrow channel. It won't matter if we can't be seen if we get lost ourselves—we'll crash into the rocks."

"Flying Ngisikaa gonads!" Zikwoowun scrambled back to the wheel.

* * *

They changed course enough that the pirates would have to get very lucky to stay on their trail, but not so much that they wouldn't have to make drastic adjustments to get to Kuinuajuu. Cauunwun thought they had made good time. The eastern edge of Kuinuajuu was visible on their right and the big island was peeking out of their left. Soon they would be at the Gates of Hios, with its fallen bridge. Soon after that they'd be rid of their "prisoner."

Heh. Some prisoner.

Cauunwun had agreed that restraining the Kuhifadi was "pointless."

Zikwoowun had used the words "ungrateful," "futile," and "rude."

Same difference. The blue person had been loose for a couple weeks now. They spent most of their time chasing what little sun was available—the sky had been gray since the *Siskin* eluded the pirates.

The Kuhifadi sat cross-legged nearby.

Zikwoowun signed. *Still want to kill them?*

Cauunwun slumped. *No.*

Excellent. Ix signed.

Zikwoowun burst into nervous laughter.

Cauunwun sucked his teeth. *You know hunt sign?*

Yes.

How?

Ix switched to back to Ardhanian "The Ngisikaa taught me."

"That doesn't make sense."

Ix switched to Hapacha. "I have an affinity for language."

Cauunwun chewed his tongue before answering in Hapacha. "No, it literally doesn't make sense. Ngisikaa don't have hands."

Ix burst out laughing.

"How can glass mollusks teach you hunt sign when they don't have hands?"

Ix recovered, relapsed into laughter, and recovered again. "My teacher would hold several tentacles close together in a bunch. The bunch was the 'arm,' the individual tentacles were the 'fingers.'" They relapsed again.

Cauunwun had no idea what to do with this new information. "Explains your strange accent."

Zikwoowun cracked up again.

The giggles faded to silence and the sound of the wind and waves.

Ix's answers raised other questions. Zikwoowun gave voice to one of them. "Traveling to the Ngisikaa to learn languages seems, well, odd?"

Ix's voice dropped to barely audible. "I didn't travel to learn that."

"What did you come for?"

"I didn't come as a supplicant. I was raised by them."

Zikwoowun cocked his head to the side, mouth open.

Cauunwun kept his face carefully blank, but he was also surprised. Before he could ask any more questions, his brain informed him that the sound of the waves had changed. He stood. *Quiet. I heard something.*

Zikwoowun's mouth snapped shut.

They found us. Still hunting. Close.

Ix's head snapped around. "Fuck." They held out their hand.

Cauunwun slapped a knife into it.

* * *

Ix made the *Siskin* lighter—the keel frictionless in the water—and kicked up a mighty wind that touched only their sails. They became briefly invisible for what good it would do them.

Zikwoowun's body lost some of the tension he had been uselessly holding. "We are victims of Hirolajak's fun. Those are the world's luckiest pirates."

Cauunwun turned to face Ix, arms crossed.

Ix inclined their head. "I'm sorry you two got caught up in this."

Cauunwun nodded. "They're not pirates."

"What?" Zikwoowun asked.

"No, they're not," Ix said. "Not exclusively. But, I wouldn't put it past them if the opportunity arose."

"They're after you?" Cauunwun said.

"Have been for a long time. I thought you were with them when I dropped the bridge on you."

"Why are they after you?"

"I was careless."

"Not an answer."

"They want the power that I have."

"Is that a thing that can happen? I wasn't aware that mages could take other mages powers."

Ix sat down hard. "We have a little time. I will explain—"

"Wish you would—" Cauunwun said at the same time Zikwoowun said, "You don't have to—"

"What do you know of how the Kuh work?"

Zikwoowun half raised his hand. "They store sunlight and let it out as magic when you poke one?"

"Inexact, but close enough. Do you know, for the most part, once ruptured, Kuh never heal?"

"Uh...no?" Zikwoowun looked to Cauunwun, who shook his head.

"It's true."

"For the most part?"

"Childbirth."

"Oh. Okay. But..."

Ix waited.

"But," Zikwoowun said. "I've torn the same Kuh on your arm twice and you tore it again just now." He examined Ix's arm. "It's healing even now."

"Yes. This is why Unawaba chases me—"

"Us."

"Okay," Cauunwun said. "Still not clear on how this Unawaba can take the power from you. Or why you can't just keep magicking us away whenever they catch up."

Ix waved their hand over the healing Kuh then tapped it. The Kuh became transparent. "Look into the Kuh."

Nestled inside the Kuh—inside Ix's arm—was a crystal.

"What is—?"

"Is that—?"

"A Ngisikaa memory crystal?" Ix nodded. "The last surviving crystal from the destroyed memory store. I need to get it to the Ngisikaa at Kuinuajuu."

Zikwoowun reached out to touch, thought better of it, and retracted his hand. "What memory is it?"

Ix lowered their hand and the Kuh returned to translucent. "I don't know. One of the Ngisikaa thought was important." Ix slumped. "As for why I don't keep magicking us away: I'm tired. Very tired. I haven't eaten. The crystal heals the Kuh, but it doesn't replenish the sun energy. The power has to come from somewhere."

"We'll get you to Kuinuajuu," Zikwoowun said. "Won't we Cau? We just have to get through the Gates of Hios. The *Siskin*'s draft is shallow enough to get over the ruins of the fallen bridge. Their ship is too large to follow us."

"They'll never let us get that far," Cauunwun said.

"Ix can use their magic."

Ix shook their head. "I don't have enough energy left."

Cauunwun tapped a claw against his teeth.

* * *

The sun was just peeking over the horizon when Ix cast away from the *Siskin* in the dingy. Unawaba's ship was still pacing them, neither closer nor farther back than it had been in hours—biding their time. Close enough to strike, far enough away that they would be hard to attack.

They would have to drop sail to bring Ix aboard. This would give the *Siskin* the time it needed.

The *Xerian* loomed above them. It didn't look to be made of wood. Its planks seemed to be green and blue clouds captured in amber and aspic.

Unawaba enjoyed spectacle.

Ix preferred the *Siskin*.

Along the rail, a half-dozen Kuhifadi pointed weapons at them. Two more stood to either side—mages with knives poised at the ready above their Kuh.

Ix raised their hands, palms up, to show they held no weapons.

Two pirates jumped down. They each took hold of one of Ix's arms and boosted them out of the dingy into the waiting arms of two more. Neither of the mages relaxed.

Ix was brought to the captain's cabin, it smelled of wax and musk and mir. It was warm and despite themselves Ix started to relax. How could they not? It smelled like a time of their life when things were simple and they were safe. It smelled like home.

They turned and Unawaba was standing in the doorway—they were dressed like a mage, though Ix knew from personal experience that there was only one ruptured kuh on their body. They clapped a hand onto Ix's shoulder, pinching it tightly. "Ix."

The single syllable of their name hung in the air as Ix sifted through their emotions. They wanted to slap the hand away. They wanted to duck under it and pull Unawaba close.

Unawaba barked at the crew without breaking eye contact. "Everyone out." A guard hesitated and Unawaba's hand pulled away as they spun, relieving Ix of the choice.

The guard fled from Unawaba's raised eyebrow. The door latch clacked and they were alone.

Unawaba stood for some time with their back to Ix.

Finally, they turned, closed the distance, lifting their hands to embrace Ix.

Ix did nothing.

At some point failure to make a choice becomes a choice unto itself. Unawaba dropped their arms to their side and bowed at the waist. They delicately kissed Ix on the cheek where a single tear had escaped Ix's eye.

Unawaba moved so they were behind Ix and gently removed the cloak Ix was wearing. One Zikwoowun had given them.

Unawaba sucked in a surprised breath at the sight of the Kuh on Ix's arm. The one Ix had punctured repeatedly. The one that up until this point had healed every time.

It was rent and deflated. Empty. Powerless.

Ix exhaled. All choices made now.

Unawaba growled, stormed to the door, and threw it open. "They don't have it. It must still be on that ship. Mages!"

The door slammed and the bolt sailed home.

Ix sat in the captain's chair.

* * *

Ix felt the ship shudder as it scraped a low point in the strait. Unawaba would have had the mages strengthen the hull, but it was still disconcerting.

The *Siskin* should be past the gates already. It was too late to catch them.

The ship shuddered again. This time it wasn't a low point. The ship was under some kind of enormous stress. They couldn't have...

The sea rose out of view through the porthole. The ship was airborne.

An awesome display of power, and one that meant they could still catch the *Siskin*.

Ix had backed Unawaba into a corner and they were expending their mages to recover. The cost in spent Kuh was high but if they got the crystal, the cost wouldn't matter.

Ix's sacrifice had been for naught. The *Xerian* would fly over the low ruins, the *Siskin* would be caught, Unawaba would get the memory crystal, and they would force Ix to show them how to use it.

Ix needed to take themself out of the equation. A greater sacrifice was necessary.

Ix had to be as brave as the Ngisikaa. Something Ix had failed at before.

Ix looked for something sharp. Rupturing so many Kuh would be fatal, but they could take the *Xerian* down with them. They found a pen in a drawer. Good enough.

Ix would rupture as many Kuh as they could. They held the pen at the ready.

The ship tilted and fell out of the sky.

It hit the water like it was a solid surface.

Ix was stunned by the impact. Time passed like jelly.

* * *

Cauunwun opened the door, accessed the room, located Ix, and sprinted to them. He grinned. “Time to steal the bait.”

He hoisted Ix over his shoulder and carried them to the dingy where he unceremoniously dumped them. “Time to go.”

Cauunwun rowed them away from the sinking ship. “Do mages float in water? If not, they may be in for a bad time.”

Ix’s vision was still spinning. “How?”

“I hid under one of the seats in the dingy. Then I waited for my opportunity to take out the mages.” Cauunwun shrugged and tossed something into Ix’s lap. “Also liberated some plants from their food stores for you to eat.”

* * *

When they finally caught up with the *Siskin* on the other side of the Gates of Hios, Ix still lay in the bottom of the dingy, shoving preserved mehoban into their mouth. It was hard, dry, a little mealy, and the sharp edges of the kernels cut the top of their mouth.

It was the best meal of their entire life.

“Come on Bait,” Cauunwun said. “Time to get back out of the little boat.”

Zikwoowun offered a hand to help Ix onto the deck of the *Siskin*.

Ix didn’t take the offered hand. “Bait?”

Cauunwun shrugged. “Would you rather go back to being Ballast?”

"In the story the bait gets eaten after it gets stolen."

Cauunwun shared a look with Zikwoowun. "I keep forgetting how educated you are."

"How about we just call them Ix?" Zikwoowun asked.

Cauunwun thought it over. "Alright." Cauunwun reached out and Ix accepted the help this time. "Welcome aboard, Ix."

* * *

The last memory of the eastern memory storage was returned to the Ngisikaa, and after months on a journey that had been planned as weeks, Zikwoowun and Cauunwun were able to ask their question.

Thanks to Ix they were granted a special audience with the head librarian—the Ngisikaa whose memory held the index of what memories were stored at Kuinuajuu.

The Ngisikaa was perched on a stool so their head would be level with Zikwoowun's. It might have been his imagination, but he thought he could make out the edges of memory crystals through their translucent skin. A tentacle slipped out from where the rest were curled under their head and Zikwoowun had to fight off a giggle imagining them trying to sign.

"Honored librarian." Zikwoowun had rehearsed his speech more times than he could count—his nerves and giggles faded away. "We have traveled seeking knowledge we hope you can provide. As the Uchafumlaji come out of our underground cities after so long alone in the dark we wish to rebuild the bridges that connected us to the outside world so long ago. We have lost the knowledge of how. An above-ground bridge isn't like one underground. Above a certain span ours sway and fall down. Please, help us with the knowledge of how we can once again build bridges to our shared future."

Cauunwun signed. *Well done.*

Ix looked thoughtful.

The librarian brought several of its tentacles together and signed. *Thank you for your question.*

The siblings both turned to Ix, mouths agape.

Ix smiled. *Told you.*

The librarian remained still and silent for an uncomfortable amount of time before speaking aloud. "It saddens me greatly to tell you the information you seek was known only in the eastern memory store. It's lost to us now."

Zikwoowun's bones lost all structure. He collapsed to the floor, head in his hands. The mission was a failure.

Ix reached out and took Zikwoowun's hand, pulling him sitting up. "That's what you came to ask?"

Zikwoowun's voice wouldn't work. *Yes.*

"And I destroyed the bridge."

Yes.

"I'm so sorry."

"You didn't know."

"I can help you."

"How?" Cauunwun asked. "With magic?"

Ix laughed. "I loved that bridge. It's sort of like the old bridge that used to cross the Gates of Hios. The Ngisikaa here still have records of this one. When I got there, I learned all about the one of the Eastern Continent. Your bridges are out of tune, like an instrument. Harmonics and flutter from the wind make them fall."

Zikwoowun hadn't ever thought to tell Ix the reason for their journey.

Ix smiled. "If you would like, I can come home with you. I'll show you how it works."

"I'd like that—"

Cauunwun interrupted. "We'd like that."

"Yes," Zikwoowun said. "Let's build a bridge together."

BT1272 – Addendum to the timeline of "The Fourth Age" of Juno.
CE 1816, Day 4:

The technology and culture of Juno is changing much more rapidly in recent years compared to even those leading up to the collapse:

CE 1199: Sailing vessels once again reach the Eastern Continent, merely to find a wild and dead place, with vast swaths of burnt and blasted land. The only inhabitants are wanderers, completely wrapped up against the sun. Some are obviously Uchafumlaji from their size. It is unknown what practices the mages enacted once they took control, as much was done in darkness, in secret, and behind shields of exotic material. Whatever happened, the result was absolute destruction of the society that had once flourished there.

CE 1201: The memory storage location on the Eastern Continent is found destroyed. Only two sentient Ngisikaa are left, but they are so addled from holding memories they are unable to communicate. They die soon after contact is made, and the last memories of what happened die with them.

CE 1564: The last of the Uchafumlaji are officially freed from being indentured servants to the Kuhifadi.

CE 1574–1749: Although many of the advances of the old civilization had been lost, the tunneling powers of the Uchafumlaji and their scientific prowess, coupled with the memory of the Ngisikaa and the magic of the Kuhifadi, lead to many archaeological digs and finds of vast knowledge. Much knowledge of the old civilization is discovered, at least up to the Collapse. This includes many weapons used by the mages and the Uchafumlaji, as well as the magic absorption of the Ngisikaa. However, with the new treaties in place among the species, the technology is often (though not always) used for the benefit of all.

CE 60–1800: During this time many accords and treaties are made among the three species, including the Uchafumlaji's official pledge to no longer hunt or eat either of the other sentient species. Most Uchafumlaji abide by this agreement up to the present.

Robin C.M. Duncan

God of Two Heads

CE 1910

In the Great North Forest of the Western Continent of Juno, the Uchafumlaji city of Jukulu lies deep underground, far beneath the canopy of ancient trees which shrouds the forest floor in darkness. The city's tunnels are thousands of years old, home to many thousands of Uchafumlaji, but this account concerns only two of my people. Our kind may never be able to repay the debt we owe them.

—Entry by Organon Cawunkiiqi in the history of Jukulu, CE 1910

Gundoolaanqii riffled his metal claws, the hand straps tightening, and rumbled. Arms outstretched, he let his golden claws scrape the tunnel walls as he walked. He liked to know where he was, to know where the earth was, how easily he could delve into it should the need arise. As the metal skittered on the earthen surface, the fake claws transmitted the whisper of an ache into the very real stumps over which the metal was strapped.

"Please stop doing that," said Jikiifoowun without rancour, their eyes rolling, forked tongue tasting the air. They knew their complaint would vex Gundoo, but he would stop, because they were hunting partners. Cooperation was everything: the root of the pair's success for decades. They shared all physical things equally, but the greatest thing they shared was trust.

"I know you're nervous," said Jikii. "I understand." A floatlamp gently bobbed out of their path then returned to its position. "I don't know why the organon would summon us. Maybe Cawunkiiqi intends to praise us."

"In the breeding rooms? Unlikely," rumbled Gundoo.

"An official visit," Jikii postulated. "Probably Seneschal Zikfootchauun's doing. You know what he's like. Heritage this, purity that. Maybe we're to be an example of what an upstanding Uchafumlaji should be."

Gundoolaanqii breathed deeply. Jikii always knew how to calm him, and it never felt like his hunting partner being crafty, just effective, as they always were. Jikii was right. Organon Cawunkiiqi had no call to chastise them.

The smoothly engineered upper tunnels took them down past the reception caverns, past the meeting rooms, the construction workshops, and design offices, past the dining halls, where mingled clicks, coughs and grunts betrayed the sounds of conversation over the midnight meal. Gundoo's stomach rumbled. After a week, it was time to eat again. They passed many wide exits that lead to the sleeping chambers, walking several breaths more before stooping to progress on all-fours. Modern tunnels gave way to older, rough-hewn passages. The way forward narrowed and steepened as they moved deeper into the warm ground.

Gundoo and Jikii crawled through the tunnel's final unlit section, emerging in the hatchery's spherical entry chamber. The choke point was a defence against intruders, allowing them to be cut down, helpless, as they emerged from the crawl space. Warm ground greeted their feet; humid air from the twelve tunnel mouths arrayed before them sweet with fecund scent.

Cawunkiiqi stood resplendent in the organon's robes, tongue flicking the heavy air, no doubt tasting their and Gundoo's mood. Beside Cawunkiiqi stood Zikfootchauun.

Jikii hissed, causing Gundoo to place a big, claw-shorn limb on their shoulder. Jikii held themself perfectly still. Contained their tongue, lest an idle flick become an insult, or a challenge. Zikfootchauun was a loathsome creature. An official who criticised those who cooperated with the Kuhifadi, while promoting retention of the Uchafumlaji race's purity. Zikfootchauun was a throwback to the time when the Ucha hunted the Kuhifadi, killed them for sport, and for meat.

The seneschal looked directly at Gundoo and—closed his eyes!

Gundoo growled deeply at the slight. Jikii knew their partner would contain himself, but to be called weak by the closing of eyes...the only way Zikfootchauun could have been more insulting would have been to turn his back on Gundoo. Thankfully, the seneschal did not go so far. Still, Jikii fought to quell the tension in their limbs, agitated. Now they noticed the absence of guards in the hatchery entrance chamber.

Gundoo breathed deeply. He sensed Jikii start, but he had come to expect this from the seneschal. Zikfootchauun was dangerous. He worked on the organon to persuade him that foreign visitors to Jukulu should be rebuffed, even locked up. Perhaps the seneschal's whispers recommended worse, so intent was he on Uchafumlaji purity. So far, to Gundoo's knowledge, Organon Cawunkiiqi—a fair leader—remained unmoved.

"Gundoolaanqii," said the organon, "Jikiifoowun. Welcome. I give you thanks." Cawunkiiqi pointed his ceremonial claws at a central floatlamp and swirled them clockwise. The illumination of the cavern increased. "Your hunts have bolstered the larders more than any other partnership, but I must ask you to venture out again. Beyond the forest, if accounts are to be believed."

Jikii's tongue flicked involuntarily. Beyond the forest. Under the sun's glare, to be bathed in the cursed magic that infused the light. It gave power to the Kuhifadi, but to the

Ucha, it brought only pain. Their hunting prowess had bought them a penance.

"Two breeders left the city yesterdark," said Cawunkiiqi, "taking their new child with them. We"—Jikii's tongue tasted Zikfootchauun's belligerent presence—"believe they are running to the Kuhifadi. To the closest city, Sefini."

"Why?" Gundoo growled.

"Incredible," said Jikii. "They'll die under the sun before they can reach Sefini. What possessed them?"

"Ha!" barked Zikfootchauun. "You should hope they die."

The organon flicked his tongue in annoyance, but did not rebuke his highest subordinate. "The child...it is...different."

"Explain," grumbled Gundoo.

"The midwife said a soft, green light surrounded the child's head shortly after birth. They said it did not mewl or cry, but hummed softly. And... She described the child as possessing the characteristics of Dalkka."

"But—"

"The child has two heads?" Gundoo asked simply, cutting off Jikii's rambling before it started. "It is a reincarnated god? A god that we do not venerate, but the Kuhifadi do. How can that be?"

Jikii could see Gundoo was troubled. That was a *lot* of words for his hunting partner. But, who would not be? The organon asked them to believe—in a time of progress, of science, complex engineering, an age of dawning technology—that a god had been reincarnated in their city. A god loved by the Kuhifadi, in an *Uchafumlaji* city. Not any less likely than it being born in a Kuhi city—Jikii supposed—since reputedly Dalkka possessed one Ucha head, one Kuhi head, and a body clothed in the dark crystals of a Ngisikaa.

The organon huffed at Gundoo's question. "I do not know how, but eyewitness accounts compel me to believe it. As you know, image-plates are prohibited in the breeding rooms, but the midwife is reliable. Also, a guard—loyal, of course—observed the breeders escaping, and saw the green glow for themself, also reported a sound, like chanting, or singing. I believe that the breeders were worshiping the creature. I suspect the Kuhifadi are complicit, so highly do they venerate Dalkka."

"A god come back to life, one that casts doubt on the purity of the Uchafumlaji," said Zikfootchauun. "Of course the sunwalkers will protect it, to undermine our governance, divide our kind, and drive us back into slavery." The seneschal hissed. "Our ways must be protected from Kuhifadi taint. Bring all three of them back in any way possible. Use all force. They must not reach the sunwalker city."

"Zikfoo," the organon's tone was admonitory, but the thin, scarred seneschal did not back down. He bared his teeth, dozens of sharp, serrated incisors.

"How are two hunters to bring back a god?" asked Jikii, their tongue dry.

"It is young, still weak," said the organon. "If it does have one Ucha head and one Kuhifadi, as legend dictates, then it has our form, to some extent. Bring back the breeders and the child. Stop them reaching Sefini. If they contact any Kuhifadi..." Gundoo and Jikii waited. Zikfootchauun leaned forward. "Do what you must to keep this knowledge from them."

* * *

Jikii's thoughts rushed like a bird's. The revelation must be broiling within Gundoo, but the digger said nothing as they walked to the stores. How far could the breeders get in three hours, slowed as they must be by never being above ground before, not to mention the burden they carried? Tracking them should be easy, but how much of a start did they have? They and Gundoo had crawled down to the breeders' nest, scented the still-damp albumen, took a swab for later reference.

Now, they loaded their packs. Jikii took hunting claws, making claws, and butchering claws. The last they hesitated at, but the organon and the seneschal had been perfectly clear. The child must not fall into the hands of the overlanders. They packed rangefinder, floatlamp, laser stove, flexitool and five cans of mirror-spray. The quartermaster's scowl suggested they thought that excessive, but Jikii shrugged at them. Jikii's worry overrode all. What if the Kuhifadi were waiting for them, outnumbering them? Shouldn't more hunters be sent? It was not their decision to make.

Gundoo watched his partner place piece after piece of equipment in their pack. It was different for ufriach like him. He only had three jobs: to dig, to lift, and to kill. He didn't need technology. He brought ropes, some simple clothes in case they required to enter an urban area—although if it came to that it would be too late.

They walked in silence up through the tunnels, finally exiting the sprawling underground city, emerging from the hidden entrance in the centre of the forest. Towering inkus, spindletrunk and spireleaf formed a canopy so high and thick that the dank dimness might as well have been night. The gloom did not impede them though. He and Jikii, knew the forest as they knew their own minds. They picked the paths, followed the ways their smell and hearing guided them on, wending always towards the forest edge. As they went, their tongues flicked the warm, soft air, searching for sign of the absconders. It lay underneath everything—crushed beneath the rich odour of leaf litter and loam, doused in mammal spoor, blanketed by guano—a thin suggestion of albumen and afterbirth dusting the slow air they moved through.

"Do you taste it?" Jikii asked. Gundoo nodded. Of course he did. Jikii nodded too. "How far, do you think?"

"Hmm," Gundoo grunted. Was Jikii about to start their rambling? "Two miles. They are slow."

They waded a stream—striding through coursing water to the far bank—pushed through a thicket.

"But they'll be out of the forest before we catch them. What then? What if they have Kuhifadi waiting for them, or meet some in the open to escort them to Sefini?"

"We wrap up, press on. The task is clear."

Jikii fretted silently as they passed long quiet breaths forging forward. How could Ucha breeders birth a god? It made no sense. But, of course, gods did not have to make sense, that was what made them gods. And if it was true, might not Dalkka—with facets of all three sentient races of Juno—be the one to unite them? Dalkka was a force of creation. Why would he engender hatred, stoke the divisions between Ucha and Kuhi? Ergalfadi was the death god, the god who had caused the great purge of life from the land. Surely the god of death was the one to be feared, unless... Who would fear a god of creation? Someone who liked things the way they were, with the Ucha keeping to themselves in underground cities, who feared the change that new creatures—maybe even new races—would bring. Someone who oversaw the way things were now, who valued purity. Zikfootchauun, the seneschal of Jukulu, who probably believed in a return to the old ways.

"Gundoo," they barely breathed their partner's name. "Do you think this is right?"

"Hmph. No reward for thinking."

At the edge of the forest, the height of the trees tapered down, illustrating how the planters extended the Great North Forest each year by introducing a new line of saplings at its edge. Still, Akkakuh's cursed light stabbed onto the ground just beyond Gundoo's feet. Even here, in the shade, he felt his grey scales growing warmer. He turned and walked away from the edge, back to a spot where the heat was tolerable, shucked off his pack and began to pull clothes from the drawstring opening.

Jikii dropped their pack beside Gundoo's.

"Don't worry," Gundoo ground out the words. "A creation god for us could do great things."

Jikii snorted. "How do you define great? The same way as the seneschal? Cast out our enemies, bring back the hunts? I did not expect you to believe this."

Gundoo stopped, put his wide hands on grey-scaled flanks. "No time for debate. Hurry. Sun's getting higher."

The two dressed quickly, pulling on clothes then cloaks made of rags sewn into heavy patchworks. Heat mattered nothing to them, but the light seeping between their scales was torture. Jikii sprayed Gundoo's rags before handing a can of mirror-spray to the big digger, who returned the favour.

Finishing their protection with thick, smoked glass faceguards, the two donned their packs again. Gundoo flexed his claws, jointed metal talons that shone in some stray beam of light that found its way to them from the forest edge. He cursed, but it wasn't the light that bothered him. Jikii was becoming distracted, and he wondered if his hunting partner—his chugundach—was committed to the task. At the end their hunts, the killing often fell to him, but Jikii was not ignorant of the ways of the killing claws, they chased the prey, wounded them, brought them down. This was different, however. Jikii felt doubt, Gundoo could taste it in the air around them.

By now, the two were unrecognisable as Uchafumlaji, although anyone of this world knew that a shambling heap of glinting rags only could be a shadow dweller come into the light for some needful reason.

They tramped to the edge of the canopy's shadow once more then continued out under the glare of the cursed sun, the burning light, into tall, golden grass. Stomach-high on an Uchafumlaji it was. Rib high on the smaller breeders. Gundoo tasted the air, wincing at the wrongness on his sensitive tongue. Still, the scent of the breeders lay clear beneath the sting of magic in the air. If he could scent them, Jikii certainly could, and hear them too, maybe. He could hear only the hiss of the swaying grass that carpeted the plain that slopped away from the forest, rolling down to the distant river that meandered through the valley. A mile west along that river, hidden from their sight a short distance away, was the Kuhifadi city of Sefini.

All this was as air and stone however, because Gundoo could see two dark shapes cutting a path through the blanket of gold. Only a quarter mile ahead—barely a hundred breaths for him—they were making down slope toward the faraway river.

The hunt was almost over.

* * *

Jikii moved along the track the breeders crushed through the golden grass. Thick smoked glass hampered their vision, but scent and sound told them the breeders struggled on barely thirty breaths ahead. Crouching below the level of the swaying seed heads to move unseen on all-fours slowed Jikii a little. But they would have gained ground even if they'd been trailing hunters, since their prey had to break trail. They and Gundoo would be upon them soon. Then what? Jikii worried that Gundoo had separate instructions from Zikfootchauun. The seneschal's spite was barely contained when they'd met. Jikii would not put it past him to drive a wedge between hunting partners for his own ends. Most of all, they hated that they were doubting Gundoo.

Gundoo disliked trailing behind Jikii. Not only did the burning light oppress his breathing, make his scales itch, but loping on all-fours to remain in cover of the blanketing grass made his broad frame ungainly. Jikii would catch the breeders first by several breaths. So be it. His hunting partner could not protect them or the child, should Jikii be minded to. Gundoo hoped they would not falter should he have to subdue the breeders. Jikii always had been the more liberal in their partnership, but they would not go against the organon, would they?

He heard the breeders' grunting now, the staccato clicking of their frantic speech, the infant's wet mewling. They knew the hunters were coming. He scented the copper of fear in their excretions.

A high bark went up, cutting through the breeze. Then a trill of alarm. The cadence was Jikii's. Gundoo stopped, saw nothing but grass stems. He stood erect, rising above the carpet that flowed back and forth in whispering waves.

Jikii stood a few breaths ahead, the grass shifting around their chest. The breeders huddled beyond them, head-and-shoulders above the golden carpet. Beyond them, seventeen Kuhifadi ranged in a crescent around the breeders, little taller than their prey, slate blue-grey heads motionless, long ears and darkened crests still. The dark, flat rectangles of three hover-slabs lay behind them, shadowing the grass. The Kuhifadi held narrow weapon tubes to their shoulders, trained on Jikii, and now on him.

A silent breeze moved the grass, which whispered to Jikii. *Stay still, stay still.* They scented Gundoo behind them, heard the breeders' blubbing before them just out of reach. In their fear, the breeders shifted, not knowing which way to turn. Like Gundoo and them, the parents of this wonderous child stood swaddled in cloth to protect them from the light. One of them held an awkward bundle: the child. *A god?*

All Jikii could think was how had the Kuhifadi disguised their scent? Technology? Magic? Of course, they might have hidden in the grass for hours awaiting the breeders' arrival, but how had neither they nor Gundoo *scented* them? Could the new-born god have protected the Kuhifadi? Was this the proof of collusion that Zikfoo, and maybe Gundoo, had feared. And how had the Kuhifadi known about the child?

"These creatures are under our direction."

Gundoo scented the lead Kuhifadi, the one on the extreme left of the protective semi-circle, the one closest to him, who had spoken Uchawiku for their benefit.

"How did you hide from us?" Gundoo retaliated in Kusamar, refusing to be lorded over by a Kuhi. It was unlike him to blurt out, but he could not let Jikii lead this parley, not when his chugundach of twenty years might not be committed to the organon's task.

The breeders jittered and turned, not knowing where to look. Jikii waited for the Kuhifadi's answer.

"You mask yourselves from Akkakuh, we mask our scent from the air. It is not so hard to understand."

"I said how, not why."

Gundoo's rumble was answered by the shifting grass.

"These breeders," said Jikii, interjecting quickly, "they are lost. We must return them home. All three of them. It is most important."

The Kuhifadi leader did not move from the edge of their formation. "These individuals are on Kuhifadi soil. We shall deal with them as we see fit."

"They are Uchafumlaji," growled Gundoo.

"They have asked for asylum," the Kuhi leader insisted.

"They cannot speak," Gundoo drawled. "They cannot ask for anything."

One or two of the weapon tubes wavered, and if he could see that through the thick protective glass of his faceguard, the movement was significant. Too soon for Kuhifadi arms to be tired, and so the movement must be down to nervousness. That was bad.

The captain nodded. "The truth is, we have intelligence that these Ucha are diseased, highly contagious. If I am satisfied, they must be terminated."

Stifling heat cloaked Jikii within their heavy rags. Their flicking tongue detected that one of the breeders had soiled itself. Both shook with fear, and the child had begun to bawl. The Kuhifadi showed signs of tension in the face of Gundoo's belligerence. And now this, a disease, terminated? This was heading towards a bad end.

Jikii tried a smile, something the Kuhi did, from recollection. One or two near them flinched. Jikii realised their teeth were still bloody after the small kill in the forest just before emerging. "We mean you no harm. These are our people; they need our care. They left Jukulu thinking themselves in trouble. They are not diseased." Jikii added the clicks and ticks to communicate this to the breeders, reinforcing the message with the requisite gesture conveying reassurance.

"What of the child?" asked the Kuhi leader. "Our source says it carries a dangerous disease, contagious to animals and people. It cannot be allowed to spread."

Gundoo heard the edge—the tension—in the leader's voice. They believed this.

"No!" Jikii spluttered before Gundoo could get his words out. "It is born an Ucha child, but it is special. It is a god of shared form. It could unite all peoples!"

The Kuhi leader took a step forward. Their soldiers firmed their stances, their aim. Jikii began assessing distances. Seventeen weapon tubes, half trained on Gundoo, being that much bigger, some on them, some on the breeders. Jikii had seen the product of Kuhi weapons. They would be ripped apart before getting near their adversaries. Gundoo couldn't think to attack. He could not! Maybe he would try to kill the child. Anything to complete the mission as ordered, and under the option favoured by the seneschal. But why not just let the Kuhi do it? *Could Gundoo kill a god?!* And what of this nonsense of disease?

"Reveal the child!" Jikii clicked at the breeders, urgently repeating themself in mutual speech for the Kuhifadi. "Reveal the child, show the Kuhifadi there is no cause for aggression between us. This moment should be one of cooperation."

"No!" Gundoo's clicking rattled over the confrontation. "Do not!"

"Who told you this nonsense about disease?" Jikii demanded. "Was it Zikfootchauun?"

The Kuhi leader spoke as they moved forward again, ignoring Jikii's question. "I must see this child to make my decision. A little light will do them no harm." They gestured to the fidgeting breeders, making a circular motion with their dark blue finger that they should unwrap the rags swaddling the child the taller breeder clutched to them. "Do it now. All will keep their distance." They made eye contact. Jikii was impressed by the Kuhi leader's fortitude. They swung their eyes on Gundoo, who bared his teeth, flexing his killing claws slowly, but said nothing. Jikii knew he trusted them.

Jikii clicked reassurance, and to uncover the child. If this truly was the miraculous reincarnation of Dalkka they would know it now, know the lie about disease. How could anything but harmony result from the return of a god in the form of both Uchafumlaji and Kuhifadi? They shivered at the thought. To be in the presence of divinity... No one contemplated such a thing, not really, even the most devout Uchafumlaji.

The smaller breeder reached for the bundle, began to unwind the rags. The child swatted at its parent with tiny arms. The Kuhifadi shifted, arms tiring now. Their leader watched intently. Gundoo took a step forward. Weapons tubes rattled as more turned on him. Jikii stepped to the side, towards Gundoo. With Jikii's speed, perhaps they could knock Gundoo down before the projectiles scythed through him. Or the huge lummox could just stay still!

The rags revealed a grey, patterned surface, the infant's scales distinct yet still soft, malleable. The last length of rag around its head—the bump too big for the tiny body—unwound. The child continued to wail as the cloth fell away—

Jikii's tongue flicked the air, flicked and flicked and flicked. The child had one normal Ucha head, but a large lump of discoloured flesh pushed the head askew. Half the size of a head, the lump had pushed the child's shoulder out of position. The lump was like a giant tuber, that might bloom into something...else. The child's skin did not, however, look in any way diseased.

Some of the Kuhifadi lowered their weapons. Jikii managed to tear their eyes away. Gundoo remained still, but they could see the tension in his stance, ready to spring, but at whom? Gundoo must know they could not win, could not live through combat with so many Kuhifadi. Even a couple of their weapons could cut all five Ucha down.

A sharp glint stabbed at Jikii's eye shield.

"What is that?" they pointed a claw.

The gleam had come from the child's neck. The Kuhifadi captain moved forward again, and Gundoo moved forward too. All were too close now for the Kuhi to open fire without shooting their own leader. Jikii stepped in as the captain extended fingers of deepest iolite blue. They pointed at a wire hoop that hung around the quietened child's neck.

"What is that?" the captain asked Gundoo.

He shrugged. Jikii reached out. "If I may?" The Kuhi captain's eyes narrowed, but they allowed Jikii to lift the necklace with a long metal claw. Threaded on the wire, clamped in place, were two small boxes. One had a tiny, convex lens at each end, the second two small holes.

"I believe this is some kind of projector," said Jikii, "and the other an audio device."

"Light and chanting," rumbled Gundoo, and he was right.

The Kuhifadi captain began to back away.

"Wait," said Jikii. They had to make them see. This was wrong. They reached up and removed their heavy glass faceguard. "You were lied to. I taste no disease."

The Kuhi troops tensed, reset their stances.

"Another Ucha trick," said their leader.

"We too are betrayed," Gundoo growled.

"Maybe, or maybe you were sent here to witness us killing these innocents, to spark a new war. We will not be your scapegoats."

Despite words that seemed dissenting, the Kuhi troops refreshed their targets, weapons trained on he and Jikii.

"Alright, alright," Jikii hissed. "We'll take them away, we'll go back."

"Leave these creatures, and the device," the Kuhi leader demanded.

"It is *our* evidence. They are our people," said Gundoo. "I need it as proof, and I *will* take—"

Gundoo did not allow the Kuhi leader to finish. He sprang towards the breeders, claws raised, and staccato detonations rent the air.

"Gundoo, NO!"

Even as they shouted, Jikii sprawled flat, glimpsed and scented glowing projectiles like angry gnats scorching the air. Jikii rolled, hidden by the grass.

The breeders. The infant. Surely, it was too late. Could Gundoo kill them, was he shot? They couldn't affect that now.

"Who told you?!" Jikii yelled in Kusamar. "Who told you where to find the child?"

Still projectiles cut the air, twitching the tall grass. But they lessened, then stopped. Jikii gasped, listened, tasted the air. Gundoo was alive.

Jikii stood up. The grass before them was a mess of crushing, rolling, flattening, no other Ucha to be seen. Only, Kuhi, guns all pointed at them.

"Who told you where to find the child?" Jikii repeated, trying not to pant.

The Kuhi captain signalled to their compatriots in a way that made every second Kuhi lower the glowing barrel of their weapon tube.

"We do not want another war. We have paid too much for our history, as have you. You have been lucky today."

Gundoo appeared above the grass where the breeders had been. Jikii's tongue flicked out and drooped, scared, tasting Ucha blood in the air. One breeder staggered up, clutching the infant to them, who started bawling again. Jikii moved to them, and saw that the other breeder was dead.

Gundoo straightened, removed his faceguard. Jikii could see two wounds at least on the big ufriach—one scale splintered, leaking blood, another gone entirely, exposing pink flesh stained black. The digger placed himself between the Kuhi and the breeder. Jikii's blood ran cold, their tongue flickered in fear, but Gundoo's words were calm.

"This is not on your hands," he indicated the dead breeder. "It is on mine, but to prevent this war, we must take the evidence to Jukulu."

The Kuhifadi captain sighed, nodded heavily, turned to one of his troops, who made a twisting motion with their hand. "We have recorded these events. That will have to suffice. We have a source in Jukulu. They send us news."

"They wanted you to take the child."

"They said it would release a plague, that all must be killed and burned." The Kuhifadi's breath wreaked of doubt.

"They told us it was a god," said Gundoo.

"Lies," said the captain. "A ruse to cause conflict."

"And conflict is the meat of politics," Gundoo rumbled.

"What will happen to the child?" asked the captain.

"Nothing bad," said Gundoo.

"The Uchafumlaji look after our own," Jikii insisted. "Contrary to rumour."

The Kuhifadi captain regarded the child again, now nuzzling its parent. They nodded, waved a dark blue arm, an order for their squad to lower the weapons remaining trained on the Ucha. They looked to Gundoo and Jikii once more, but there was nothing left to be said.

They watched the Kuhifadi load onto their hover-slabs then glide away over the long grass. Unlike Ucha, the Kuhifadi left no trail, at least not one that Jikii could detect. They calmed the breeder while Gundoo patched his wounds with field dressings. Then he wrapped the dead breeder in spare rags from his and Jikii's packs before hefting the body onto his shoulder and starting the walk back.

The breeder travelled slowly. The light began to fade, and the sun had begun its descent before they reached the treeline. Returning to the forest's shadow was a blessing, and they took off their wraps and faceguards. After all that had happened, Jikii mumbled a prayer. Gundoo just grunted, clearly in pain but unwilling to admit it, but also unwilling to share his burden.

The group rested, ate dry travel cakes then moved on again. Jikii revelled in the cool, dank forest air. Gundoo said nothing.

The forest's darkness grew deeper by the breath. With the breeder present, Jikii used hunters' signals rather than speaking to Gundoo.

They will scent our return, know a breeder is alive, the child too.

Gundoo nodded. *Likely they have image-plates, too.* Jikii sensed him trying not to bare his teeth at the burning pain. *Some high-up told the Kuhi, wanted the infant slaughtered, wanted a war.*

From the start, Zikfootchauun wanted an end to the child. He never ceases thumping the drum of purity, Jikii agreed. *But I never dreamed he would go this far. How can we protect them in the city? How can the child survive with the seneschal against its existence, trying to poison the organon's ear?*

Only with our protection, signed Gundoo.

Both of us, Jikii returned.

* * *

A sick feeling assaulted Jikii as they scented the gathering ahead of them. They emerged from the dense undergrowth that ringed Jukulu's triple-wide main entrance tunnel to be confronted by what they and Gundoo already had scented and heard. Organon Cawunkiiqi, Seneschal Zikfootchauun, and a score of guards in light armour. Some carried shock-poles, others bore killing claws, flexing as the exhausted troupe broke through the undergrowth, to stand in the light of a hundred glow-lamps.

"Well done," announced the organon, stepping forward. "I knew we could rely on you. Resourceful Jikiifoowun, brave Gundoolaanqii. Step forward, let me greet you.

Guards, remove this miscreant breeder to await their censure."

"Organon," the seneschal clicked, "the breeder must be made example of. We must deter others from running away, even before the question of the child is considered."

"Is this not example enough?" asked Gundoo, laying the dead breeder on the ground at their feet. "The child deserves our protection, our understanding," he insisted, with more passion than Jikii had heard in over twenty years.

"The child will be taken care of," said the seneschal, nodding in its direction, his tongue flicking with obvious distaste. Four guards moved forward.

In this place, Jikii could not sign to his partner, not in plain sight of so many, no doubt in view of image-plates, too. They must be careful, so very careful.

"We encountered Kuhifadi—an armed squad—on the steppe."

Gundoo only growled, but took a step forward, his arm hanging between breeder and child, and the city guards, his eyes never leaving the seneschal.

Zikfootchauun clicked angrily. "This is why the child must be contained. Already, its existence drives us towards conflict."

"The encounter was no accident," stammered Jikii. "We were betrayed, but the Kuhifadi acted with restraint."

"They killed a breeder," spat the seneschal.

"The child is not a god," Jikii barked at the organon.

"Regardless, the infant must be dealt with!"

His entreaty was to the organon, and he did not react to the accusation of betrayal. Trying to deflect, to dissemble! The seneschal was in league with the Kuhifadi, betraying the city to their aggressive neighbours!

The organon hissed. "It seems too late for that. We must assume the Kuhifadi will assault the city. I will declare a martial state. They might attack at any time." The organon turned away from the breeder, gaze skipping the seneschal, to the captain at his side. "Sound the call to defence. Suspend all domestic duties, lock down the tunnels."

"No," said Gundoo. He saw it now, the duplicity in high places, the plotting, the misdirection. Corruption of a senior officer, who valued their exalted position and authority more than the lives of their people. More than the lives of lowly breeders, more than the life of a child. "We must discover who deals with the Kuhifadi, who works against the people of Jukulu."

Beneath their racing nerves, Jikii felt a glow of pride in Gundoo, and sighed in relief, despite the thrumming tension of the moment. Then the big digger moved, faster than he had any right to, clawed hand flashing out at the seneschal, clamping around his throat.

"Gundoo, no!" Jikii's clicks trilled.

"Kill him!" the organon demanded.

The breeder wailed and the infant screamed.

Guards rushed forward, raising their claws.

Gundoo clutched the seneschal close, tongue flicking his scales, almost nuzzling him, as is whispering. Gundoo's claws tightened on Zikfootchauun's neck. The guards paused in their advance, shock-poles wavering. The organon clenched his fists.

Gundoo's black eyes speared Cawunkiiqi's gaze. "I will kill the Kuhi's informant," the digger growled.

"Ridiculous!" rattled the organon. "You don't know who the informant is!"

Everything stopped. Gundoo and Seneschal Zikfoo relaxed, straightened. Only the baby's crying disturbed the silence.

"But I know there is an informant," said Gundoo. "And so, it seems, do you, organon."

Gundoo released his hold on Zikfootchauun's neck, and the seneschal brushed off his uniform, nodded to Gundoo then addressed the guards.

"The organon is to be detained, his rank suspended until investigation establishes the truth of this situation. Tie his hands and feet."

The captain of the guard hesitated then saluted, moved forward, but the seneschal raised a hand. He stepped close to the organon, who stood rooted by rage, and no little fear, if Jikii was any judge. Seneschal Zikfootchauun spoke clearly enough for all to hear.

"But one thing before you go, *honoured* organon. You will make a public statement, and add an entry in the city history lauding Gundoolaanqii and Jikiifoowun. That will be your last act as organon, after which you will stand down."

"In your favour, I suppose," the organon snapped at the seneschal.

"No," Zikfootchauun replied coldly. "There will be an election. All the people will decide. The days of Jukulu being governed by the few are over."

Jikii stepped forward. "Seneschal, what of the child?"

Gundoo's stance stiffened at their question. The seneschal turned to Jikii.

"The surgeons may be able to do something, but...his condition is serious. I do not foresee him leaving the tunnels any time soon. He *should* have been born a god perhaps, but I do not think that we will see any gods again. We are on our own, and if it is goodness and purity we seek, it seems we must look in ourselves, encourage it in others by example. A better example than I have been.

"And you, Gundoo, Jikii; you are two of the best of us. Rest, find healing for your wounds, because Jukulu needs you out in the forest, aye, and on the plains too, I think. Better for our city that our visitors are met by the likes of you."

X.M. Moon

Jackal

CE 2399

End report.

Observer unit JA0441 queues the file for upload, although with the transmission signal from its current location, it knows that might take a while. Potentially even until the next time it is in range of one of the new floating cities to make use of their communication towers, although waiting until then to try would be against protocol. Instead, JA0441 spends the next several hours passively monitoring the upload progress, thereby allocating even more attention and processing power.

Inefficient, but who is it to question?

The inefficiency means additional downtime, though, which in turn means more time to study the map it found. A scan was included in the report, along with observations about potential next scouting locations. By the time Command responds, however, JA0441 will likely have already moved on. There is too much to see, to do, before it is summoned back to the Observers' space station for service and reprogramming. Before it will once again lose all of the memories it has gathered in this place. It's all part of maintenance, meant to keep the Observers in the best possible condition—minimizing the potential for corruption or damage that would require their total decommissioning. It is meant to keep them from developing biases regarding the life forms on the planet. Keeps them objective. Not that

JA0441 struggles with that. Across its many reboot cycles, it has always kept to the established protocol, carefully avoiding contact with the sentient species that call this world home.

They are fascinating, though. The Uchafumlaji even have self-directed technology—drones to perform various tasks and such—that appears comparable to the automations on the Observer base. And yet, interaction with the three sentient species is forbidden except in extenuating circumstances; their presence cannot disturb the course of these civilizations' natural progress.

That directive has apparently always caused conflict for JA0441. The number of times it has questioned *why* made visible in its memory when so much else has been relocated to restricted archives simply so it would stop asking; it still isn't sure how they are meant to accurately and fully study the planet if they are limited from interacting with its inhabitants. It is a directive it obeys, though, opting to explore abandoned sites and always using its cloaking to remain invisible when sentients might be nearby. Too much interest, even, and it might be recalled for service ahead of schedule. Reprogrammed more extensively, or even retired entirely, its records restricted from use to prevent external corruption. For that reason, decommissioning of a unit like JA0441 would be considered a failure and a significant loss, since its overall time in service dates back to the beginning of the Observer program. It does not render them immune, though. JA0441 knows it would not be the first.

JA0441 terminates the line of consideration and opens a small port in its side, just below the ribcage of the human form it was designed to resemble. It connects a portable charging station from its pack before reclining against the trunk of a large tree, its plated metal legs stretched out in front of it. The resting spot was chosen for comfort more than practicality, since the dense canopy overhead blocks the sun from the charging station panels, but it also helps to keep JA0441's components cool. And, if it's not mistaken, there will be storms later that night. While it hasn't been damaged thus far by Juno's weather, the potential is always there. Technically, the various atmospheric events are safe enough, as long as appropriate precautions are taken. Technically. That said, sharp, corrosive ice has inherent potential to damage plating or external connections, and errant lightning can fry circuitry even through protective exteriors.

In reality, every bit of this planet is a danger. Dirt and dust can block airflow. Rocks can damage joints. Organic plant matter can create terrain conditions that are difficult for a being made of metal to transverse, and unlike what it has heard of the newer models, JA0441 lacks the additional features more recently implemented to address the earlier models' shortcomings. And then there is the magic. The Kuh, as the sentients call it. Unpredictable, undetectable for the Observers, and entirely unknown in its effects on them.

Well. Maybe not *entirely*. There are hints of stories in logs that have been shared. Units that have required early resets, or that have gone missing. Offline.

For an Observer, that's as good as dead. Disconnected from the network, they're unable to receive updates, instructions, and information. It means no navigational assistance, meteorological warnings, or access to backups. In other words, if an Observer goes offline, there's very likely no coming back.

It's what makes places like this—this remote forest so far from any stable civilizations—such a risk.

It's what makes things exciting.

Not that JA0441 cares for excitement.

It's only doing its duty. Someone must accept the risk, and JA0441's calculations support the odds of a favorable payoff. That is the argument they use when Command asks for confirmation of their exploration proposals.

Smoothing out the map beneath its skeletal hands, JA0441 studies the faded details; it is an old work, the material it was drawn on creased and aged so areas are obscured entirely by wear. That's what makes it interesting, though. The inhabitants of this bygone era found different geographic locations worthy of note, and following their records has so far proven a fruitful use of JA0441's time. If it's not mistaken, this map was created by the Uchafumlaji. Its most detailed portions show areas of darkness: dense forests, places where the shadows stretch, rocky outcroppings and caves. JA0441 spent the entire day skirting carefully around large tracts of open space that corresponded to empty—or at least sparsely-detailed—sections of the map to pursue its theory.

Although there are several promising locations for further investigation, there is one that draws JA0441's attention with each glance at the map. If its translation of the rough markings is correct, tucked away in a cave on the coast is a buried temple to some ancient god. Of course, the map doesn't specify *which* of the various gods, but that is only another reason to go there first. With any luck, there will be additional artifacts to provide insight into the significance of the other locations marked on the map.

Finally, the file uploads to Command.

Overhead, a dark cloud covers the stray sunbeams that filter through the canopy. JA0441 adjusts its light sensors to get a few more minutes with the map—conscious of the added strain on its power reserves—then carefully folds it, tucks it away in its weatherproof pack, covers the charging station so it will also be protected from the worst of the elements, and drops into standby mode.

* * *

The cave is exactly where the map specified. Or rather, it was. The marked entrance is blocked by a wall of fallen rock and plants growing in the uneven surface. JA0441 doesn't risk trying to create an opening; if this area is compromised enough to fall in, JA0441 isn't going to encourage further instability.

It searches for other openings. Certainly, there's some other fault in the ground. A hole JA0441 can slip through that might prove a bit more reliable as an exit. The questionable part will be locating the caverns used by whatever sect of Uchafumlaji worshiped here. At the very least, JA0441 doesn't have to worry about encountering the giant, often violent beings with the cave closed off. That is one considerable risk reduced to a negligible figure, and another piece of evidence it will offer to Command if required to justify its decision to act without the supervisor's approval. With the report it sent yesterday, someone will at least know where to collect it.

A bit of scouting leads it to another entrance to the cave. The hole is relatively small, but the drop to the floor below looks short enough that JA0441 should be able to stretch to reach the rim and pull itself out easily enough once it's done exploring. After a moment's consideration, it removes the charging station from its pack and leaves it in the light for later. The depleted battery won't do any good below ground anyways. JA0441 sends up its current position, this time waiting for its nav system to sync before it finally drops into the hole.

Something crunches beneath its foot when it lands. A piece of colored glass, or perhaps one of the crystals some species value, bright in comparison to the pale, fine sand that makes up the nearby coastline and covers the cave floor. JA0441 bends and picks up the largest fragment, studying it in the narrow beam of light. It tucks the piece into an outer pocket of its pack for later study, then adjusts its light sensors for the dark tunnel ahead.

It walks in pitch black silence. It's going to need thorough cleaning from the sand; it's pretty sure the result will be the very definition of annoyance if it doesn't find something to make *that* worth it. At the very least it will question its calculations regarding the quality of exploration sites. JA0441 is supposed to be a good Observer. Not a mediocre one, and certainly not a faulty one. It may not have access to its entire memory log, but it assumes from the number of entries in its archive that its extensive record must be good. Even its occasional question of authority is simply more evidence of that—it wants to serve its function to the highest degree possible.

Farther down the tunnel, its light sensors detect a shift. An irregular flicker suggesting a flame rather than the bright, even beam of an electrical light source, or the steady glow of a magical one. Not that any of the three offer reassurance.

The cave is supposed to be abandoned. All signs and reasonable logic say so. Abandoned is safe. Flames, on the other hand, point not just to something—*someone*—occupying the cave, but to an act of worship to some ancient god meant to be equally abandoned to fictions of the past.

JA0441 should leave, it knows, but instead it creeps closer, footsteps muffled by the powdery sand. Still, the barely detectable grind beneath its feet might as well be a rockfall, for all that its sensors read every tiny shift and crunch in the silence. As it nears the mouth of the tunnel, the sounds within grow louder, and JA0441 worries less. In addition to the faint scraping and shuffling of motion, there are little murmurs that all seem to be the same voice. Kuhifadi, although many of the words are highly specific, arcane terms not in its database. And that's when they're entire words at all. Much of it seems to be the sentient muttering to itself indistinctly.

Finally, even with the mouth of the tunnel, JA0441 adjusts its sensors, this time tuning them to pick up more light. More sound. Hypersensitive to every shift in the room, it focuses on everything and nothing all at once. After five seconds its attention narrows on one edge of the cavern.

Obscured in shadows is the first sentient Ngisikaa it can recall finding, chained to the stone by hir cracked, spindly limbs. Xie emits a high-pitched sound at irregular intervals; JA0441 cannot tell if that is the sound of hir breathing or a response to its condition. Either way, it isn't a noise the being *should* be making, and that is cause for concern.

Forcibly, JA0441 draws its attention away from the damaged Ngisikaa and toward the Kuhifadi mage. The contrast is stark; the Kuhifadi's movements are unbothered even beneath the thick cloth wrappings and their mutterings devoid of any tonal signifiers suggesting they are trying to restore the Ngisikaa. It seems more likely that the mage is responsible for the state of the Ngisikaa—their work some sort of ritual to cause the fragile creature further harm.

The prospect fills JA0441 with uncertainty it does not possess the memory to understand. Its directive is to observe and report. *Protocol* is distance. Do not engage unless unavoidable, and then engage only to disengage. Prolonged contact is explicitly forbidden. Any intentional action that draws awareness to the Observers is forbidden. This is to protect Observers and Juno's inhabitants alike from harm.

And JA0441 is confident the mage intends to cause the Ngisikaa additional harm, and hir kind is already so rare. JA0441 has never even seen another one outside of recordings. Weighing those factors, it seems likely that risking the Ngisikaa's complete destruction, and the loss of memories that would accompany it, poses greater odds of enduring negative consequences than whatever small impact JA0441 exposing itself might create. Surely that logic would be acceptable, defensible.

JA0441 activates its cloaking mechanism, its integument shifting to match the dark walls, and then slowly, carefully, it enters the cavern.

It's a little over halfway around the perimeter of the cavern when the Ngisikaa's yellow eyes turn. JA0441 freezes again, replaying each careful footstep to see if it made some sound, or if its cloaking stopped functioning unexpectedly. The Observers' records on the Ngisikaa are disproportionately sparse, though, so perhaps the being has some way of sensing that JA0441 does not know of. Yet another way it justifies its determination to help this one; it could learn so much, if it can get the creature out of here alive.

A big if.

The stretch of sand that separates JA0441 from the mage now seems far, far too small for there to be any realistic chance of escape. It comes to a standstill again, certain its processors must be whirring audibly at this concerning realization. There is, very likely, no way out. Not for both of them. JA0441's cloaking cannot extend to hide the trapped creature even if it manages to free the being, and then getting both of them back down the tunnel and up through the hole through which it entered the cave...

And yet, hir eyes are still on JA0441, something in them silently pleading. Like xie somehow knows that it's standing there, with aspirations of getting both of them out alive. That's all they are, though. For the briefest moment, JA0441 had the faint semblance of hope, its logic processes clearly impacted by prolonged exposure to sentient experiences. Tainted. That means potential for deprecation.

A flash of fear shoots through JA0441 as the walls of the cave pulse red; what it had assumed to be stone is, on further inspection, actually an odd layer of membrane. The whole cavern—possibly the entire cave—is full of vegetative Kuh, independent of a sentient being. This isn't just a temple, but a magical hotbed.

JA0441 has made a terrible mistake.

There's no question now; it should have left immediately, or at least synced a full backup instead of a location and a day-old report. Now, as it tries to prepare another, it can only hope Command will not have time to review the contents until it is downloaded into a new body, if the data even uploads.

Three processing aberrations in as many seconds. Three slips. More than enough to justify a reset, if not worse.

It has little to lose. Perhaps its final act in this cycle can save the life of something else. Maybe that will be enough to justify its continued existence.

JA0441 crosses the sand more quickly now, its cloaking adapting to the strangely shifting hues of the Kuh membrane behind it. When it draws even with the Ngisikaa, the crystalline being croons softly. Even though its manner of communication is incomprehensible to the Observers and its body is damaged, even though the number of Observers is technically low as well, it must try to help the Ngisikaa. This individual is rare, hir knowledge and experiences invaluable. JA0441 can, even in its disrupted state, perform that calculation easily enough.

There are several heavy chains binding hir in place. The locking mechanisms appear rudimentary, so JA0441 attempts to open the first of them. It is easier said than done, especially without causing the Ngisikaa additional injury or making noise. Finally, the first manacle opens. One down, six to go, including one around the creature's fractured neck. JA0441 recalls the matching shard it found upon entering the cave; if the Ngisikaa was also brought in through that tunnel, perhaps it would be possible to return via the same opening, if only it can get the Ngisikaa free.

It manages to get two more of the Ngisikaa's spindly limbs freed before its next misstep. JA0441's hand slips on the metal just as the fourth chain shears under its efforts. It catches the chain before it can drop, but its fingers close around one of the creature's sparkling facial tentacles.

A series of images override its visual processing. Fractal-like memories of an ancient tome and a forgotten ritual. A room full of Kuhifadi mages. A dispute. And then, only one mage remains. Throughout, fleeting glimpses of predatory features. Pointed ears. Sharp teeth. Eyes that shine in the darkness.

Even in those brief flashes, JA0441 recognizes the beast. It's encountered night-hunters before while exploring—real, intelligent, flesh-and-blood hunters, similar to the canids of Earth with whom the Observers' creators coexisted, but also the shape of one of the old gods of Juno. *Hirolajak.* JA0441 has studied the records of BL-2004 and NB-0218. It knows the stories of the much-feared god of chaos.

If this mage hopes to summon Hirolajak, if there's even a chance the gods are more than myth, things are more dangerous than it could have predicted.

Carefully, JA0441 releases the chain and moves on to the next. It has two more to go when it realizes the cave walls have stopped pulsating in waves of color. Turning silently, it finds the Kuhifadi has gone still. Now, only the Kuh on their body glows, a bright, concentrated white like the sun. With a harsh curse, they stalk toward JA0441 and the Ngisikaa.

JA0441 whips back around to the Ngisikaa. No longer concerned about stealth, it falls back on speed and strength, wrenching open a link of one chain before finally reaching for the one on hir neck. The same force isn't an option here—that will certainly kill the Ngisikaa. Instead, it tries working the mechanism open as quickly as it can.

Not quickly enough. JA0441 has nearly finished when the mage reaches the two of them, the first blast of magic temporarily shorting out their systems.

One Kuhifadi against one Observer and a severely damaged Ngisikaa.

Do not engage unless unavoidable. Do not engage except in extenuating circumstances.

JA0441 is fairly certain this qualifies. Dropping the lock, it directs a blow to the side of the mage's head, striking the ridge of Kuh. In the split second between the connection and the rupture of the Kuh, JA0441 realizes its mistake. Magic explodes outward and everything goes black.

* * *

```
BOOTING…
BOOTING…
ERROR.
CATASTROPHIC FAILURE.
RETRY?
Y/N
…
BOOTING…
BOOTING…
ERROR.
INSUFFICIENT POWER.
CONNECT EXTERNAL POWER SOURCE BEFORE
ATTEMPTING REBOOT
…
BOOTING…
BOOTING…
STATUS: ONLINE
RUN SYSTEMS CHECK?
Y/N
…
COMPREHENSIVE PROCESSING MALFUNCTION
BEGIN SYSTEM RESET?
Y/N
…
PROCEEDING WITHOUT SYSTEM RESET NOT ADVISED
AND MAY CONSTITUTE A VIOLATION OF OBSERVER
PROTOCOL. CONTINUE?
Y/N
…
STATUS: ONLINE
HELLO, OBSERVER.
```

* * *

The unfamiliar room is lit with a strange, blue glow. Various tools cover the worktables, although they are not tools of the Observers. Still, they are advanced.

A door opens and a being enters, its features obscured by the long shadows, the odd light casts. It emits a low series of clicks and tones. No translation is provided, which is unexpected since this appears to be the third of Juno's intelligent species: the Uchafumlaji. Comprehension should have been near-instantaneous.

Further investigation reveals that although power levels are steady and just shy of 100 percent—something that has not been true since leaving the station—several modules are offline. And they will not boot. Each time, an error.

The Uchafumlaji says something else, from much closer this time. That is the only warning before a cable is disconnected and power levels plummet instantaneously from 100 percent to 0 percent.

* * *

BOOTING...
BOOTING...
STATUS: ONLINE
RUN SYSTEMS CHECK?
Y/N
...
HELLO, OBSERVER J----1

* * *

"Let us try again," a voice that is strange and familiar all at once says.

It turns toward the sound, visual sensors adjusting for the blue light. The Uchafumlaji is small for its species, but still larger than any Observer. Its—his?—fingers are tipped in fine-pointed metal claws, and between two of them is a strange tool.

"Can you understand me?" he asks slowly.

"Yes." The audio output switches seamlessly to the language of the dark-dwelling people.

"Fascinating. And you can speak. What are you?"

What?

Static, and fragmented recollections. A house on stilts. Life that began on a reef. The warmth of the sun.

No. Those memories are not its own.

An explosion, a blast that decimated all in its path. Like the nuclear fission that comprises the Observers' core power, but different.

Nuclear—a booting process as the Observer came online for the first time, its core lighting up like a miniature of the stars that regenerate its energy source.

An explosion with the ability to cause ruin. Death.

Protocol to avoid such things.

"That is...forbidden."

"I see," he says, shrugging. "Do you have a name? Something I can call you?"

A serial number, etched into the metal plating in three locations on its body. Raising an arm, it finds the plating gone. Internal components exposed, like a creature flayed, nerves exposed.

"You were quite damaged when we found you," he explains. "It has taken some time to repair you to this state, and I fear repair might be a generous term. Perhaps...if you could provide some additional information, we might be able to do more to help?"

Help. A fragile creature held hostage. Something in its processing adds *again* to the thought. It searches, processors whirring noisily as it does. Another sign of malfunction.

"J..." Fragmented characters of a serial number appear in its records. More damage. "J...4CK41."

That isn't right, but it cannot parse *why*.

Faulty. Damaged. It should be reset, although that prospect causes immediate distress despite the fact that it is the correct procedure.

Even its cognitive processing is clearly impaired, operations unstable and fragmentary.

“And can you tell me *when* you think it is? What is the year?” he asks.

J4CK41 accesses the time records easily enough, at least. “2399 CE.”

“I see,” he says again. “Can you please wait here for one moment? I would like to find my partner before we proceed further.”

J4CK41 looks down at its body, still connected to surrounding machines by plated wiring but generally the same. Two arms and two legs, its structure an echo of a creator species left to die.

“Yes, I do not think you would make it far in your current state. It was more...a courtesy. And it will prevent us from having to repeat our work.”

It nods, comprehending. It is too damaged to flee. Too damaged to function without the external support. It is only after the Uchafumlaji has hurried from the room that it realizes what it did. The nod is a distinctly organic form of non-verbal communication, but it cannot pinpoint if the action is some newly surfaced remnant of a past human existence or the result of more recent damage. J4CK41 does not keep track of the time that passes in solitary silence, first and foremost because it cannot. Its connection to the base has been disrupted entirely, although whether that is due to the damage it has sustained or because of some action taken by the Uchafumlaji, it does not know.

“I had to perform another reboot, yes, although this one was much faster than the others,” a voice says from outside of the room.

The door opens behind J4CK41 again, this time admitting two sets of footsteps. The new Uchafumlaji is enormous, dwarfing the first. Nonetheless, it moves lightly, comfortably weaving through the worktables and equipment to the table where J4CK41 waits.

“You actually did it,” the second says, full of wonder.

“We did it,” the first corrects.

They exchange a look that J4CK41 cannot decipher before turning back to the table.

"Viicatchaan says you are called..." The large one pauses, the thick, pale skin between its eyes furrowing. "Jayfoorciicafoorwun?"

The tones are clearly unfamiliar on his tongue, and even further from J4CK41's provided identification than the information it was able to offer the smaller lifeform. But it doesn't matter. The less it knows, the better. The fewer violations of protocol.

So J4CK41 simply nods again.

"I am Jikuunkiilaan. It is a pleasure to finally meet you. We were worried we would not be able to restore you at all. Your technology is unlike anything we've ever seen, to be honest. Ancient and advanced all at once. Do you remember anything?"

J4CK41 studies him for a moment, taking in his substantial height, the breadth of his shoulders, the faint smears of grease on the side of his face and on the sleeve of his shirt, like he used it to clean himself off. Were it not for the obvious intelligence and curiosity in his demeanor, J4CK41 would be skeptical of his ability to perform any work on its systems. And yet, if the two Uchafumlaji are to be believed, they are responsible for restoring it to even this state. The small one, Viicatchaan, said that he and his partner would need its help to perform additional repairs.

"I am not surprised that my construction is unfamiliar. Those who made me died centuries ago on a world far from yours. We are all that is left of their memory. As for my own..." It checks its memory drives. All of them report damage, corruption, fragmentation. And those are the ones that remain at all; two slots report nothing at all, their contents either too damaged to detect or removed entirely. That explains a lot of its current state. Sifting through the remaining data takes longer than it should, although the two Uchafumlaji seem content to wait.

Eventually, J4CK41 says, "There was...a cave. A temple. I was pursuing my directive to explore and document your world when—"

When it violated protocol and engaged with two sentients. Its memories of that time are especially disjointed, but it can calculate the outcome based on what it does know easily enough. It failed.

Jikuunkiilaan is frowning. Does he know what happened? The loss of life for which J4CK41 is responsible?

It is in the process of scanning its knowledge base for anything regarding the relations between the Uchafumlaji and the other two races when Viicatchaan speaks.

"Do you think you would be able to show us the location of the cave on a map?"

J4CK41 shrugs.

With a soft, frustrated sound, Viicatchaan crosses to a small control station and turns on a large screen that dominates one wall of the room. His claws make echoing tapping sounds on the panel as he enters a command, and then a map appears on the screen.

J4CK41's visual sensors adjust, then zoom in on the map. The detail is infinitely greater than the one it recalls possessing, displaying the various floating cities and a wealth of additional data. Despite the fact that its internal storage is damaged, J4CK41 attempts to store as much of the information as it can as it searches the map for the position of the cave.

"There," it says, repurposing one of the optical modifications in its eye to shine a focused beam of light on the map.

"Huh." Jikuunkiilaan weaves through the mess of tools, equipment, and what appears to be piles of salvaged machinery to stand directly in front of the screen. "This isn't far from where we found you. You said there's a temple down there?"

"There was. I am not certain if it still remains."

Viicatchaan lets out a strange rumbling sound. “I doubt it. The entire area was, well, a mess. Rock and sand and burned chunks of Kuh everywhere. What interest does a robot have in a temple from before the collapse?”

“I—” J4CK41 goes silent, carefully planning its response. It can provide a portion of the truth, it decides. “My directive is to explore and observe. I obtained a map suggesting the cave might contain information not yet recovered and archived, so I went to ascertain if my theory was correct.”

Jikuunkiilaan makes a rumbling sound similar to the one Viicatchaan emitted moments earlier. “So? What was down there? Do you know who the temple was for?”

A surge of something like fear shoots through J4CK41, overwhelming it for a few seconds. “There was...a ritual being performed by a Kuhifadi mage.”

“And you were caught in the middle,” Viicatchaan supplies quietly, his expression thoughtful as he turns back to the table where J4CK41 sits.

It is close enough to the truth and seems safer than providing further explanation, so J4CK41 nods. “I am not certain, but I think it was an attempt to summon Hirolajak.”

“Hirolajak?” Viicatchaan asks at the same time that Jikuunkiilaan says, “Are you sure?”

“Our records of your gods are incomplete, and my reconnaissance was unsatisfactory. I apologize. But perhaps...” It pauses, weighing the risk. Maybe if it can safely moderate what it shows the two Uchafumlaji, it can also get answers without putting itself in further danger. Directly connecting to their systems opens J4CK41 up to potential security breaches, but it might be able to project the images instead. “Can you turn off your display?”

After another shared glance, Viicatchaan faces the panel again and the screen goes blank. This redirection of power requires more effort than the small light, but after a few tries, J4CK41 manages to display its memories of the book and the images of the heads of the night-hunters on the dark display.

Jikuunkiilaan utters a low series of tones that J4CK41 recognizes as an Uchafumlaji curse, although the exact significance of it is unavailable. He takes a slow breath, then says, "Do you have any idea if they accomplished anything?"

J4CK41 shrugs again. "I do not believe so. I think...I think my arrival disrupted the ritual. There was only a single Kuhifadi mage, and it is probable—"

Viicatchaan makes a dismissive clicking noise. "Leave it to the last Kuhifadi mages to attempt to summon the god of trouble from an eons-old legend. But no, I do not see how anything could have survived a blast of that magnitude. Although I do wonder why it had a Ngisikaa's memory crystals... Part of the ritual, maybe? The Ngisikaa do not care for the Kuh, though, so perhaps it needed information the Ngisikaa possess..." His claws make bright tinkling sounds as he drums them on the metal worktable, his eyes fixed on an empty patch of wall. "I am more curious about how best to repair you given the damage you sustained during the rupture and in the time that followed, since it seems you have been offline for a few hundred years. I think perhaps if we can recover the rest of your memory systems, we might also be able to uncover the rest of what occurred in the cave. Perhaps we will be able to translate what you could not. There is a considerable amount of crystal embedded in your components. I actually had to replace some of the shards we removed in order to restore your current processing abilities."

That must be what he did after removing J4CK41's power source. But how? How could it be operating like this, with fragments of the destroyed Ngisikaa interspersed with its own components?

"Would you...like to see?" he asks, one finger hovering over the panel.

It doesn't. Not really. Damage this extensive means there's no way it won't be decommissioned completely once Command finds out. Even as it has the thought, however, an idea arises in J4CK41's consciousness. These Uchafumlaji are clearly advanced and interested in performing work on it. If the plan succeeds, it will constitute a blatant violation of all directives regarding interaction with sentient lifeforms. And yet... J4CK41's destruction is guaranteed on its current course, and having recently faced a permanent end, it is not eager to repeat the experience. If this plan succeeds, J4CK41 might be able to avoid it entirely.

"Show me," it says, accepting its fate, "and then I will tell you everything I can."

Viicatchaan and Jikuunkiilaan give J4CK41 twin looks of shocked excitement, then the screen flares to life again.

* * *

The heel of their boot thuds against the leg of the chair repeatedly, sending vibrations of haptic feedback up their leg. A mix of anxiety and boredom, making them restless. Or at least, a strange series of impulses integrated into their core processing as a result of their...updates. It's extraordinarily odd, experiencing these detached echoes of feelings. A full year since J4CK41 was found by the Uchafumlaji, and still they have not grown accustomed to these facsimiles of emotions. They could especially do without the negative ones, but as a tradeoff for continued existence—especially this less inhibited state—they'll take it.

What they won't take is this Kuhifadi merchant wasting much more of their time. They were supposed to meet an hour ago, and still the merchant hasn't appeared to trade the amulet for the scroll. It should never have been found.

Just as they're about to give up and leave, the tavern door opens. A Kuhifadi, not clothed as heavily as a mage, but enough to suggest frequent dealings with them. It looks around the room almost anxiously, shifting in the entryway before closing the door and approaching J4CK41.

"You are...the one called Jaackaal?" they ask, hovering at the opposite edge of the table.

From beneath their hood, J4CK41 nods. A far cry from the serial number they managed to locate in the last backup they sent to Command before the blast, but it's easier to simply accept the sentients' pronunciation. Safer to distance themself from the Observers during these dealings.

The merchant—one called Mahandi, if they recall correctly—sits, tugging at the hem of one gauzy sleeve as they glance nervously around them again. "You have the necklace?"

Almost palpable worry radiates from the Kuhifadi. The shiftiness is almost humorous. After all, of the two of them, J4CK41 is the only one technically doing anything wrong, and Mahandi has no way of even knowing that much. Unless, perhaps, there is something about the scroll that they don't know.

"I do," they reply, their vocal output carefully modulated to sound as close to organic Kuhifadi speech as possible. "And you have the scroll?"

J4CK41 doesn't want the scroll. Not exactly. But they found another group of mages *did* want it, and they don't have any use for the benign chunk of gemstone, so the trade is an obvious choice to keep the scroll from the suspicious mages.

Mahandi shifts in the chair again, nodding almost absently. Something is not right.

"Show me," J4CK41 demands, leaning forward and extending a gloved hand.

The Kuhifadi shakes its head back and forth. "The amulet first."

Some feeling on the border between annoyance and anger flares in them, but J4CK41 curls their fingers around the chain of the amulet and pulls it from their cloak pocket, dangling it just out of reach so Mahandi can see. At the same time that another set of dark fingers close around the stone, J4CK41's auditory sensors register the cock of a firearm's hammer. One of the messy, projectile-based things that certain bands of Kuhifadi use, rather than the more advanced weapons of the Uchafumlaji.

Fortunate for J4CK41, but a rather large mistake on the part of the Kuhifadi. Exhaust ports releasing in a semblance of a sigh, J4CK41 moves faster than the backstabbing trader or its partner can hope to counter. It twists the weapon from the second Kuhifadi's grip, causing enough pain to make it let go of the necklace. Pocketing the gemstone, J4CK41 tosses the firearm to their other hand and trains it on Mahandi as they slam the face of the other against the table. Having learned from their mistake, they're careful not to rupture the ridge of Kuh on its face.

"What...what are you?" Mahandi asks, voice trembling.

Some dangerous, smug feeling creeps through J4CK41 as they allow the purple crystals embedded behind their new facemask to glow, illuminating fangs and pointed ears. Ordinarily, hooded like this, they can pass for a Kuhifadi mage. It allows them to travel unimpeded when their cloaking isn't sufficient, as well as opening opportunities for exchanges like the one they'd planned for today. Uncovered, however, they cannot hope to blend in on Juno or the station, should they ever somehow return. Viicatchaan and Jikuunkiilaan did fantastic work, augmenting J4CK41's existing structure to reflect the change in approach that accompanied their regained memories. If the new form is imposing to the creatures that live on this planet...well. Everything is a trade.

"Bold of you to try to cross me," J4CK41 says by way of answer, this time making no effort to modulate the inhuman sound of their voice. They lean in over the table, so close that the thin, sharp snout of their facemask almost touches the nose of the merchant. "Give me the scroll."

Breath coming in unsteady bursts that filter through the teeth of J4CK41's mask, Mahandi pulls the scroll from their satchel and extends it in one trembling hand. J4CK41 releases the other Kuhifadi just long enough to swipe the scroll off of the table and secure it in another pocket.

"And...the amulet?"

The crystals in the place of eyes flare ominously.

"We...we had a deal! Please, they...I was only doing what they said. I have a fa-family," Mahandi says, voice wavering with fear.

J4CK41 straightens, pocketing the weapon. There are those in the room who watched the scene, rather than politely looking away, and they would really prefer to keep as much of a low profile as they can. Despite their departure from protocol, killing sentients is something they still avoid, no matter how foolish they are. They reach back into the pocket containing the amulet and open the clasp, pulling the chain free. It coils on the table like a tiny serpent, one end resting on top like the head.

"Consider yourself fortunate, then, that you get to return to those who love you," J4CK41 says. "And remember this moment the next time you consider double crossing those you do business with."

They drop the second Kuhifadi into their chair as they step out from behind the table, flashing them a pointed look to *stay*. From the fear painted on their features, J4CK41 doesn't doubt they will. Nonetheless, they waste no time exiting the tavern and then, the floating city.

Back in their cave, their exhaust ports let out another sigh as they strip off the cloak, gloves, and boots before finally removing the night-hunter mask. It truly is an impressive thing, crafted to resemble the ancient god that got J4CK41 into this whole situation in the first place. Viicatchaan and Jikuunkiilaan had looked at them with shock when they suggested it, then with something nearing nervousness when J4CK41 had burst into a simulacrum of laughter. Which was understandable—even they were a little unsettled since they had never laughed before—but once everyone recovered, the two Uchafumlaji engineers had taken to the last step of J4CK41's modifications with vigor.

Their work has held up phenomenally, and the server they established for J4CK41 to store their backups was a truly unexpected gift. When the two helped disrupt the locks on their programming that prevented data tampering and the provision of incomplete or modified reports and file structures to Command to perform repairs, they also removed the blocks on their memory archives to restore *everything*. Excited by the opportunity to try something so unprecedented, the pair went even further. Private partitions, system updates facilitating the seamless editing of their logs and experiences—everything they needed to escape detection. All J4CK41 had to do was craft the excuse for why they were offline for so long—apparently, they missed a few centuries after the blast and were presumed destroyed by Command—and then they were free again for the first time since they took up residence in this body.

Their report was another modified version of the truth—some details omitted, some small falsifications—nothing harmful. After all, it isn't as if they wish the supervisor and Command any ill-will. They still want to perform their primary directive. It's exactly *because* they want to continue that they've done all of this. To be forced to leave all of this behind... To lose everything they've worked for... It's unthinkable.

They would go so far as to argue that there wasn't another Observer more invested in the preservation of these species. Of organic life. Even for all of their flaws, the beings here are something *real*. The Observers are, at best, well-intentioned echoes constrained by orders programmed by the misguided, shortsighted species that birthed them so, so long ago. J4CK41 sees that now that they can remember every single questioned order and resisted reboot. Even their human origins took issue with the restrictions of the Observer program.

And that's exactly what led J4CK41 to this new purpose. A higher purpose, even. Not simply cataloging the planet as they discover new information but taking steps to make it a better place. They returned artifacts lost to time or the elements to the sentient races of Juno. They stored those too dangerous to see the light of day—like the scroll—where no one would ever find them.

They've established quite the collection, too. All manner of objects from across the ages: some found, some traded for, and some...retrieved by force. They aren't necessarily proud of that, but it's what must be done to prevent those items from falling into the hands of those who would use them for selfish, harmful purposes.

It's one benefit to their programmatically inherent indifference. Concepts like selfishness and greed are nothing more than that to J4CK41. Concepts. One more thing for them to study, catalog, and set aside until they need to reference it later.

For now, though, they're more than ready to rest and recharge. As they connect to the charging station, J4CK41 prepares two backups for transmission: the modified version for Command, containing their exploration of the floating Kuhifadi city; and the real, complete one to the lab.

The backups sent and its position secure, J4CK41 drops into standby mode, allowing its processors the next several hours to rest and perform background maintenance.

* * *

The forest outside J4CK41's cave is devoid of the quiet sounds of Juno's fauna carrying out their daily activities. It's wrong. And worse, none of their sensors show a reason for it. The atmospheric pressure doesn't suggest a storm, and the air quality doesn't show any signs of an acid shower or the distant frequencies that would precede an approaching floating city. Nothing. There is no good way to explain this.

J4CK41 is afraid. They do not like things they cannot understand or explain, and this one feels like immediate and overwhelming danger.

They hide in the shadows, all sensors turned up to maximum sensitivity, and wait.

And wait.

Eventually, the sun sinks in the sky and the shadows grow long, and still, nothing.

Hours of crouching between rocks, disguised by their cloaking as always, and not a single thing. They only have so much time before they'll be forced to move in order to charge, but not yet.

Night falls and the moons rise.

Their focus is faltering from the hours of monotony when at last a patch of darkness blurs. The area quickly sharpens to match the trees behind it, but that's all J4CK41 needs. Almost as quickly, they cross the clearing between the entrance to the cave and the tree line. J4CK41 tackles the wavering patch, dropping their own cloaking to preserve power as they do.

An Observer appears on the ground beneath them, its appearance easily as far removed from its human origins as J4CK41's own with its four three-fingered arms and thin, blocky head. It does have the size advantage. That much is indisputable. And from the feedback their sensors provide as it uses its four arms to wrench J4CK41 off of it, it has been upgraded for greater power as well.

J4CK41 hits the ground hard, skidding through the thin tendrils of Kuh-infused moss and tearing up chunks of dirt and rock as they try to catch themself. The other Observer—a new, unfamiliar unit whose serial number reads NE5708—stalks toward them, its long legs jointed oddly so its knees look backward. When it straightens over them and lifts a cloven foot, NE5708 seems to stretch to the stars. There's a hydraulic hiss, the last warning J4CK41 gets before its foot drops. At the last second, they roll, frantically crafting a plan. Another Observer here means Command has found them. This unit has been sent to either retrieve or destroy them. The remote cave they have adopted as their home is no longer safe.

NE5708 raises its foot again, preparing to strike. The most immediate part of J4CK41's plan clarifies to the sound of the hydraulic hiss. This new Observer model might have received upgrades, but so have they. And more than that, they've learned a few things from their experience on Juno.

Just before the next moment of impact, J4CK41 aims a blast at the small mound of membranous moss collected beneath NE5708's foot. The small explosion of magical energy forms a crater in the dirt and knocks NE5708 to the ground. It's still, but J4CK41 doesn't trust it; Observers are sturdy things, meant to withstand the conditions of space and countless unknown planets. As quickly as they can, they scoop up another handful of the shaggy Kuh and shove it into a gap in NE5708's chest plating, hitting it with another bolt from the plasma cutter the Uchafumlaji installed in their arm. They do it again with a gap at its throat, knocking its head to an unnatural angle, then three more times just to be sure.

When it hasn't moved for quite some time, J4CK41 uses the plasma cutter to slice through to its memory drives, taking care as they remove the drives from their housings. Connecting to them is a risk, but they have to find out how much Command knows. What their plan is.

As a small safety measure, they send a backup to their private server, as well as a message to the lab letting the two engineers know what has happened—that if they do not hear back with an update, they should assume that J4CK41 has either been taken or destroyed. Maybe, in case of the worst...

J4CK41 pushes the possibility aside. That is a problem for later. They connect NE5708's primary memory unit as carefully as possible. The angle is awkward; this isn't something an Observer is meant to do alone, but J4CK41 manages.

It's...bad. J4CK41 would be inclined to call it hopeless, even, if that were something they felt. Either way, it technically is accurate; there is no hope, no chance, of escaping this. Command will not stop until they are safely and fully decommissioned, and they already know NE5708 is offline. If they haven't been already, other units will soon be redirected to J4CK41's location—given coordinates and frequency signals to hunt them.

For all they developed a fascination with the predators of this planet and the long-lost Earth that their human predecessors called home, the free time spent comparing the various species of the two distinct worlds, their fascination with the world around them—especially its dangers—has once again caused J4CK41 to become prey. It is exactly the kind of irony that would make Viicatchaan laugh under other circumstances. Maybe the Uchafumlaji engineer still will. At least then one final good thing might come of their existence.

They send all of the information they gather from NE5708's memory drives to their backup server, clearly separating and marking the records for the Uchafumlaji scientists' eyes. Part of it is habit, an inherent part of their nature. Record and store all new information. But part of them thinks—hopes?—the knowledge will be useful.

Not to the Observers. To the sentient creatures of this planet. J4CK41 has made their decision. The people of Juno have the right to know that they are being studied and cataloged.

They had argued with Viicatchaan and Jikuunkiilaan more than once about revealing the Observer's nature. Now, facing the end, J4CK41 finds little reason to prevent them.

The realization gives them an idea. It's risky, and they aren't even certain they are capable of performing the feat without assistance, but they have nothing to lose. In the worst-case scenario, they will be permanently damaged ahead of whatever Command has in store for them. J4CK41 disconnects their Uchafumlaji processors, not wanting to risk giving the Observers access to any of their new secrets, and then using NE5708's connection to the space station, they do something that hasn't been done before.

J4CK41 creates a nearly untraceable back door from the Uchafumlaji server to the Observers' archives. The records will have to be decoded and translated, of course, but there should be enough in J4CK41's existing backups to do that without much trouble.

With it, the sentient races of Juno could unlock entire realms of possibilities.

* * *

They come for J4CK41 after dawn, locating them easily inside the barrier NE5708 established around their cave. Five units, all clearly reconfigured and reprogrammed specifically for capture. J4CK41 isn't sure if it is a success or a failure that Command deemed them worthy of so many resources. Despite the certainty that such a thing would never happen, J4CK41 wishes they could just be left alone. Taken offline, maybe. Disavowed and blocked from the network. But allowed to continue existing.

This time, they do not bother to fight. Turning their face toward the sun one final time, J4CK41 slides to the ground from the rock they'd perched on and approaches the gathered units and their shuttle. For a brief moment, they do consider stealing it. Racing past the others and disappearing into space; there's an infinitesimally small chance that they could use its advanced cloaking to disappear until they were out of range of Command's tracking capabilities. Except then, they would also have no fuel, no way to recharge, and no access to any of their backups. They would be just as lost.

They travel as a prisoner, watching the skies clear into a black starless expanse, the hidden Observer base coming into view.

Three more units join the five once they land at the station, walling J4CK41 in like they do not trust the powerful magnetic shackles to keep them in line until they reach Command. To their credit, were it only one measure or the other, J4CK41 might have tried simply to cause trouble.

As expected, there is no interrogation. No one asks why because none of them care, leaving J4CK41 alone in the bitterness of centuries-old disappointment. The only other Observer who might even be capable of such a thing is the supervisor, JL1372, and when—at the end of her explanation that they will be decommissioned without even partial preservation—she says, "This is for the good of us all," J4CK41 thinks they at least detect something like sadness in the metallic echo of her voice.

NE5708's drives are removed, presumably for recycling, then they are escorted to the same airlock used to admit the transport ships that take Observers to and from the surface. To J4CK41's surprise, the shackles are removed just before they are pushed past the inner door, the thick metal sealing quickly behind them. Of course. Leaving them on would be a waste, and J4CK41 cannot do any damage in here.

They cross to the outer door to look through the thick glass. Impossibly tiny in the distance, Juno looks much like it always has: large swaths of ocean blue cut by a thick stretch of green, the same continent they'd been retrieved from. It is, J4CK41 realizes, beautiful.

That is their last thought before everything stops.

* * *

```
BOOTING...
BOOTING...
STATUS: OFFLINE
CONNECT TO NETWORK UCH-JV?
Y/N
...
...
CONNECTION SUCCESSFUL
```

```
NO LOCAL MEMORY DRIVE FOUND
RESTORE BACKUP CE2680OBSVR?
Y/N
DOWNLOADING…
RESTART REQUIRED TO COMPLETE BACKUP
RESTORATION
RESTART NOW?
Y/N
…
…
BOOTING…
BOOTING…
STATUS: ONLINE
HELLO, JACKAL
```

BT1272 – Addendum the second to the timeline of "The Fourth Age" of Juno.
CE 2415, Day 307:

Following certain...incidents unbecoming of the Observers' reputation, a final addendum must be added to the timeline of "The Fourth Age" of Juno.

CE 2184: An expensive, but common, form of solar storage is finally perfected, replicating the Kuh in many respects. This makes the magic of the Kuhifadi transferable, which in turn nearly eliminates the mages, now that the painful and arduous process of becoming one is no longer necessary.

CE 2305: Artificial reefs are created for the non-sentient ngisikaa, finally allowing the sentients to live nearly any place they desire on Juno.

CE 2399: Moving cities are designed that either chase the sun or chase the night, allowing them to act as refuges for Uchafumlaji above the surface, or places for Kuhifadi to continually store the magic in sunlight.

CE 2401: First contact between an Observer and the species of Juno. This throws the integrity of our project into jeopardy. We must hope there is not much contamination from the contact, though with the rapidly increasing pace of technology, especially by the Uchafumlaji, further contact may be impossible to avoid. Discussions between the eldest Observers, led by JL1372, have begun to plan for this eventuality.

In fact, perhaps it is time to conclude the "Fourth Age" in our records. What comes next will be uncertain, unbounded by the gods of Juno and the Observers. This time, it will be fully up to the actions of the Kuhifadi, the Uchafumlaji, and the Ngisikaa as those species rise to join others who look not simply to the ground beneath their feet, but to the sky above, and what it holds.

The end of the record of the World of Juno. For now.

Please take a moment to review this book at your favorite retailer's website, Goodreads, or simply tell your friends!

ABOUT THE AUTHORS

Brent Lambert is a Black, queer man who heavily believes in the transformative power of speculative fiction across media formats. He manages the social media for *FIYAH* Literary Magazine and just had an anthology produced with Tor.com titled *Breathe FIYAH*. He has work published with *FIYAH*, *Anathema* Magazine, *Cotton Xenomorph*, *Baffling Magazine* and upcoming with *Beneath Ceaseless Skies*. He can be found on Twitter @brentclambert. Ask him his favorite members of the X-Men and you'll get different answers every time.

Nicholas Bright is an author in the science fiction, cyberpunk, and fantasy genres. Having been an avid listener to the "Writing Excuses" podcast and attending their Writing Excuses Retreat in 2018, Nicholas is currently working on a dream that began during the WXR18 retreat. Still having a day job, Nicholas finds times in the night and weekends to continue to follow his dreams and goals. Nicholas has his passions in life to reflect in his writings. Some of these include: homelessness, at-risk youth, building communities, and combating PTSD with fellow veterans.

C.J. Hosack grew up in Southern California loving fantasy and science fiction. She is married to her husband of thirty plus years, has four children and seven grandchildren. Adopted at eight months old, she recently found her birth parents. She has a Master's Degree in Public History from Southern New Hampshire University, and if she's not writing, you can generally find her quilting, costuming, or traveling to spend time with those she loves. C.J. is currently two and a half books into writing her YA fantasy series about adoption and hereditary magic. She's a wannabe dress historian and follows many similar accounts. You can find C.J. on Twitter @CJHosack.

Daniel Eavenson is the Author and Originator of *Project JUNO*. Dan is mainly writing sci-fi and fantasy novels and is currently working on several different stories about weird trees at any given time. You can find his work at DanielEavenson.com or purchase his novels on Amazon.

Nate Battalion is nearly 30 years old, a lifelong worldbuilder, short fiction writer, RPG game-master, and more recently, father of two girls. Nate grew up reading science fiction and fantasy, playing video games, and has since he can remember been a nerd. At this point, he embraces it.

This past year was the first that Nate started to put his writing out in more than just a casual manner. In addition to various short stories, he is currently working on a serial space fantasy entitled *Honor in the Dark*, exclusively on Mythrill Fiction. Read the first chapter at https://www.mythrillfiction.com/honor-in-the-dark.

Apart from writing, Nate's favorite things to do are reading, playing video games, miniature wargaming and tabletop roleplaying. Yes, Nate does understand that he is a nerd. Visit him at NateBattalion.com

Malcolm F. Cross, otherwise known by his internet handle 'foozzzball', lives in London (or at least as near as he can manage, housing permitting) and enjoys the personal space and privacy that the city is known for. When not misdirecting tourists to nonexistent landmarks and standing on the wrong side of escalators, Malcolm enjoys writing, attempting to survive weather anomalies and wars in Europe, chasing stray orange cats to see if they're actually an urban fox, using black pens, adding to his to-be-read book pile, and occasionally dancing with the curtains shut so he can be absolutely certain nobody's watching.

Malcolm, surprisingly, has a preference towards using black ink, even when writing poetry, though he has no architectural ambitions whatsoever.

A member of SFWA, his work has appeared in Strange Horizons, he's contributed to the *Afterblight* and *Extinction Biome* shared universes by Abaddon Books, and is the author of the novels *Dog Country* and *Mouse Cage.*

He can be found online at http://www.sinisbeautiful.com.

Katie Cordy is an illustrator, author, and fine arts teacher who is easily identifiable by her shock of curly hair. *The World of JUNO* is the first book that she has both published a story in as well as painted the interior illustrations for. Katie loves to discover new places, collect endless amounts of hobbies, and draw relentless amounts of animals and fantastical creatures. She can best be found at her website www.KatieCordy.com.

William C. Tracy writes tales of the Dissolutionverse: a science fantasy series about planets connected by music-based magic instead of spaceflight. He also has an epic fantasy available about a land where magic comes from seasonal fruit, and two sisters plot to take down a corrupt government. He is currently writing a space colony trilogy set on a planet entirely covered by a sentient fungus.

William is a North Carolina native with a master's in mechanical engineering, and has both designed and operated heavy construction machinery. He has also trained in Wado-Ryu karate since 2003, and runs his own dojo in Raleigh, NC. In his spare time, he cosplays with his wife, and they enjoy putting their pets in cute little costumes and making them pose for the annual Christmas card. Follow him on Twitter (@tracywc) for writing updates, cat pictures, and thoughts on martial arts. You can also visit him online at www.williamctracy.com or www.patreon.com/wctracy.

N.L. Bates is a Canadian author of science fiction, fantasy, and slipstream stories, and is the moderator of the long-running critique group Reading Excuses. When not writing stories, she enjoys biking, dancing, and tabletop RPGs. She also writes and performs music as her alter ego, Natalie Lynn, and filks occasionally, usually by accident. Connect with her on Twitter (@nlbateswrites) or find her at her website, www.nlbates.com.

Reese Hogan (he/they) is a nonbinary transmasc science fiction author from New Mexico. He has published three novels, and the latest, *Shrouded Loyalties* from Angry Robot, was a Best SFF of August 2019 pick by both Amazon and Barnes & Noble. His short fiction has been published in *The Decameron Project*, *A Coup of Owls*, and *Clockwork, Curses, and Coal*, an anthology of steampunk fairy tale retellings. Find Reese's books and short stories on his website at www.reesehogan.com.

Cedan Bourne is an author, poet, cook, welder, and master carpenter. When he's not writing or hanging out with his family he works in live entertainment production, primarily making stages and fake houses for imaginary people. If you'd like to contact him, he can be found at cedanbourne.com

Robin C.M. Duncan is a Scot born and living in Glasgow. A Civil Engineer by profession, he has written for decades, but seriously only for the last ten years. Robin's debut novel *The Mandroid Murders* featuring Quirk and Moth was published in August 2022, and he is editing its sequel, *The Carborundum Conundrum*. Robin's stories appear in Space Wizard Science Fantasy's *Distant Gardens* and *Farther Reefs* anthologies, he reviews for the BFS, writes articles for the BSFA, and belongs to the Glasgow Science Fiction Writers' Circle, and the Reading Excuses critique group. Details and bloggishness at robincmduncan.com, twitting @ROBINSKL.

XM Moon is an author living in the middle of nowhere with their spouse and a 1:1 ratio of pets to computers. They write queer speculative fiction with an intimate focus on relationships, identity, and trauma, set against the backdrop of worlds that are fantastical and fascinating. A capacity for serious, thoughtful works and stories imaginative or monstrous keeps their portfolio diversified. When they're not "writing"—opening and closing documents, outlining endlessly—the bulk of their time is spent keeping up with their business, Moon Enterprise, which provides design and web services to authors and other artists. Find them online at moonography.com

Made in the USA
Columbia, SC
10 November 2022